THE GREAT DETECTIVE: HIS FURTHER ADVENTURES

Borgo Press Books by GARY LOVISI

Battling Boxing Stories: Thrilling Tales of Pugilistic Puissance
    (Editor)
Driving Hell's Highway: A Crime Novel
Gargoyle Nights: A Collection of Horror
The Great Detective: His Further Adventures (Editor)
Mars Needs Books!: A Science Fiction Novel
*Murder of a Bookman: A Bentley Hollow Collectibles Mystery
    Novel*
Violence Is the Only Solution: 3 Vic Powers Crime Tales

THE GREAT DETECTIVE

HIS FURTHER ADVENTURES

GARY LOVISI, EDITOR

THE BORGO PRESS

MMXII

THE GREAT DETECTIVE

DEDICATION

To the writers in this book, whose
stories have made it so special.

CONTENTS

INTRODUCTION

BY GARY LOVISI

Sherlock Holmes!

That magical name conjures up all that is thrilling and exciting about the classic mystery short story. The Great Detective, created by Sir Arthur Conan Doyle, is without doubt the most well-known and popular fictional character ever created—and with good reason. Doyle's Sherlock Holmes stories are fascinating excursions into scientific detection with interesting, well-formed characters, offering intelligent, thoughtful mysteries that all men and women can relate to—and all enjoy. Quite simply, Doyle created magic with his Sherlock Holmes stories.

Writers over the last hundred years have been desperately trying to capture and recreate that magic, and I feel that the authors in this book have done just that. These are well-crafted stories by writers whose love of the original Holmes stories by Doyle clearly shows in their work. While some of our contributors hail from as far away as Australia and New Zealand—or right back to old-time professionals like Morris Hershman who lives a stone's throw away from me in Queens, New York—what they all have in common is that each of their stories keep to the traditional Holmes and Watson as created by Doyle.

These stories feature our heroes in a variety of cases set in various stages of their career together. In this book you will encounter stories that recreate our Sherlock Holmes in all new adventures, some of which continue or expand upon earlier cases. One story takes an endearing look at Holmes in his old age, another looks at the mystery surrounding a race horse that could match Silver Blaze for speed; murder and betrayal figure in many tales, and even good old Inspector Lestrade has a bit of say-so in one tale. In my own contribution, our heroes take an unusual interest in the game of golf!

However, any anthology of Sherlock Holmes stories worth its salt is marked just as well by what it does *not* contain as by what it does contain. You'll find no distaff tales in this volume; no variants on our heroes, no unlikely personality traits, nor supernatural flummery. None of that nonsense, thank you very much, but I could not resist just one exception! This is Holmes and Watson the way they were meant to be, the way Doyle wrote them. I believe what these stories really are, are rather personal love letters by each author to Holmes and Watson, and to their creator Arthur Conan Doyle. It is good to have them all together in this one volume.

I am sure you will enjoy the stories in this book. I chose each tale especially for its unique qualities, and I know each one will not fail to entertain and thrill you as much as it did me. So now sit back in your comfortable chair and let the fog of old Victorian London swirl around you, or perhaps the smoke from Holmes' own pipe, and take a trek with us to the front door of 221B Baker Street. Holmes and Watson are there waiting, and we can see that once again, the game is afoot!

—Gary Lovisi
September, 2012
Brooklyn, New York

THE MYSTERY OF OGHAM MANOR

BY STAN TRYBULSKI

I had been away from our lodgings for several days, setting up my new surgery on the High Street in Putney, and on my return I found a noticeably thinner and unshaven Holmes packing his small travel valise.

"Aha, my missing colleague. I was about to conclude I would not have the pleasure of your assistance."

"You are working on a new case, I take it." I knew that my old friend had been in need of money recently, for he had been spending inordinate sums on matters of which I disapprove so strongly that I am not disposed to discuss them here. That he had been fasting did not disturb me for I was quite used to this manifestation of his periods of intense intellectual activity, but that his cat-like fastidiousness concerning personal hygiene had apparently been abandoned placed me on my guard.

"Yes, one that will be quite lucrative and may also prove to be a professional challenge." There was a strange glow in his eyes and I feared he had slipped back into the grip of the demons that once had so fearfully possessed him before he underwent what his brother Mycroft called "the cure."

I sat down in my wing chair and studied him carefully as he continued packing. There had been a time in his career, and not so long ago, that only the challenge to his superb intellect would have mattered. I decided not to chide him and sensing the opportunity for another good story that I could submit to a new American magazine, I only said, "Well, are you going to tell me about it?"

"I have been retained by the Anglo-Hibernian Life Assurance Company, Ltd., of Galway, Ireland, to ascertain if the shooting accident of a businessman Ethelbert Wolkner on his Dorset estate three days ago was an accident or suicide."

"This doesn't seem to be your type of case; it should be a simple forensic decision by the local coroner."

My good friend snapped his valise shut. "Ah, yes, a forensic decision to be sure. But simple? That, I am afraid, will be quite another matter. For only last month, Anglo-Hibernian insured the life of the late Mr. Wolkner for the tidy sum of £75,000. A sum they are not anxious to pay out if they can avoid it." He stared at me, his eyes almost feverish. "You had better get packing, Watson; with your knowledge of gunshot wounds from your Army days in the Hindu Kush, I am sure you may be able to render valuable assistance to the dear country doctor. And to my clients, of course."

"How on earth did this Irish insurance company come to retain you?" As I asked this question, my eyes drifted around the room but stopped when they fell on two empty cut glass tumblers resting on Holmes' laboratory table. The glasses contained a small residue of brown liquid on their interiors and next to them stood a nearly full bottle of Jameson's whiskey.

Holmes smiled. "Very observant, old chum. Yes, I have had company and not long ago. Perhaps your packing can wait a bit. Sit down and rest while I tell you a little story." He walked over to the table and poured some of the whiskey into the glasses and handed me one. I sat in my favorite wingback chair and waited.

My colleague sat opposite me and raised his glass in salute. "You have been as good a companion as any man could ask for. Both trusted colleague and friend. So let us first drink together." He quickly swallowed the whiskey in his glass while I sipped mine. I waited while he refilled his glass.

He took another large swallow and stared at me, his eyes still feverish. "I have been mysterious for good reasons about the years I spent in hiding after my confrontation with Moriarty at the Reichenbach Falls, but I can tell you this much, that I spent several of those years near Galway, on the tiny island of Inis Oírr, studying the Erse language and literature. It was there that I met a Mr. Sean Carroll, President of Anglo-Hibernian."

"Why, dear friend, even after all these years, you continue to amaze me. Erse? Why on earth Erse?"

Holmes poured some more of the whiskey into my tumbler and then filled his glass half full. I had never seen him drink like this, yet I held my tongue lest he mistake any comment as a reprimand and cease to recount what might just be the best story of our career together.

"Why on earth not? To study one of the world's most noble languages, of course. All the while hiding in Moriarty's back yard, where he would never think to look for me." He drank some more of the whiskey.

"But how on earth did you wind up in Ireland?"

"When I fell into the Reichenbach Falls, carrying Moriarty with me, I must have hit my head on a rock. When I came around, I could barely see, for blood from a cut had seeped down my brow and into my eyes. I found myself in the water at the base of the falls, with one arm draped over a fallen branch and Moriarty nowhere to be found. I hoped the fiend had drowned, but I could not take the chance that he was still alive. So I had to go into hiding.

"With my free arm, I maneuvered myself and the log through the roiling water to the bank where I climbed up into the forest. Finding the necessary ferns and plants, I managed to staunch the bleeding and dull the pain.

"Fearful of falling asleep and being surprised by Moriarty or his henchmen, as soon as my clothes were sufficiently dry, I made my way to Zurich. After a quick meal of sausage, potato salad, and a *pichet* of a young white wine, I felt restored and paid a visit to a small, very discreet private bank where I kept a secret account. Upon giving the agreed pass code to the clerk,

I was ushered into the vault where I took from my private safe box a substantial amount of pounds, francs, marks, and dollars, along with several passports, a handful of diamonds, and a dozen or so small gold bars. Enough wealth to take me to South America where I would live very comfortably while continuing my study of exotic poisons.

"After leaving my bank, I went by train to Locarno, where I spent a week recuperating at a lakeside hotel. Thus refreshed and fit enough for a long journey, I crossed the border into Italy. My plan was to take a steamer from Genoa to Brazil, but in order to make sure that I was not being followed by Moriarty or his assassins, I spent several weeks traveling around Italy. I moved through Venice, Padua, Siena, Rome, doubling back and forth, using the different identities my passports provided. It was in Florence that I chanced upon the opportunity of a life-time. The opportunity to purchase a rare Amati violin."

He walked over to his wardrobe closet and took out his battered violin case and tapped it. "This violin."

"You mean that old instrument you are constantly fiddling on is an Amati?"

He nodded and if I had not known better, I would have sworn that his face had flushed slightly with embarrassment.

"Let us say that this is just another little secret between us. An indulgence that cost me much of the money I had intended for my new life as Senhor Gustavo Peres of Salvador, Brazil. Still, I had other passports in other names and other interests that would take me to other countries. If I could not slip half a world away from Moriarty, why not then hide in his own garden? So I made my way to Galway, this time as Gerard Murphy, and on the Aran Island of Inis Oírr, I hid away while all the world believed Sherlock Holmes was dead.

"Yet, it wasn't enough to just burrow on that tiny rock in the Atlantic, monkishly pouring through ancient tomes. I had to complete my identity as Murphy. And reclusiveness among that small band of clannish people would only raise suspicion. I could not afford wagging tongues. So every few weeks, like the other islanders, I would take the ferry to Galway to buy provisions and books and read the newspapers. I had to watch out for any diabolical crimes that would indicate Moriarty had resurfaced."

"God, Holmes, you could have contacted me, your old friend who always helped you."

"I could not take the chance, for I feared that Moriarty, if he had also survived the fall at Reichenbach, was having you watched. Besides, I had my studies, not only was I reading ancient Erse, but I was writing poetry in that most wonderful tongue." As he spoke, for the first time I saw true emotion on his face. Wistfulness, at least.

"And then there were the Saturday nights. When the weather wasn't foul, I would take a fishing boat to a little village called Doolin and go to O'Connor's Pub and fiddle." He opened up his violin case and took out his prized Amati. "With this, dear fellow. The one thing I brought to Ireland with me."

"You mean you played Irish reels and such with that magnificent instrument? Suppose it had become damaged?"

"Not I, old friend, for Sherlock Holmes no longer existed. It was Gerard Murphy, bearded and speaking Erse like a true son of County Clare or Galway that drank his pint of stout and dram of whiskey by a roaring fire and much to the delight of everyone, especially myself, fiddled away while the wind and rain howled outside. I was a new man, in body, soul, and identity. For Gerard Murphy was no longer just a name on one of the passports I carried with me when I escaped into Italy. He was a hard-fiddling, hard-drinking Irishman who could compose a poem in Erse as quickly as he could recite an old one." He emitted a deep sigh.

"But alas, even old bearded Murph is no more. The reasons for my reemergence as Holmes are well known to you and I shan't waste time going over them. Suffice it to say that an end had come to the happiest period of my life."

A thin smile suddenly crept over his lips and disappeared so quickly that I wasn't sure that I had actually seen it. He picked up the Amati and expertly rosined his bow and struck off such a jolly tune that I wanted to get up and dance. When he finished, he set the instrument lovingly back in its case, poured another dram and continued.

"It was during a night of fiddling at O'Connor's that I first met Sean Carroll. He was also a fiddler and while we were playing he kept glancing at my Amati. 'That's a strange fiddle, Gerard,' he said when we were done playing. 'Perhaps it is more suited for the London Symphony.' He then explained to me that he owned an insurance company and was well-versed in the value of rare musical instruments, and that he knew the violin was quite valuable but did not know its provenance. When I whispered that it was an Amati, he asked to play it. 'Just a little,' he said, and I let him. He swore he would tell no one and in that island of deep secrets I and my violin became just one more."

"So he never knew who you were? Then how did he contact you?"

"Dear friend, have you never heard of newspapers? Or magazines? Such as the *Sherlock Holmes Mystery Magazine* in which you tirelessly promote my cases. Do they not have photographs and etchings of me for the entire world to see?"

"But you said you were wearing a beard in Ireland."

"That little subterfuge was only meant for the villagers on Inis Oírr, it would never fool a clever man like Sean Carroll, nor was it meant too." Holmes looked at the clock on the mantle and suddenly stood up. "You had better get packing, our train leaves from Paddington in thirty minutes. I'll fill you in on the rest of the story during the trip." He looked quickly around, jammed the cork back into the whiskey bottle and unsnapping his valise, placed it inside.

"The night could be cold," he said. I did not argue with him.

* * * * * * *

We were only five minutes out of Paddington when my colleague opened his valise and produced the bottle of Jameson and the two cut-glass tumblers. He half-filled one of the glasses and handed it to me, then half-filled the other.

"A gift from Mr. Carroll," he said, raising his glass in salute. "Up the Irish." He drank.

"If you say so." I sipped my whiskey.

"And so I do." A thin smile crossed his lips. "Now, are you ready for the rest of the story?" Without waiting for my answer he reached into an inner pocket of his coat and withdrew his pipe and a pouch of tobacco. When he filled the pipe and stoked its flame with a few hearty puffs, he sat back and began to relate what can only be described as a very strange tale.

"About two months ago Mr. Carroll, while in London on business, was approached at his hotel by a rather tall man with a clipped military moustache named Cyrus Murdoch. Murdoch introduced himself as the president of the Lombard Street Associates, an investment firm based in Geneva, Switzerland, but with substantial interests in Great Britain. It seems that Murdoch's firm wanted to insure the life of the late Mr. Wolkner, the head of their London branch. When Mr. O'Connor said that the premium on a £75,000 policy would be quite high, this man Murdoch did not even blanch."

"And you found that suspicious?"

"Not at all, dear fellow. It appears the insured Wolkner was worth every farthing of the premium. From London, he directed much of the Lombard Street firm's overseas investments, which are quite substantial. A grand cru vineyard in Bordeaux; trading in world currencies; gold and diamond mines in Rhodesia and South Africa, among others. He was making a lot of money for the firm.

"Moreover, Mr. Wolkner was the second son of the Earl of Putney, and as such mingled among the highest circles of the realm. Many high personages became clients of the Lombard Street Associates, which is why, as Murdoch explained to Mr. Carroll, the insurance policy on Wolkner had to be initiated very discreetly, and engaging a Galway-based firm was more appropriate to maintain secrecy."

"Perhaps we should speak to this Murdoch fellow?"

"So we shall—when the time is ripe. For now, let us speak to the good country doctor and the grieving widow and view the scene of the tragedy."

"The grieving widow?"

"Yes, dear fellow, the widow. Did I forget to mention her? I really must be getting on in years. A woman who is said to have considerable charm...or charms, as one might put it. At least in days past. The mistress of Ogham Manor."

"Ogham Manor? That is a strange name for an estate."

"I imagine it draws its name from the Ogham stones which can be found throughout Cornwall and Devon. Apparently they are also present in Dorset."

"What on earth are Ogham stones?"

"Pillars, dear fellow. Pillars carved with an ancient Erse alphabet called Ogham. In the dawn of our British civilization warlike Irish tribes rampaged through Wales and then invaded southwest England. They marked the borders of their conquests with these pillars."

As Holmes talked, I took out my pen and paper and wrote as if I was back in Cambridge, listening to my history tutor.

The story that Holmes related to me on the train made me forget the trip and before I knew it we had reached Dorchester, where my good friend had already reserved a hansom cab to take us the ten or so miles further into the hinterland.

"This is wild lonesome country for the south of England," I said as the cab took us through a maze of narrow lanes that were bordered by high hedges that separated the properties of the small holders from each other. The bleak solitude placed me on edge after the hustle and bustle of London.

Holmes nodded.

"It is a place for deep meditation and contemplation."

* * * * * *

The home of Dr. Sedgecombe was outside the village of

Beaminster, set back from a lane even more narrow and twisted than the ones we had just driven over. A large farmhouse whose ancient stone and timber appeared to be badly in need of repair, it was surrounded by high hedges and an iron gate stood guard over the drive. We found the gate unlocked and open and Holmes told the driver to go directly to the house. There was a small open carriage on one side of the drive, its horse tethered to a stone hitching post. A man, apparently the driver, was lounging against a tree. Our driver eased our hansom cab next to the carriage and got out and opened the door for us.

Alighting from the cab, Holmes told the driver to wait and we then walked up to the front door. With a surprising vigor Holmes seized the iron knocker and slammed it against the frame several times. Even as the sound still echoed, the door opened and a woman, her head covered in a veil, rushed past us, bumping into me in the process. She entered the open carriage and waved the driver forward. Behind us in the doorway stood a slightly-stooped man. His face was ruddy as that of a country gentleman and adorned with a thick walrus moustache.

"A distressed patient. I apologize for her rudeness," he said.

Holmes introduced himself, and explained that we had been retained by the Anglo-Hibernian Insurance Co. to investigate the death of Mr. Wolkner. "Merely routine," my colleague added.

"Oh," said Dr. Sedgecombe, surprise evident in his voice. "I shouldn't have thought that Wolkner would be insured for a large enough sum to warrant an inquiry."

"You consider him to be financially improvident, doctor?"

"No, it's just that here in the Dorset countryside, I've found the people to be of plain state, regardless of their economic status, not given to valuing themselves in high monetary terms."

"He was insured by his firm, Lombard Street Associates, who indeed did place his monetary value rather highly. By the way, doctor, have you heard of Lombard Street Associates?"

The latter shook his head. "I'm afraid not. I've relegated myself to a simple country practice in semi-retirement. I've not spent much time in those types of circles."

"Really? I take it then that you are not from Dorset, that you have had a practice elsewhere?"

"Yes, I had a surgery in Leeds, but as I grew older, I decided to sell the practice and relocate to Dorset. I find the weather more hospitable than in the north and the countryside rather peaceful."

Holmes nodded. "Were you the attending physician for Mr. Wolkner?"

"No, I only met the deceased, I'm afraid, after he was deceased. As the nearest physician to Ogham Manor, the Dorset constabulary asked me to examine the body and give the coroner my opinion."

"Was there any possibility of suicide?"

Dr. Sedgecombe laughed. "By shotgun? There was no way he could have pointed the gun at his head and pulled the trigger, his arms were far too short."

"What if he had used his feet?" I interjected.

"Of course, it could be possible, but he would have had to have had the most practiced toes I've ever seen. Moreover, his boots were on when he was found."

Holmes took his pipe out of his coat and rubbed it in his hands. He placed the unfilled pipe in his mouth and looked the doctor straight in the face. "Was there any evidence of foul play?"

"None that I saw. The body was found lying next to a fallen log, and Wolkner's hunting breeches and one elbow of his jacket were covered with damp soil. It was obvious that he had tripped over the log and fell, the shotgun accidentally discharging."

Holmes took the pipe out of his mouth. "One or both barrels?"

"One. Good Lord, that was enough."

"Who found the body?"

"The old housekeeper, Essie O'Brien. Mrs. Wolkner had sent her to the shoot to fetch her husband as it was getting on tea time. Even though they were residing in the country by themselves, she insisted they continue the proper social formalities."

"And just what did the O'Brien woman do next?"

"I gather from what Mrs. Wolkner told me that she ran, or rather hobbled, straight back to the manor house to inform her mistress of the accident."

"And the way you saw him was the same way the housekeeper found him?"

"That's what she told me."

"Could there have been any other cause of death?"

"With half his head blown off? Not bloody likely. Excuse the expression, but it is rather appropriate. My dear Mr. Holmes, I hardly think so."

"He was definitely shot then?"

"There was a spent shell in one of the barrels of the shotgun, a faint smell of gunpowder and more than a dozen pellets imbedded in what was left of his face and skull. Yes, he was definitely shot."

"Could he have suffered a heart attack? Or perhaps there was medication in his system?"

"Perhaps, but that would not have changed my conclusions. He died of massive brain trauma and hemorrhaging. But death was instantaneous."

"And were there no other visible injuries to his body?"

"Nary a one," said Dr. Sedgecombe, his voice turning cold. "If there had been, I would certainly have included them in my report to the coroner. Now gentleman, if you will excuse me, I have to ready my surgery. There are patient visiting hours this afternoon."

"Yes, doctor, we do not wish to detain you any further." Holmes's voice had turned quiet. "But I do have one more question. Did you conduct an autopsy?"

"Absolutely not. He had a widow in a grievous state and with the cause of death so evident, I saw no need." The doctor's face suddenly flushed. "Now, good day." He angrily shut the door.

As we walked back to our carriage, Holmes asked. "What do you make of our Dr. Sedgecombe?"

"As a physician, I can understand his attitude. After all, you seemed to be questioning not only his medical conclusion but also his professional judgment."

"Perhaps with good cause."

I said nothing further on the matter, for I knew Holmes's intellect and deductive reasoning in past cases had proved me wrong much too often. Nevertheless, I still felt discomfited by the assault on a medical colleague's integrity.

When we arrived at Ogham Manor, we were greeted by an elderly woman whom I took to be the housekeeper, Essie O'Brien. Holmes handed her his card and the letter of inquiry from the insurance company and asked to see Mrs. Wolkner. She led us to the library, a large room just off the entrance hall, and whose walls were adorned with various hunting weapons as well as book cases. There was a desk and chair facing the window and a large Chesterfield sofa facing a fireplace. The housekeeper left to inform her mistress of our presence. Instead of sitting while waiting, I inspected a set of hunting rifles affixed to one wall in a crossed position, while my colleague amused himself over some books.

We did not have long to wait for Mrs. Wolkner. She soon appeared at the library door, her presence announced by the housekeeper. I turned from the gun rack to see a woman of late middle age but still somewhat attractive, with long white hair done into two thick braids that hung all the way down her back. She wore a long black dress that showed off what appeared to be a handsome figure, but what my medical experience had taught had more to do with the abilities of her undergarments and the tailoring of her clothes than the bounties of nature.

"Mr. Holmes?" Her voice had a quaver that I put down to her emotional condition, for she was twisting a handkerchief with her hands.

My colleague suddenly turned away from the bookcase and faced her. "Mrs. Wolkner." He approached and gently seized her hand with a gallantry that was most unusual for him. "This is my colleague, Dr. John Watson. I am so sorry that we have to disturb you in this time of bereavement."

She looked briefly at me and dabbed at reddened eyes with the handkerchief. "Mr. Holmes, these business matters are a terrible imposition, but if you must.... Well, let us sit then."

Holmes led her to the large Chesterfield sofa and sat next to her, still holding her hand.

"I don't quite understand, Mr. Holmes. I had no idea my poor dear husband had ever taken out insurance on his life."

Holmes patted her hand. "Indeed, he did not. He was insured by his firm, Lombard Street Associates. Were you not aware?"

She shook her head. "My poor dear Bertie never discussed business matters with me." She dabbed at her eyes again. "Well, if the policy does not concern me, Mr. Holmes, cannot this matter wait until I at least place poor Bertie in his final resting place?"

"I fear not, dear lady. But it may not be necessary to disturb you much further. We would need to speak to your housekeeper, Essie O'Brien, of course, as she was the one who discovered your unfortunate husband."

"Yes, of course, I'll send her to you straight away."

"And the place where this tragic event occurred. We will have to inspect that, as well."

"He maintained a private shoot adjacent to the manor's woods. He and some other gentlemen from his firm owned it jointly. He loved to shoot, ever since his Oxford days. He said it helped reduce his stutter."

"Ah, yes, his stutter. I understand he acquired that due to his childhood nurse trying to 'cure' him of left-handedness."

"Yes, but he still wrote left-handed although he shot with his right, and all she gave him in return was that horrible stutter. When it would reach the point that it interfered with his work, he would go off to the shoot. There's a small hunting lodge, really just a cabin, where he could be alone. Sometimes he would even stay overnight if he wanted to hunt early in the morning."

"May we see it?"

"Of course, Mr. Holmes. I'll get you the key. And Essie will show you the way."

Holmes waited until she left the room and then asked, "What do you make of her?"

"An aging beauty."

"Well, we're all getting on in years, old boy. What I meant was, how did you assess her psychological state?"

"She seems to be keeping a stiff upper lip over the death of her husband."

"Yes, she does seem so."

Our conversation was interrupted when the old lady appeared at the library door. "You wanted to see me, sir?" Her question was directed at Holmes.

"Ah, Mrs. O'Brien. Your mistress said you would direct us to the shooting cabin. And I would like to ask you a few questions on the way."

"It's Miss O'Brien, sir, I've never married." Despite her age, the housekeeper spoke with a firmness of voice that indicated that she was still not only of sound mind but of body.

"Tell me, good woman, other than yourself who else is in service at the manor?"

"Only Throbble, the gardener. He's a little dimwitted, but he manages to muddle through his chores."

"I'm afraid I haven't seen him here."

"You won't, it's his day off. Is there anything else?"

Holmes smiled at her. "No, you've been very helpful."

"Please follow me then."

Outside, Holmes went over to our driver and spoke a few words, and then scribbled something on a piece of paper and handed it to the man. He rejoined us and the old woman led the way. She moved at such a brisk pace that I, with my war wound still aggravating my leg, had some difficulty keeping up. As we passed out through the main gate, she pointed at the stone columns that stood on each side of the drive, silent and sturdy as if they were sentinels. Strange markings that appeared to be horizontal and angular slashes were cut into them.

"Ogham stones, sir," she said, quickly blessing herself. "You will see another, a larger one, by the cabin. I believe Mr. Wolkner understood them; that was why he had the cabin built there."

"And you, Miss O'Brien? Can you make anything out of them?"

"I fear not, sir. They may have something to do with ancient Erse, that's all I know." She started walking through the fields and we followed. After about a quarter mile, she stopped and pointed at a spinney in the distance. "You'll find the cabin there, Mr. Holmes. At the edge of the spinney. I'll return to my duties now."

"Your duties can wait. I need you to show me exactly where you found the body." Holmes gripped her elbow and gently urged her forward but she shrugged him off and retreated a few steps.

"I can't, sir, it's too horrible. Please don't make me."

"I'm afraid I must. You found the body and your presence at the scene is absolutely necessary." His voice had turned cold as ice and hard as steel.

"Heavens, Holmes," I said. "She has already described all this to the Dorset constables."

"That would be like you describing Isaac Newton's laws of motion to a cat."

And quick as a cat, he bounded alongside the poor woman and seized her arm. "Now come along, Miss O'Brien, there is nothing to fear." It was clear, however, that she feared plenty, whether imagined or real. Yet she held herself erect and took a step down the path.

"Very well then. But I certainly have no need of an Englishman to guide me."

As we walked, Holmes continued to question the woman, his voice and manner no longer hard but casual.

"Did Mr. Wolkner hunt often?"

"Many mornings in the spring and fall. Often he would stay overnight in the cabin so he could be out at the crack of dawn."

"But this is midsummer?"

"Yes, sir, but he said he had spotted some grouse the other day while walking in the fields."

When we neared the spinney, I saw a large cabin with a porch that looked out over the meadows and some low rolling hills beyond. Next to the cabin was a thick pillar about five feet high with carved markings like the Ogham stones back at the manor.

"Where was the body when you found it?"

"Over there." Miss O'Brien pointed at the edge of the spinney where there were some downed trees. Holmes set out towards them, the woman following behind him. I brought up the rear in case she tried to run off. After a hundred or so paces, we reached one of the fallen trees.

"There," she said. "On the other side of that log was where the body lay." She made no move toward the spot. Holmes again gripped her elbow and prodded her forward until they were standing in front of the log.

"How did you come to find him?"

"My mistress sent me to fetch him for tea."

"Yes, yes, we know that. But how did come to find him in this exact spot?" As he asked the question, Holmes was not looking at the woman but instead was gazing intently into the spinney.

"I called for him but there was no answer. I went into the cabin but it was empty, so I walked into the fields and called again. There was no one, not even a bird. I walked all the way around the edge of the meadow and as I made my way back toward the spinney, I almost tripped over him."

"Was he face up or face down?"

"Face down."

"And where was his head and where were his feet?"

"His feet were by the log and his head was pointing toward the meadow."

"And his shotgun?"

"Lying on the ground, next to his right arm."

"Did you touch the body?"

She shook her head.

"Then how did you know he was dead?"

She shuddered but said nothing.

Holmes turned his gaze away from the trees and looked

directly at her for a long moment. "What did you do next?"

"I ran back to the manor and told my mistress."

"Told her what, exactly?"

"That Mr. Wolkner, her husband, was dead."

"How did she react?"

"She had one of her fainting spells."

"I take it she was not in good health?"

"On, no, she is really quite fit for her age, if you know what I mean. It's just that she's given to what she call the 'vapors.' She would often collapse and gasp for breath when she became overexcited."

"Poor woman," I said. "Is she under medical care?"

"Dr. Sedgecombe treats her."

Holmes smiled thinly at her. "I have no further questions at this time, thank you, but I will trouble you for the key to the cabin."

She reached into the pocket of her dress and produced a sturdy brass key and handed it to him. Without saying another word, she turned and starting walking back in the direction from which we came. She had gone only a few steps when she stopped and turned once again toward us.

"It was the blood, sir. There was so much of it everywhere. On the grass, on the log, on poor Mr. Wolkner. That's how I knew he was dead." She turned again and walked away.

Holmes nodded at her receding figure and walked up the steps to the cabin door and unlocked it. Inside, we found a large room with a stone fireplace and a few chairs and a small dining table. There were smaller rooms on either side of the large room. One was fitted as a kitchen with a stove, a wash basin, a counter, and some cupboards. The other room contained a large bed.

"Seems like something out of one of those American wild west dime novels, podnuh," I said to Holmes, trying to make a small joke.

"Very much so. What do you make of those?" He pointed to a wall with a series of hooks from which a conglomeration of clothes hung. There was an army uniform with unpolished buttons hanging from one hook. Army boots and a pair of Wellingtons were beneath it on the floor.

"Sloppy soldiering," I said.

"Not at all, dear friend. There were not to be worn at tattoo but for hunting. If the buttons were polished, their brightness would scare away the birds."

I also saw a patched woolen loden hunting jacket, its bright green long faded from use.

"What do you deduce from the hunting jacket, dear fellow?"

"That our late Mr. Wolkner was not a man to spend money unnecessarily. It looks like something one would find at the old clothes market on Gloucester Street."

"Quite so. Anything else?"

"I hadn't thought he was that smallish," I said, noting the jacket's size.

"Precisely." He took his pipe out and filled it. "I want to sit outside for a while and calculate. Would you be good enough, old boy, to rummage around and see if there's any tea and put a kettle on?"

While I ransacked the cupboards. Holmes dragged one of the chairs out onto the porch. When I brought him his tea, his pipe was lit and he was lost in thought. Without saying a word, I set the cup down next to him and went back inside and poured myself a cup. I had brought a recent treatise on gunshot wounds and blood poisoning to read on the train, but the tale Holmes related was so fascinating, I had left the little monograph untouched. Sitting in one of the chairs, I now pulled out the treatise and began to read. Some time had passed, I knew not how much for I had become as lost in thought as my colleague, before I noted his presence back inside the cabin.

"Watson, I have considered much here and there is still much more to consider. I think I'll have a short lie down." He walked into the bedroom and closed the door behind him. By the time he awoke, the afternoon had grown late and we immediately set off for the manor. When we reached the house, it was almost dusk. Our driver and the hansom cab were nowhere to be found.

Anger flooded through me. "Good lord, Holmes, how on earth are we to get back to Dorchester? And our luggage? It is gone. What are we to do?"

My colleague appeared unperturbed by the matter but I persisted. "Perhaps someone in the village can drive us? Let us ask Mrs. Wolkner."

Essie answered the door and ushered us in. I saw our bags resting on the floor and immediately felt relieved. "Look Holmes, our bags. Perhaps the driver has not left us after all?"

"I'm afraid not, sir," Essie said to me. "When I returned from the cabin, the driver and the cab were gone. Only the bags were there, sitting on the ground, so I brought them inside."

"Thank you, dear woman," I said to her. "But how are we to get back to Dorchester? Is there anyone in the village who can drive us?" As I asked the question, Mrs. Wolkner came down the stairs, hobbling slightly and assisted by a splendid looking brass-topped walking stick.

"I am afraid it's too late to return to Dorchester. You will not find a coachman willing to navigate these treacherous country lanes at night. But there are guest rooms here at the manor, and it would not be an inconvenience to put you up. In the morning, I will send Essie into the village to find someone to drive you."

Holmes gave a little bow to the woman. "That is very kind of you, Mrs. Wolkner, but the hunting cabin will be sufficient. There is a fireplace and wood outside."

"Very well, Mr. Holmes. I will have Essie pack some food for you and prepare a lantern, for the walk at night is not easy." She gestured at her ankle. "As you see, a turned ankle can happen anywhere."

Holmes smiled thinly. "Yes, I do see. Thank you, you are most generous with your hospitality."

* * * * * * *

"That blasted coachman." Anger had flooded me because of the situation he placed us in. Mrs. Wolkner was right. Even though the path was clear and we had trod it only an hour or so ago, the walk was dangerous in the pitch black night. And carrying our luggage and the basket of food made it even more dicey.

"Now, dear fellow, is that anyway for a physician of your stature to speak?"

"If you twist your ankle like Mrs. Wolkner, ask me that question again."

My anger was soon tempered, however, by the delicious food Essie had prepared for us. In the basket was a roast chicken, boiled potatoes, and a wedge of Stilton cheese, two bottles of beer and a bottle of port. While I set out the dishes, Holmes prepared a fire and we ate and drank as fine a meal as Mrs. Hudson had ever prepared for us at our lodgings.

Afterwards, I made tea and Holmes poured the last of the Jameson into our cups and we drank.

"What do you make of Mrs. Wolkner?" he asked after a long stretch of silence.

"You already asked me that."

"No, I mean her state when we saw her tonight."

"She seemed to be holding up well; nerves calm considering the death of her husband and now the injury to her ankle. I must say, that was an exquisite walking stick she was using. I have never seen one like it. With a brass top. Oriental, I gather?"

"Quite so. Teak with Buddhist carvings, but its head is gold-plated."

"Fascinating."

"I agree, Watson, I agree. Fascinating." Holmes finished the last of his tea and Jameson and stood. "I think I will take a walk outside and look at the Ogham stone."

"It's a shame that Essie O'Brien doesn't understand them. For your curiosity about them seems rather high."

"Not to worry, Watson. For during my self-exile on Inis Oírr I met the most wonderful and delightful intellect I had ever come across, an erudite monk named Brother Kenneth who, when in his cups, wrote the most lovely Erse poetry. There were many the stormy nights when Brother Kenneth and I sat by the fire with cups of hot tea and Jameson and discussed Ogham and the Ogham stones. Not only did my knowledge of that ancient language expand, but by delving into the mysteries of the Ogham Stones, I was able to satisfy my ongoing interest in codes and ciphers. And the Ogham Stones proved to be the most difficult ciphers of my career. Yet, as I expected, I eventually cracked them. I certainly shall have no trouble understanding this one."

Holmes went out and I stoked the fire and finished the monograph before retiring. I awoke the next morning to a steady drumbeat of rain on the roof and the comforting sound of the kettle on. Holmes was already up and had shaved and was pouring our tea. He drank his tea quickly, oblivious to the heat, and stood. Seizing an umbrella that was by the door, he thrust the portal open and looked outside.

He then turned back to me. "The rain is bearable. Finish your tea, old boy, and come take a walk with me. I have something to show you and I would like your opinion about it."

"My opinion? Is it a medical matter?"

"Not in the least. Nevertheless, any conclusions you draw may prove to be invaluable."

Always ready to render assistance to my colleague, I followed him out the cabin door, and hunching up next to him under the umbrella we headed toward the spinney. Once inside the grove, Holmes shut the umbrella and plunging ahead, used it to poke back the branches in our path. We soon reached a small clearing where in the center stood a wooden pole.

"What do you make of that?" he asked me.

I walked over to the pole and examined it. It had long perpendicular striations carved into it, and there were horizontal and slanted slashes running through the striations and from their sides.

"It looks like an Ogham stone, but the pillar is made of wood and the cuts are recent."

"Excellent observations. Anything else?"

"It is crudely carved."

"Jolly good observation."

"What does it say?"

The thin smile reappeared on his face. "Like the stone pillar, it contains a message. But this message is gibberish."

"Gibberish? Why on earth would someone carve gibberish in the middle of a Dorset spinney?"

"Let me give you a rudimentary explication of Ogham, dear fellow. The alphabet is based on the twenty trees that were sacred to the ancient Irish druids. Each slash or combination of slashes stands for one of the Ogham alphabet. Now let us return to the cabin, for I wish to have another cup of tea and wait."

"Wait? Good lord, Holmes, wait for what?"

"Not what, Watson, whom!"

When we reached the cabin, there was a folded note pressed into the door. Holmes snatched it and began to read. "Aha. We must return to the manor house immediately. There is no time to lose lest we allow the murderer of Mr. Wolkner to escape."

"Murder? How...when did you deduce his death was a murder?"

"I will explain later. Did you bring your service revolver?"

"It is in my bag."

"Good. Fetch it and follow me. Quickly now." Holmes pushed open the umbrella and set off down the path toward the manor house.

"But the umbrella...," I yelled after him for he had left me with nothing to protect myself from cold drizzle. But he did not stop and soon he disappeared from view. I went into the cabin and retrieved the Colt. I tried to catch up but it was no use with my bad leg. By the time I reached the manor house, the front door was open and I plunged through it without knocking. I could hear voices in the library, and I slid open the door to find my colleague and Mrs. Wolkner, sitting and leaning on her walking stick, being served tea by Essie.

"Ah, Watson, Just in time. I was about to relate an interesting tale to our hostess, and it should interest you as well."

"Won't you join us for tea, doctor? I am sure you are as interested in what Mr. Holmes has to say as I am."

I sat and waited while Essie poured my tea. When she had finished Holmes began.

"My story starts two decades ago in America. It is a tale that should curdle the blood of any decent human being. A story about a vivacious young woman. A woman who wanted and expected everything that a life of leisure could give her. She was an actress. No, not the kind that appears on the stage to delight audiences. For this woman's stage was the boudoir, and her audience consisted of rich young men, sons of successful Southern planters. Have you ever heard of Miss Annabelle Portia Perkins?"

I shook my head for I hadn't the foggiest notion who he was talking about.

"Perhaps you might remember her by the infamous name her notoriety bestowed upon her. The Black Widow of Virginia. Does that jog your memory, Watson?"

"Yes, I do remember something about a woman called that, but that was some years ago, wasn't it?"

"Yes, many years ago. This actress of the bedchamber managed to win the heart of Eustice Broyhurst, the scion of a rich Virginia tobacco company. As Annabelle Broyhurst, she became the toast of Southern society. And then her young husband tragically died, shooting himself for reasons no one could quite fathom at the time. There were rumors that there had been a scandal involving his wife, and soon she was referred to as the Black Widow. There was also talk of prosecuting her for the man's death, but his family was said to have hushed it up, paying her a substantial sum to leave the country.

"In Paris, as the story goes, Annabelle dropped her first name and called herself Portia. After squandering her fortune on a series of handsome but rather vapid young paramours, she left the City of Lights for Nice on the Riviera, where she met an elderly Bavarian aristocrat, Otto, Freiherr von Schritter zu Adelberg. It was not long before she had also drawn him to her evil bosom. In a matter of weeks she was the Baroness Portia von Schritter zu Adelberg and the mistress of his family's vast estate and castle. That marriage, like her first, did not last long and also ended in tragedy. It seems the good old Freiherr, perhaps after indulging in a little too much schnapps, stumbled over a log while out hunting in the woods and accidently shot himself."

"Incredible. What a coincidence. Both husbands killed."

Holmes suddenly sprung to his feet. "Coincidence? Watson, your naivety amazes me. Having witnessed my tragic affair with the woman, have you learned nothing about the wiles and cunning of the female species?" His voice was wrought with emotion.

I knew Holmes was talking about Irene Adler, the only woman he had ever loved and who had betrayed him, only to later seek him out in New York and give her life to save his.[1] Because of the pain and anguish he felt, he could never say her name, and would only call her "the woman."

"I'm sorry, dear fellow. I didn't mean to upset you. Please sit back down and continue."

"It seems that the old Freiherr had a son, a cavalry officer who was a favorite of the Kaiser. Given the feudal laws of primogeniture and the Kaiser's influence, the estate went entirely to the young man. He apparently kept his stepmother around for a temporary dalliance, but then quickly tiring of her, he sent her packing with little more than the clothes on her back. But the story doesn't end there, old chum. No, Watson, the baroness Portia was not going to allow herself to be consigned to the Hades of jaded beauty, to be dismissed from society, sent away with only a trollop's *pourboire*. It was at the spa in Baden that she came upon the late Mr. Wolkner, second son to the Earl of Putney, whom she took to be wealthy enough for her to ignore

---

1. In another story, *Be Good or Begone*, I related how Irene Adler died trying to save Sherlock Holmes from being poisoned in New York by Professor Moriarty.

his pronounced stutter."

Holmes looked over at Mrs. Wolkner and smiled thinly. "Have I related the story correctly?"

"It is your story, Mr. Holmes, so I shall let you tell it without comment for now."

"It seems my trusted colleague Morrell has wired me from Switzerland with some interesting news."

"Morrell? You mean that scruffy little bootblack who used to shine shoes outside the Theatre Royal in Haymarket until he earned the price of a standing-room ticket? That Morrell?"

"Exactly, dear friend. That Morrell who became the most talented and trusted of my Baker Street Irregulars and who carried out some of the most daring feats in that capacity. The lad I sent up to Sydney Sussex, where he did a double first in Classical Languages and in Modern History."

"I can't believe it."

"Who, upon leaving Oxford, was no longer the humble drudge of his childhood and became employed by The Crown in matters as sensitive as those that I had tasked him with."

I sat back in my chair.

"And who along with my brother Mycroft is also a stalwart member of the Diogenes club. Upon my instructions yesterday, our coachman took the train to London and went to the club and left a note for Morrell. A note in which I asked the man to make a very urgent and specific inquiry for me. Mycroft, for whom Morrell also undertakes sensitive matters, made sure that the message was wired immediately to Geneva. I have the reply right here." He smiled thinly once more and withdrew the folded piece of paper that had been jammed in the cabin door.

"What does it say?" My curiosity was now at a fevered pitch.

The smile disappeared from his face. "Perhaps Mrs. Wolkner can tell you?"

"I'm sure I have no idea," she said, her voice tense.

"Very well then; I shall enlighten you." He turned back to me. "As you know, the Lombard Street Associates is a Swiss-based firm. I asked Morrell to make inquiries through his contacts in the Swiss government and find out who the owner was."

"You mean the owner was not that man Murdoch?"

"Murdoch was only a pawn in this evil scheme. To be used and disposed of when no longer needed."

"But used by whom?"

"The mastermind who controls Lombard Street Associates."

"Who?" I cried. "Who?"

He put the folded piece of paper back in his pocket. "I shall come to that in a while, but for now I would like to turn your attention to the mystery of the Oghams. Remember the gibberish on the wooden pillar? Well, it took me almost an hour before I realized that it wasn't just gibberish, after all. Not if you looked at the message as numbers instead of an alphabet. After another hour, I had deciphered enough to discern that I now possessed the combination to a safe and the pass code to a bank account. A pass code not unlike the one to my safe box in Zurich. I walked back to the manor while it was still dark, slipped inside and found the safe behind this bookcase."

I watched as Holmes walked over to very same bookcase that had intrigued him only the day before. He reached up to a corner and pressed the wood. The panel next to the case slid up to reveal a wall safe. Spinning the combination dial quickly, he yanked the steel door open and withdrew a thick packet of papers that was bound with a red ribbon. Turning toward Mrs. Wolkner, he said, "Shall I read the contents?"

"That will not be necessary." Using her walking stick as a crutch, she forced herself to her feet and hobbled over to where Holmes was standing.

"You are very clever, Mr. Holmes."

"What on earth is she talking about? What are those papers that you have?"

"Evidence, Watson. Evidence that Lombard Street Associates is owned and controlled by the Baroness Portia. Who is none other than this evil creature you see standing before me." He gave a slight bow to Mrs. Wolkner.

She nodded back.

"Baroness?" I cried, looking at the woman. "Good heavens, Holmes, do you mean...?"

"Yes, Watson. She is none other than the Black Widow of Virginia."

Mrs. Wolkner nodded again. "Please continue."

"When I said her husband had made a lot of money for the firm, it was the truth. But at the expense of his clients." He undid the ribbon on the packet of papers and waved the top sheet at me. "It is all here, Watson. How the firm was looted, their clients' money siphoned off and deposited into a secret bank account in Geneva. An account controlled by this poisonous creature."

"Do you mean Wolkner stole from his family and friends? But he was from one of the finest of families. A British aristocrat would never commit such foul deeds!"

"No, Watson, Mr. Wolkner did not participate. These crimes were solely the work of his employer. Somehow, he stumbled onto the embezzlements and also learned that he was merely a dupe for the woman he was married to."

"But why did he keep the papers in his safe?"

"Guilt, Watson. Guilt and love. The two emotions most common to our male species."

"So he did kill himself?"

"No, dear fellow. The poor man may very well have contemplated it, for he was faced with either handing over the woman he loved to the law or betraying the trust of clients. Either way, he would have been ruined."

"I don't understand why he carved the numbers on the wooden Ogham pillar? Who was it to be a code for?"

"No one, Watson. He was not intentionally leaving a clue, only trying to work it out in his mind by writing things down. He was tormented by his moral dilemma and did not know what to do, so he set about writing it out but in a way that he thought no else would stumble upon it." Holmes stared at Mrs. Wolkner.

"I suspect that the original plan had been for our Black Widow here to disappear, leaving her husband, as the Americans like to say, holding the bag."

Mrs. Wolkner laughed. "The stuttering fool actually confronted me about the thefts. If he had only left well enough alone, he would be alive today."

"Yes, his honor and decency of character required that he inform you of what he had learned. Did he plead with you to return the funds to the firm's accounts? Of course he did. Did you play along with him? Of course you did. But you had no intention of doing any such thing. So the plan had to be changed. Now, the poor man would have to be disposed of. That is where your accomplices came in."

"You have proof of all this?" I was incredulous, for we had been at Ogham Manor for less than twenty-four hours and Holmes seemed to not only have found a murder where there was none, but to also have solved it.

"Inspector Gregson has Dr. Sedgecombe in custody. His full confession is not necessary, for we have enough evidence to hang him."

"Gregson? Sedgecombe? How on earth did Gregson become involved? And what evidence?"

"Our valiant coachman also delivered a message to him at Scotland Yard. Gregson then made inquiries about Sedgecombe with his colleagues in Leeds. It seems our country doctor had been forced to sell his surgery to settle some very large gambling debts." He turned to Mrs. Wolkner. "Sedgecombe was always in need of money, a weakness that someone of your cunning would have seized upon. Am I not correct?"

The woman said nothing.

"Your silence will change nothing. An autopsy will reveal slivers of rock imbedded in Mr. Wolkner's face. For he was rendered unconscious with a savage blow before being dispatched by a shotgun blast. The force of the pellets tearing through his face would have pushed the rock fragments deep into the bone and pulp. But any good pathologist with a knowledge of war wounds would have found them. My colleague, Dr. Watson, for example."

"So Dr. Sedgecombe killed Mr. Wolkner?"

"Not at all, dear fellow. Nor did the other accomplice, the slow-witted gardener, Throbble. The murder was left to another.

"Yes, the doctor and Throbble were only pawns whom this evil woman lured into her honey trap and easily convinced to do away with her unsuspecting husband.

"She concocted a story for Throbble. How her husband had discovered that she loved the dimwit, and he was going to have the poor man dismissed from service, beaten, and jailed. There was only one way Throbble could save them. He would have to hit Wolkner with a rock and kill him, she said. It would look like a fall and then he, they, would be safe to continue their affair.

"Of course, she knew better. A face smashed by a rock would never be taken for the result of a fall. So she watched from the cabin as Throbble approached her husband and struck him down. After she sent the dimwit back to the manor, she went over and placed the shotgun's barrel next to the unconscious man's face and pulled the trigger."

He stared down at the woman, a look of distaste spread across his face. "Is that how you killed your first two husbands?"

"Oh, with that twit Eustice, it was suicide all right. I made sure he had plenty of reason. It wasn't difficult to arrange it so he would come upon me while I was in a compromising position with one of the plantation overseers. I knew he couldn't handle it emotionally. It was risky, though. He might have killed me as well." She gave a little laugh.

"As for Otto? I had him teach me everything he knew. He thought it was a lark to have his wife fence. The epée, the saber, the foil, I learned them all. And when I became as good a fencer as he was, I killed the swine.

"Yes, Mr. Holmes, it was easy to kill the old fool. While we were hunting one afternoon, I asked if I could use his shotgun instead of mine. So we switched weapons. And then just a push as he stepped over a log while going down a slope and I shot him with his own gun and took mine back. A tragic accident. Everyone agreed." She gave a venom-filled laugh.

I was shocked by the bitterness of the laugh that came from

such a pretty mouth. Even Holmes drew away from her, horror on his face. The woman laughed again. "Don't be so surprised, Mr. Holmes. After all, Irene Adler played you for the utter fool."

Rage suddenly flooded into Holmes's face. I had never seen my colleague so angry. He reached out and grabbed the Black Widow's braids and twisted them so roughly that the evil wench was forced to her knees.

He yanked on the braids, forcing her face upwards. "If you even utter as much as syllable of her name again, I swear I'll garrote you with your own hair."

"You'll do no such thing." With a sudden move, she hooked one of his legs with her walking stick and upended him. Springing to her feet, she twirled the stick as if was a baton. "Oh, did I forget to mention that Otto also taught me the art of single stick before he had his accident?"

At the mention of that ancient and noble art of *canne de combat*, which my colleague was also an aficionado of some repute, I was curious to see if the Black Widow's prowess with cudgel could best him.

Holmes rolled over on his side several times until he reached the chair where he had rested his umbrella. He snatched it up and held it in front of his face just in time to parry what might have been a lethal blow from the gold-plated head of the walking stick. The Black Widow danced away, and then with a spin of her body she danced forward, thrusting her stick at his groin, only to have him parry it once more.

He had not yet been touched but clearly he was on the defensive in this combat. On her toes, the evil woman circled him and then once more thrust the stick toward his manhood. Holmes managed to parry again, only to have her twirl the stick like a baton and bring it down upon the center of the umbrella, which snapped like a twig.

"I have you now, Mr. Holmes. And I assure you, I will make your demise as humiliating and painful as possible." She thrust once more at his groin, but Holmes managed to deflect most of the blow with a shard of the umbrella. But with a flick of her wrist, she sent the other end, the one with the gold-plated knob, crashing against his left knee. Holmes fell to the floor, trying to ward off further blows with his left arm while jabbing at her with a piece of the umbrella in his right hand.

It was no use. I could see he was tiring and it would be only a matter of time before the Black Widow delivered an incapacitating blow which surely would be followed by others until my colleague was no more.

"Stop!" I cried, taking my service revolver out of my pocket and pointing it at her. With a motion so fluid and so fast that I did not even see it until it was over, she knocked the gun out of my hand, dropped her stick, snatched the gun up and waved back and forth at Holmes and myself.

"One more murder or two, it matters not," she laughed.

"You'll never escape," Holmes said.

"We'll see." She turned to the housekeeper. "Essie, fetch my walking stick and go harness the carriage."

The old woman picked up the stick but did not move further. Finally she spoke. "I knew you were evil the day I first laid eyes on you. But to kill your husband, who was only good to you...?" Essie suddenly lashed out with the walking stick, knocking my pistol out of her evil mistress's hand. As it clattered to the floor, the Black Widow dove for it. Holmes, just as quickly, rushed toward her and buried his head between her thighs and gripping her buttocks, upended her before she could the reach the weapon. She kept bucking her hips while clawing for the pistol as my colleague pushed his head further between her thighs. Suddenly, with a violent twist, she managed to break free and sprang to her feet.

Holmes was on his hands and knees, gasping for breath, but was now between the killer and the gun. She stood in front of him and laughed. "You think you are very clever, don't you, trying the French trick on me. Did you really think you were the first man to try and subdue me in the Gallic manner?"

She dashed for the doors to the garden before Holmes could reach the pistol. She turned back and glared at us, her eyes dark pools of hate. "I'll have my revenge, Mr. Sherlock Holmes; we'll meet again." Then she disappeared through the doors.

"Holmes, she's getting away."

"Let her go, Watson, I have what we need. The law will soon catch up to her."

* * * * * *

Such was the sad case of Ethelbert Wolkner of Ogham Manor, Dorset. How Holmes used his prodigious mental talents of deductive reasoning to discern the plot by the dead man's wife, the erstwhile baroness Portia von Schritter zu Adelberg and her true identity as the "Black Widow of Virginia," and the complicity of her paramour, Dr. Sedgecombe, was revealed to me on the train ride back to London.

"The clues were all there, Watson, as many as the stars in the sky, but you had to look up to see them."

"When did you first deduce that Mr. Wolkner's death was the result of murder?"

"When we first arrived at Dr. Sedgecombe's farmhouse. I deduced it from mere observation. You should have done the same."

"Observation. Just what was I supposed to have observed?"

"Do you not remember the description of Murdoch that was given to me by Mr. Carroll of the Anglo-Hibernian Insurance Company?"

"Of course, a tall, pale-faced man with erect posture and a military moustache. What has that got to do with Dr. Sedgecombe?"

"That is exactly the question I would expect from someone as inobservant as you apparently were. Old chum, Dr. Sedgecombe was stooped with a ruddy face covered by a walrus moustache, was he not?"

I nodded agreement while taking notes.

"Imagine if he stood erect and his face was not ruddy from the country air, and the walrus moustache was trimmed to an officer's measurement. What would you see?"

"Why, Murdoch, of course."

"And what about the state of the farmhouse? Surely you noticed that?"

"It was badly in need of repair."

"And what did you deduce from that observation?"

I stopped writing. "I must confess, Holmes, that I had not deduced anything."

"And now?"

"That Sedgecombe either did not have the funds to make the repairs, or that he had no plans to stay long at the farm and would leave the repairs to the next owner."

"Excellent. A day late but an excellent deduction. For as Inspector Gregson's inquiries in Leeds had proved, Sedgecombe had impoverished himself through gambling and had to sell his surgery to cover his losses. A rundown farmhouse in Dorset was all he could afford. Now let us progress to his patient, the woman who so rudely bumped into you as she hurried away from the farmhouse."

"What about her?"

"Did not the doctor say that he had patient hours later that afternoon? So why was she there? And who was she?"

"You mean she was the Baroness Portia, I mean Mrs. Wolkner?"

"Yes, and the driver was Throbble. While I was investigating last night for the safe, I also looked into the carriage house and spied the very same carriage that was outside Sedgecombe's place. And that Throbble was driving his mistress on his day off led me to deduce that their relationship was something more than mistress and gardener."

"And did not Essie say that Sedgecombe had been treating the woman for the 'vapors?' Yet, he swore he had never met her husband until the man's death. Moreover, I suspect that if we question Essie further, we will learn that the 'vapors' only came about after Sedgecombe moved to Dorset.

"Furthermore, one who was observant would have seen that

while Mrs. Wolkner was dabbing at her reddened eyes with her handkerchief, there were no tears."

I took this as a reprimand by Holmes concerning my talents of observation, but I was so impressed by his deductive reasoning that I could only urge him to continue.

"These clues were enough to raise my suspicions, so I had Morrell confirm them with his inquiries in Geneva. Meanwhile I was consumed with deciphering the Ogham inscription on the wooden pillar in the spinney. Remember, you commented that the slashes were rather crude. That was because they were right-hand writing done by a left-handed man. And that could have been none other than poor Mr. Wolkner.

"And then there was the hunting. One never hunts grouse in mid-summer. It just isn't done, old boy. No, Wolkner was going back to his Ogham pole. Topping that off, there were clothes in the cabin. It was you, Watson, who clued me while remaining clueless yourself."

"However do you mean?" I asked without looking up for I was scribbling my notes as fast as I could.

"The size of the green loden hunting jacket, of course. A Bavarian style, I might add. You commented how small it was. That was because it did not belong to Wolkner, but rather to his wife, the Baroness Portia. And from that one could deduce that she was knowledgeable about hunting and weaponry. Yes, dear fellow, once the clues marked the trail, I only had to follow it."

"And what will become of Essie? At her age, it will be hard to place her in service elsewhere."

"I believe that when I inform Mr. Carroll of the valuable service she rendered and the money we have saved the Anglo-Hibernian Insurance Co., there will undoubtedly be a generous stipend to be paid, and perhaps a small cottage on the coast."

"And then you could go and fiddle for her by the firelight." I laughed at my little joke.

"Perhaps I shall, Watson. Perhaps I shall."

THE DENTIST

BY MAGDA JOZSA

I.

It was mid-October of the year 1883. Life was comfortable. I had recovered from my war wounds (except for the occasional twinge), and was now doing locum work to supplement my meager pension.

I took over the practice of Dr. Peter Morley while he was away on holidays. His practice was located in Epping, and, as part of the deal, I was to live in his house—to save commuting daily. It also made me more readily available for his patients after hours.

To familiarize myself with the clients of his practice, I made a habit of reading up on his case notes of past patients. I don't know what it was that made me delve into his deceased files, perhaps it was just the desire to see if there had been any epidemics in the area, or perhaps it was the unwitting influence of my friend Sherlock Holmes. No one could live with such a man and not lose some of his naiveté with regard to human nature. Whatever the reason, I made a curious discovery.

His case histories were filed in order of year. I began with checking the deaths for the past year. There had been three deaths in the last six months. One was Dr. Morley's own wife, Beatrice, and two other ladies—a Mrs. Kate Boyce, and a widow, Mrs. Elsie Presnell. Dr. Morley—in their case notes—had described all three as presenting with acute nausea, vomiting and impaired respiration. Rapid in onset, culminating in heart failure and death. All three were in their late thirties to early forties. They had died within hours of the first symptom. I found this rather singular. What disease would cause such symptoms? In the back of my mind I could hear Holmes's clipped tones saying: "Poison, Watson, poison."

Could it be? Surely an experienced doctor of Morley's years would have been able to detect if the victims had been poisoned—especially as one was his own wife? I wished Holmes were here. It would be good to talk to him about this. My tenure here was only for eight weeks. I had already served four and hadn't seen Holmes since. I had invited him to come visit me in Epping; only he was in one of his lethargic moods and could not bestir himself.

I was disturbed from my ruminations by the arrival of a patient, and found myself busy for the next two hours. Just as I was thinking of having some lunch, a maidservant came hurrying in.

"Doctor, you're urgently needed at the Hurley house—Mrs. Hurley is ill something dreadful!" she cried.

I grabbed my bag and followed her. She had a carriage waiting. At the house, the sick woman's sister, Gloria Hobson, met me. As she hurriedly led me to the sick woman's bedroom, she explained that Mr. Hurley was out of town on business.

We entered the tastefully decorated room, but I must confess I did not pay much attention to my surrounds. The woman in the bed caught my attention immediately. I surmised that she was a fairly attractive woman under normal circumstances. Now she bore the waxy pallor of the very ill.

"Mrs. Hurley, I'm Dr. Watson," I said, taking her hand and automatically checking her pulse. It was rapid. "Can you tell me your symptoms, please?"

Her voice was weak and barely audible. I had to lean close to hear her.

"And I can't see clearly," she said. "Things are blurry, and can't keep anything down. I feel so sick." She stopped talking to catch her breath, which was coming in short, rapid gasps. "M-my tongue's numb."

"What have you eaten today?" I asked.

She shook her head. "Nothing," she muttered softly.

"We were on our way home from the dentist when she started feeling sick," said Miss Hobson. "I helped her home and sent for you."

I must confess I was rather mystified. What struck me as most significant was the similarity between this lady's symptoms and those of the three cases I had read about earlier. Could she have been poisoned? The sister seemed genuinely concerned for her welfare and I thought it unlikely that she was the culprit. Dr. Morley had not recorded numbness or blurred vision in the other cases, but the speed of the patient's deterioration was the same. I was highly suspicious. It was fortunate the husband was away, or he would have been my first suspect.

If it was poison, how was it administered? She had not ingested it. I examined her arms for signs of a needle prick, but her skin was blemish free. I was baffled. This bemusement did not stop me from acting though. I considered using an emetic on her, but decided against it. She was too weak and had already been vomiting. Any digested substance would have been evacuated long before now. Instead, with the help of her sister, we forced her to drink charcoal. This substance has a highly absorbent quality and is especially good for neutralizing noxious substances in the stomach. It was all to no avail. I tried everything I could think of, yet her condition continued to decline. Without actually knowing what the substance was I could hardly administer an antidote, even if I had a supply of it. In the end, in desperation, I called in the housemaid who had fetched me and wrote out a telegram to Holmes, asking her to dispatch it immediately. After which I returned to my patient.

II.

Holmes arrived within the hour. His eyes were bright with curiosity and the eagerness of a bloodhound about to be given a scent. His prominent nose and long, lean torso seemed to quiver in anticipation of this scent. He arrived ten minutes before Mrs. Hurley died.

"So, what is the emergency, Watson?" he asked, his eyes going to my patient.

'She's dying, Holmes, and there is nothing I can do. I think she's been poisoned. She hasn't ingested anything. There are no needle marks on her arms, yet to all intents and purposes she has the symptoms of poisoning. I would bet every penny I had on it."

Holmes moved across to the woman, whose breathing now came in ragged gasps. "How long has she been like this?"

"The first symptoms started three hours ago. I've been here for two of them. She lapsed into a coma within the last half hour."

"What was she doing prior to her collapse?"

"Nothing. She was on her way home from the dentist. She hadn't stopped to eat anything. Her sister was with her. She collapsed when she was halfway home."

"The dentist?" Holmes leaned forward eagerly and opened the woman's mouth. He studied her intensely. "Looks like two fillings."

"Surely you don't think it's from the dentist?"

"I don't think anything yet, Watson. I'm just gathering data." Holmes examined her arms, and also her feet and in between her toes.

"What are you looking for?"

"Injection marks. If you inject someone between the toes no one will ever think to look there. There are none though." He sniffed the air and asked: "Did you keep some of her emesis?"

"Yes, in a jar. I meant to have it tested later."

"Good. I can do that. There are various alkaloids around that can cause similar symptoms to what she is exhibiting. You should read my monograph on poisons." He stepped away from her. She had not responded to his examination. Indeed, she was not conscious of his presence.

"Holmes, the reason I called you so promptly is that this is the fourth case in the last six months."

"What?" Holmes turned a surprised face to me.

"I was reading some of Dr. Morley's past histories and came across three similar cases to this. One was Morley's own wife. All three died rapidly."

"Had they been to the dentist?" asked Holmes with interest.

"The notes didn't say."

"I want to talk to the sister. Where's the husband?"

"Away on business. Not expected back until tomorrow. Husbands are always the first to be suspected, but he's in the clear this time."

"Hmm." Holmes looked at my patient, his eyes thoughtful. At that moment the sister entered. She looked askance at Holmes.

"Miss Hobson, this is Mr. Sherlock Holmes," I introduced.

Her eyes widened in surprise. "Sherlock Holmes, the detective?"

"Yes," said Holmes. "Can you tell me exactly what happened today—from the moment you arose until her collapse?"

She appeared startled, but answered readily enough. "Not a lot happened. We had breakfast at seven. Dorothy always invites me to stay over when her husband is away. She feels scared when she's alone."

"Why?"

"Oh, ever since some burglars broke in and attacked her. Fortunately there was a constable passing the house. He heard her screams and came to the rescue."

"How long ago was this?"

"Six, maybe seven months ago."

"Continue."

"Well, like I said, we had breakfast, then we went into town.

We did a little shopping, filling in time until it was time for Dorothy's dentist appointment. She'd been troubled with tooth-ache lately. The dentist—Mr. Carlyle is new to the area, but I hear he is very good."

"Did you both eat the same food for breakfast?"

"Yes. It is served on a platter and we just helped ourselves."

"Who made the appointment for the dentist?"

"Her husband."

"What does Mr. Hurley do for a living?"

"He is an insurance investigator. That is why he has to travel occasionally."

"I see. She was well until she visited the dentist?'

"Never better."

"How long was she with him?"

"Nearly an hour."

"Was she alone with him?"

"Oh no. I was there. She hates going to the dentist. I always have to go with her. Same with doctors."

"Did he give her any injections or fluid to drink?"

"No."

"She had two fillings?"

"Yes. He said he didn't have to pull the offending tooth out."

"He was in your sight the whole time?"

"Yes."

"You saw him mix the fillings?"

"Yes."

"Did you notice anything unusual during this procedure?"

"No—not really. Why all these questions?"

"Bear with me please, Miss Hobson," said Holmes. "Dr. Watson here has reason to suspect poison, and I agree with him."

"Poison!" she gasped, her eyes turning to her sister in horror.

"So you left the dentist after an hour. What happened then?"

"We thought we would walk home, it being such a nice day. We were halfway here when she complained of feeling sick and dizzy. She said her mouth was numb. She couldn't go on. I hailed a cab, and as soon as we got home I sent for the doctor."

"What were relations like between your sister and her husband?"

"All right, I suppose. They had their differences, but all married people do."

"Was she happy?"

The woman's face clouded a little. "I'm not sure. She really didn't discuss her married life with me...although, once or twice, she did say that I didn't know how lucky I was to be single."

"Did her husband ever physically hurt her?"

"Not that I am aware of."

"What do you think of him—personally?"

Her lips tightened. "I can't say I am over fond of him. I only meet Dorothy when he is away, or she visits me. He has always resented our closeness."

"What company does he work for?"

"United Kingdom Insurance."

Suddenly the patient convulsed, white froth bubbling from her mouth, and then she became still as she stopped breathing. I hurried forward, but there was nothing I could do.

Miss Hobson let out a wail of distress and ran to her side, clutching her sister's hand.

I patted her on the shoulder comfortingly. "I'm sorry."

Her eyes burned with grief as she turned to face Holmes. "If Hurley is in any way responsible for her death, I want you to get him, Mr. Holmes. Spare no expense. I want you to get the villain responsible for this."

"I'll do my best, Miss Hobson." Holmes left the room whilst I did my best to comfort the grieving woman. He was outside in the street by the time I joined him nearly half an hour later.

III.

"I'd like to see the records of the other dead women, Watson," he said, as soon as I joined him.

"Um.... I don't know if I can do that, Holmes. They're confidential."

"But if you suspect poisoning in all four cases, then the law can subpoena those records. I need more information, Watson."

I hesitated a moment and deliberated. Finally I decided that as the women were dead, quite possibly murdered, then I owed it to them to supply the information to Holmes. "All right, we'll go back to the clinic."

As we walked, Holmes said: "I spoke to the servants while you were occupied."

"Anything interesting?"

"Yes. Seems Mrs. Hurley was not happily married. She and her husband argued often. She was driven to tears many a time."

"But the husband couldn't have poisoned her, he is out of town," I pointed out.

"Hmm," was his noncommittal reply.

Back at the surgery, Holmes took up the histories and began to study them. After a long while, he said, "I'm surprised Dr. Morley didn't suspect poison. It is also curious that his own wife died of the same symptoms."

"Well he couldn't have poisoned Mrs. Hurley, he's in Switzerland."

Did he tell you why he was going there?"

"Yes. He told me his wife had died recently and he needed to get away for a while."

"I see." He turned back to the files, then after a moment muttered, "Interesting...I wonder...." His eyes took a faraway introspective look as he became lost in his thoughts.

I was loath to interrupt him so I busied myself with some paperwork.

Abruptly Holmes woke from his reverie and came over to me

saying, "Punch me in the jaw will you, Watson."

"What?" I stared at him, startled by his request.

"Punch me in the jaw. I want to have reason to visit the dentist."

"Can't you just pretend to have a toothache?" I asked, reluctant to punch my best friend.

"No. If he is a good dentist, he will know I'm faking it. If I've been punched, I can claim I'm worried about a loose tooth."

"I don't want to punch you Holmes," I replied.

His lips quirked into a grin. "I am glad about that, but for art's sake, realism and all that sort of thing, I beseech you to do it. Otherwise, I will have to go out and start a brawl with some innocent."

I sighed, drew back my fist and punched him. The hit turned his head slightly.

"Call that a punch?" he jibed. "A five-year-old girl could hit harder than that. Call yourself a man? You really are a pathetic excuse for a...."

I struck again, much harder this time. Holmes took several steps back from it I was pleased to note.

He rubbed his jaw. "That's better. I don't know that I'd really want to get on your bad side, old chap. You've got a punch like a mule kick." He was still feeling at his jaw, and then checked his teeth. "I'll be damned!" he exclaimed.

"What?"

"I think you really have loosened a tooth."

My eyes widened. "Oh, I am so sorry, Holmes. You shouldn't have said those things."

"That was the whole idea."

I shook my head. Who could ever figure Holmes? Anyone else would have been furious. He was happy.

"Well—I'm off to the dentist, after having been attacked by a brute of a doctor." He grinned at me.

I would have liked to have gone with him, but there were patients in the waiting room.

IV.

After Holmes left, I had little time to fret, as I was busy attending to the patients. The last left by half past five and I was becoming rather anxious. What was keeping Holmes? I wondered if I should close the office and go home, or wait here for him. Also, my belly was growling. I had missed lunch. I decided to wait another half hour, and then return to the Morley residence. Holmes could always find me there.

I was just locking the door when I heard Holmes's voice. "Have you got the vomit, Watson?"

"The...?" I turned around in surprise. Then it clicked. "Oh, in the office." I unlocked the door again and collected Mrs. Hurley's specimen.

"Feel like some dinner, Watson," he asked, rather cheerily I thought.

"Well and truly," I handed Holmes the jar.

He looked at it and added, "Perhaps you could put it in a bag? I don't think the restaurant would approve our having a jar of vomit on the table."

"I don't think I am much taken with the idea, either," I said, finding a paper bag.

* * * * * * *

We discovered a quaint little Italian restaurant, found a table by the window and ordered. As we sat sipping our aperitifs, I said, "So how did it go? From your manner I am assuming you have had a successful day."

"It certainly wasn't a waste," he agreed.

"So?" I prodded.

He smiled. "Well, I went to the dentist holding my poor aching jaw and told the receptionist it was an emergency. I got in to see him fairly quickly. Dr. Thomas Carlyle is a rather personable man and skilled at his work. He fixed my tooth quite expertly.

"'So, Mr. Witherspoon,' said he, 'how did you loosen your tooth?' I looked up and told him I'd had an encounter with a tradesman when he tried to overcharge me. The lout had struck me when I was unprepared, I said. He commiserated with me. We had a nice little chat. He told me he used to have a practice in Hampstead, but wanted to live closer to London. He's been in practice in Epping for the last six months. I asked him if he had settled in and made friends in the area and he said he had—other professional gentlemen. He asked me what I did. I told him I was a jeweler. That was pretty much it. He was very quick in his ministrations. Gave me a large bill and sent me on my way."

"Is that all?" I asked, surprised. This seemed rather paltry. Hardly worth being punched in the jaw.

"Almost. As I was paying my bill, I chatted with the receptionist. I asked her if Mrs. Morley, Mrs. Boyce, and Mrs. Presnell had visited the dentist in the last six months. She was surprised by the question but answered yes to it anyway. I mentioned, just in passing what a nice fellow Mr. Carlyle seemed to be, and how I hoped he wasn't too lonely settling into a new territory. She told me that he wasn't in the least bit lonely as he had been keeping company with Mrs. Presnell quite a bit—she was a widow."

"'Have you seen her around lately?' I asked. The question made her think. 'No, not lately,' she said. At that moment another customer came in and I took the opportunity to leave."

"Did they die the same day that they visited the dentist?" I asked.

"Not sure. I could hardly ask the girl for the exact dates. I will pay the office a visit later on. Care to join me?"

"If you like," I agreed. "So is the dentist the murderer, Holmes?"

"If the other three had visited him on the day of their deaths, it will look highly suspicious for him. However, I still need method and motive."

"Yet, if he did do it, what possible reason could he have for murdering those four women? It is all a mystery to me," I said.

Holmes smiled faintly. "And a suitable brain teaser for me. Thank you, Watson for bringing it to my attention. I was dying of boredom in Baker Street."

"That reminds me, what took you so long? I'm sure you weren't at the dentist's this whole time."

"No, I paid a few visits. I once handled an investigation for United Kingdom Insurance. They promised to look up some information for me. They think very highly of Jack Hurley. He is definitely away on business by the way. He sent them a telegram around eleven this morning. His wife took ill around twelve-thirty. There is no way he could come from Dunsmead to here in that time, so he is in the clear as the actual murderer. Certainly in this instance, anyway."

"In this instance? What do you mean?"

"Watson, Watson, Watson. You have heard what I have heard. You have seen what I have seen. Try and figure it out for yourself," said Holmes, refusing to say anymore on the subject.

We enjoyed our meal, after which we went to Baker Street so that Holmes could test the specimen. Whilst he set about organizing his equipment, I helped myself to his monograph on poisons, deciding now was as good a time as any to familiarize myself.

V.

Holmes worked quietly for an hour, and then grunted with disgust. He turned off his burner and came over to join me by the fire. "Nothing! Not one ounce of any known poison."

"Perhaps she expelled it with her first vomit," I suggested.

"Then she would have recovered. "No," Holmes shook his head, "there still should have been a trace." He took up his pipe and threw himself down into his armchair, lapsing into a brooding silence.

"Well, I didn't think she ingested it anyway. Perhaps we

should have taken a blood sample," I suggested.

"I wouldn't be surprised if that came up negative as well. After all, she wasn't injected, either."

"There are various ways for a person to absorb something," I began, in my best medical lecturer tone. "Through the skin, the mucous membranes, the...."

"That is it!" cried Holmes; his eyes alight with sudden excitement. "What a sluggish goat I've been. She complained of tingling in the mouth did she not?"

"Yes."

"The mucous membranes in the mouth are amongst the most absorbent in the human body. The poison was in the fillings. We'll have to get them."

"Are you mad? You cannot go pulling teeth out of a dead woman—why, that's sacrilegious!"

"I'm not about to pull *all* her teeth out—just two," argued Holmes. "I need them to test. If I hadn't been so abysmally slow, I could have got them earlier. Do you know which funeral parlor they have taken her to?"

"No."

"Never mind, it should be easy enough to work out. After all, she is likely to be at the closest one."

"Are you forgetting you were planning on breaking into the dentist's office tonight?" I said.

"We can do both." Holmes's eyes glinted. "Are you game, Watson?"

Like a fool, I said yes, even though I did not relish the idea of breaking into a funeral parlor.

"Do you have any tooth pulling tools?" asked Holmes.

"No."

"Never mind, we'll steal some from the dentist's while we're there."

I sighed. This was getting worse by the minute.

We changed into our burglar clothes—dark trousers, polo neck jumpers and dark coats. Holmes checked his lock picks and dark lantern, whilst I carried a jimmy, just in case force was needed. Holmes was grinning. I secretly thought that he enjoyed these forays to the other side of the law. He loved the thrill and excitement of such nerve-wracking endeavors. There is many the time that he has said that he would have made a good criminal, and I have no doubt of it. He would have been a formidable foe indeed. I sometimes wondered if he ever regretted being on the side of the law. In fact I asked him once.

"The only problem with my being a criminal is that I would have no incentive. The lure of riches does not appeal to me," he had said. "It is hardly worth risking life and liberty for material gains if one does not care for them. And to steal for art's sake is a poor motive for a life of crime. I'm afraid I couldn't work up the enthusiasm to break the law just for the sake of it. I have to have a reason for my actions."

We made our way back to Epping, stopped the cab two streets away from our destination, and walked to the dentist's surgery. At the back door, Holmes made short work of the lock. Inside, I went to the surgery to collect a pair of tooth-pulling forceps, while Holmes examined the appointment book.

"Any luck?" I asked, joining him.

"Yes indeed. All four visited the dentist the same day they died. I would sat that it is more than a coincidence. Now I am even more convinced that the poison is in the fillings."

"So it's the funeral home next?"

"Mmm. There are two in this area. The nearest is The Eternal Rest funeral parlor."

VI.

At The Eternal Rest, we had to take a risk and enter the front door, as the back was barred. I kept lookout while Holmes picked the lock. It was a rather complicated one and he had difficulty with it.

"Why are they so security conscious?" I whispered. "It's not like anyone would want to steal their merchandise."

"Not the coffins perhaps, but many customers are buried with jewelry on. They are easy pickings for thieves."

"How ghoulish."

"It's a living," shrugged Holmes. Considering that he was about to rob the dead woman of her teeth, I supposed that he was hardly in a position to criticize other grave robbers.

I was breathing heavily by the time we entered as I had spotted a constable on his beat up near the end of the street. The last thing I wanted was to be seen breaking in. We passed through the reception area and crept towards the back rooms. There were two empty tables and one that was occupied. Holmes pulled back the sheet—it was Mrs. Hurley. He had guessed right—sorry, deduced correctly. He claimed he never guessed.

"Rip out the teeth, Watson," ordered Holmes.

"No, I can't," I replied, feeling suddenly squeamish despite having seen numerous dead bodies both in my practice and in the army. I just felt that this was a desecration.

Holmes threw me a curious glance, and then took the forceps from me and handed me the dark lantern instead. "You hold the light then." He bent to his task and located the two teeth with the new fillings.

I grimaced at the noise he made as he wrenched the teeth out. Lucky she was dead, I thought, otherwise she'd be screaming blue murder.

Holmes dropped the teeth into an envelope and pocketed it.

"Shh," I hissed, just as he was about to speak. "I heard something." I quickly extinguished the lantern as Holmes moved silently towards the door. He peeked out, then hurriedly closed the door.

"It's the constable," he whispered just as softly.

I looked around the barren room with its tiny windows that we could never fit through. We were trapped. Holmes also glanced around, but unlike me, his fertile imagination came up with a solution.

"Quick, up on the tables."

We grabbed a sheet each and jumped up onto the hard

wooden tables, throwing the sheets over us as we lay down. Not a moment too soon, either. I had barely covered myself before I heard the door open. I held my breath, absolutely petrified of being caught.

I could hear his heavy footsteps as he clumped around the room. I saw the light of his lantern through the sheet as he shone it around. It seemed to rest on me for an eternity. I could feel my nose itching and a sneeze startling to well, when suddenly there was the most gosh awful moan.

It was chilling.

It was eerie.

It sounded like a fiend from hell. I nearly leapt up and ran for it, dredging up all my nerve to remain still.

The young constable gave a howl of fright and ran from the room.

I pulled my sheet down to see Holmes sitting up, sheet still over his head, and moaning like a banshee with abdominal pains.

"Holmes!"

He pulled the sheet down and laughed heartily.

"You and your practical jokes," I said, climbing down from the table. "Honestly, you are worse than a schoolboy sometimes."

He just grinned at me.

We left by the back door this time and had to walk several blocks before we found a cab willing to take us to Baker Street. Most were on their way home for the night. It was nearly two a.m.

* * * * * * *

Back at Baker Street, we fortified ourselves with a sherry, and then I settled down before the fire, while Holmes went to work on the teeth.

I must have dozed off, for the first rays of light were shinning through our window when I woke to the feel of Holmes's hand on my shoulder. He looked bright-eyed and rested, despite having been awake all night.

"You *are* right, Watson," he said. "She was poisoned. I have found traces of Aconitum napellus, or Aconite as it's known."

"What is it? I've never heard of it?" I blinked the sleep from my eyes and sat up straighter.

"It's a common garden plant, also known as monk's blood or wolf's bane. Its leaves look like parsley and its roots look like horseradish. It's an alkaloid and extremely poisonous. Symptoms can appear within eight minutes of absorption and death occurs in several hours. A large dose kills instantly."

"It sounds deadly."

"It is deadly. It is one of the oldest known poisons. Very popular with the Greeks and Romans of ancient times. Look at this—" Holmes motioned me over to his chemical bench.

He held up a tooth under the light. "See this discoloration, that is the aconite. He cleverly made a paste of it and applied it to the base of the filling so that when pressed down into the tooth, it would be rapidly absorbed into the bloodstream. That's why I couldn't find traces in the abdominal contents. That is also why you wouldn't have been able to save her, even if you had an antidote. Although, to my knowledge, there is no anti-dote to this poison."

"What about the other women?"

"I'd say they died the same way. They all visited the dentist on the day of their deaths. No doubt they had fillings. Perhaps we should...."

"No!" I cut in adamantly, reading his mind. "It was bad enough going to the funeral parlor. I am not going to dig up the other ladies and pull their teeth out."

Holmes smiled faintly and countered, "It would conclusively prove cause of death."

"But we already have him on one charge of murder. That's enough to hang him. Besides, once it is brought to their atten-tion, the police can always exhume the bodies legally," I argued.

Holmes shrugged. "I suppose."

"No suppose about it."

"You're just worried that they'll rise out of their graves," he teased.

"With you around, it wouldn't surprise me," I rejoined caustically.

He chuckled. "All right, you win."

"Are you going to report him to the police today?"

"No. I still need a motive. It is easy enough to deduce why he murdered Mrs. Presnell, but...."

"Easy? No it's not. Why did he kill her?"

"You always want everything handed to you on a platter, Watson. Think. Use your mind. Use your imagination. You said you wanted to become a writer; well, you need imagination for that. Exercise your brain cells."

I sighed. It was easy for him. "I suppose you've got the whole mystery solved already," I grumbled.

He smiled. "Just about. Still need to tie up a few loose ends. It is one thing to theorize, but one cannot take theories to court. I can convict Carlyle, but not the others."

"Others?"

Holmes ignored the question. "Still, it is quite an interesting little plot. Thank you for introducing me to it, Watson."

"You're welcome. What's this about the others?"

"Think about it, Watson. It really is too easy. Elementary even."

It was so irritating when he was being smug. I just sighed with frustration.

VII.

I had breakfast at Baker Street, and then returned to Epping to put in a weary day's work. By four o'clock, my eyes were drooping. I did not know how Holmes could stay up all night and day and look so chipper. At eight o'clock that evening I was thinking of turning in for an early night, when Holmes turned up.

"Though you might like to know the latest developments," he said without preamble.

"Yes, of course." I offered him a cigar and we made ourselves comfortable.

"I went out to Hampstead today. Carlyle told the truth. He did have a practice there. Left after his wife died—suddenly."

"Oh!" My eyes widened with surprise.

Holmes nodded grimly. "I'd say he perfected his technique on her. Her life was insured with guess who?"

"United Kingdom Insurance?"

"Spot on, and the investigator was none other than Jack Hurley."

I thought for a moment. "That doesn't make sense, Holmes. If Hurley became suspicious of him, why would Carlyle kill his wife? Surely it would be more logical to kill Hurley himself?"

"Oh, Hurley was suspicious all right, but he approved the policy. He had no intention of turning Carlyle in. You are forgetting that other attempt on Mrs. Hurley's life."

"What attempt?"

"The burglars, Watson. That wasn't a random attack. It happened seven months ago. Hurley tried to have his wife killed and make it look like strangers did it. All employees of United Kingdom are given policies for themselves and their spouses. He made a deal with Carlyle when he investigated his claim. 'Come to Epping and kill my wife, and I'll approve your policy,' he probably said."

"That's outrageous!"

"But plausible. It also leaves the husband in the clear, as he was out of town when his wife died. He has the perfect alibi."

"All right, I grant you that your theory works for Hurley and Carlyle's wife, but what about Mrs. Presnell, Mrs. Boyce, and Mrs. Morley?"

"Ah, that's a little more complicated. All the ladies had policies on them with United Kingdom. Mrs. Presnell was also independently wealthy. When she died, Carlyle was her beneficiary. Now do you have any guesses as to why she was killed?"

"He wanted her money."

"Correct. He ingratiated himself with the widow, and then killed her. Probably offered her free dental services."

"That still doesn't explain the other two," I reminded him.

"Surely it is obvious?"

"To you maybe, but not to me."

"That is because you are too trusting in human nature," said Holmes, but the way he said it made it sound as if this trait was more a failing than a asset. "Any doctor worth his salt would suspect poison, just as you did. They might miss one patient, but not four. Coincidental deaths would make an honest doctor suspicious. They would report their suspicions to the police, unless...."

"He was in on it too!" I exclaimed excitedly, finally seeing the way Holmes's reasoning was going.

"Exactly. He certified the deaths as heart failure. Hurley approved the insurance claims, and Boyce, the lawyer, ensured that the wills were in the husband's favor—or as in Carlyle's case, in his favor. I've seen Mrs. Presnell's will, it is a forgery and a fairly poor one at that, but as she had no relatives, there was no risk of anyone contesting the will. He probably did it as payment for Carlyle killing his wife. All four were in it together."

"That's incredible." I was shocked by the thought of a group of supposedly respectable men joining forces to murder their wives systematically. "They're all pillars of the community—a lawyer, doctor, dentist and insurance investigator. Who would have thought?"

"Greed doesn't discriminate," replied Holmes a trifle cynically. "The four are good friends, and are often seen together."

"Have you told the police yet?"

"No, I'll go tomorrow."

Congratulations, Holmes," I said warmly.

"No, it is you who should be congratulated, Watson. If you hadn't picked up on it and noticed the other details these scoundrels would have got off scot free."

I smiled. "It's living with you, Holmes. Your suspicious nature has rubbed off on me."

"I wish I could say the same. Your trustful nature has not rubbed off on me," he replied, smiling faintly.

* * * * * * *

Boyce, Hurley, and Carlyle were arrested the next day. The bodies of their wives were exhumed and their teeth checked. All had been killed by aconite poisoning, with the poison secreted in the fillings. I finished my eight-week stint and when Dr. Morley returned home, reported his return to the police. I could barely keep a straight face when he greeted me. It was extremely difficult being civil to the blackguard.

In due course, all four were hung, and Miss Hobson paid us a visit to thank Holmes. The papers made much of the case. I was rather touched when the first story came out. Holmes had been interviewed and he insisted that the case was solved largely due to me. I knew this wasn't exactly true, but Holmes always was generous, and it made me feel proud to be associated with him.

As to becoming a writer? Well, I have decided that I will set some of Holmes' extraordinary cases down on paper. It is the least I owe him. The world should be told about this most remarkable man. I will report the facts as I encounter them and let the readers form their own opinion.

THE FURY

BY LYN McCONCHIE

We were at breakfast when we heard a loud voice, the thump of footsteps towards our door, and a familiar figure appeared.

I rose in surprise to greet our visitor—while Holmes, who tends to the phlegmatic, especially around breakfast—remained seated.

"Colonel Ross!" I exclaimed. "What are you doing here, has something happened to Silver Blaze again?"

The Colonel shook his head. "No, he is still at stud, producing some excellent foals but it's a strange business—and has to do with his son."

I was somewhat perplexed. "Whose son, Colonel?"

"Why, Silver Blaze's colt of course. The Fury."

I was horrified. The colt was in his third year now; a magnificent animal and bidding fair to beat even the records set by his sire. The previous year he had stormed down tracks all over the country, winning again and again, so that the name of Colonel Ross was spoken of with awe at his good fortune in possessing first the sire, and then the colt of so great a line.

"Don't say something has happened to The Fury?" I protested. "It would be the greatest loss to horse racing England has seen. A horse like that should—must—carry on his line."

The Colonel slumped into the nearest chair and mutely accepted the cup of tea Holmes passed to him, and accepted also a piece of toast that he loaded with butter and marmalade and began to eat absent-mindedly.

"It is worse than that. If I cannot recover what has vanished then The Fury is useless to me. He will not race, he refuses to allow any jockey to remain on his back, and he does not eat well and is losing condition."

Holmes finished his toast, drained the last drop of tea from his cup and thrust back his chair. "It seems you have a story to tell, Colonel. Begin."

The Colonel squirmed. "It is not easy to confess, but The Fury is Silver Blaze's first colt. I was there at his birth and the moment he fought his way to his feet it was clear he was born to race. Every line was quality, from every angle he was a champion. An experienced horseman can see the potential in a newborn foal, just for the few minutes after the animal's birth. That is why I was present. My trainer and I could only stare and know that Silver Blaze had bred true. But there was one problem."

"What was that, Colonel?" I asked.

"The Fury's dam was Maid of Athens. She comes from a line notorious for their savagery. Her sire killed two stable lads, Maid of Athens crippled another and injured several during her racing career and it was her intractability that caused her owner to retire her early to the breeding paddock. Silver Blaze is without that sort of vice but a foal learns from his dam. We racehorse owners have a saying, 'speed from the sire, temper from the dam' and it proved to be true.

"As he grew older The Fury became more difficult to handle until finally, in a battle between the animal and my trainer who was endeavoring to break him to saddle. The Fury pulled a tendon and was put out to rest in a small paddock at the back of the stables. This is screened from the stables themselves by a tall solid hedge and as the animal had a three-sided shelter in the paddock, he was normally seen only once a day, in the evening, when a small amount of hay was brought to him.

"I was staying in the area and unexpectedly drove over to talk to the trainer, a James Hammond. After the business with Hammond I cleared out the staff and took on this man together with his family. He is a good man, married to a woman whose father was a trainer so she knows and understands horses herself, and his son too, while currently a stable-boy there, bids to be a promising jockey and I had it in mind for the lad and The Fury to be trained together.

"In addition, Hammond had hired on two extra stable-boys, both of whom I may say were terrified of The Fury and quite useless in handling him. I had spoken with Hammond and while at the stables wished to see The Fury, so Hammond and I walked down the property and passed through the hedge, not at the usual gate, but through a convenient gap at the far end— since we had been that way looking at another of my horses. Thus the lad we caught had no idea of our presence."

"Caught, Colonel?"

"Aye, caught. But doing something I would have believed no one could attempt and be unharmed. He was standing directly behind The Fury, disentangling burrs from his tail while the colt stood placid as an old donkey, and when the job was finished the boy walked to The Fury's head and that savage beast dropped his head into the lad's shirt and stood there as if communing with a friend. I was astounded—but I am no fool, though I say so myself. I caught back Hammond by the arm, cautioning him to silence, for it occurred to me on the instant that here was the perfect stable lad for The Fury.

"Find out who he is, and hire him." I hissed to Hammond.

"Sir, he looks to be very young."

I looked at the boy again and had to agree. He appeared to be perhaps twelve years of age and of very slight build, yet I have seen other lads no larger and if he could handle The Fury so confidently I cared not if he be a babe in arms and no bigger than a dwarf.

"Find him, hire him," I ordered Hammond. "I think he is a whisperer, and if he can deal with The Fury as it seems, pay him a good wage. I want him to have no reason to change stables."

"And your man found the boy." Holmes said, "The lad has now gone missing, and The Fury will not work without him."

"That is most unhappily true, sir. He vanished two weeks ago and since then The Fury has never cleaned up a meal, he has attempted to savage anyone who approaches him and no jockey, not even my trainer's son is able to stay on the animal. He is entered in one of the major races in two month's time. If we do not find the boy and return him to The Fury, the horse will be in no condition to race, I will lose a fortune and I will be a laughing stock for I have wagered heavily on The Fury in private bets as well as public ones."

"But have you not asked the lad's family?" I questioned the Colonel.

"Of course," he snapped. "That is, we could not find them, but we have looked for them."

Holmes nodded. "I think you had best go back to the beginning of your tale again and tell me how your man found the boy and persuaded him to work for you, if your man told you of that?"

"I have the tale from Hammond indeed. According to him he followed the boy across several fields until he reached a broken-down gypsy caravan. As you know, the moor is sometimes home to a number of gypsies. He presumed the lad was one of them and, as they are usually poor to starving, and the offer of a well-paid job would be seized, he approached the caravan confidently. He was met by an old woman who glared at him.

"'What's thee want hereabouts, mester?'

"'I want to hire your grandson,' Hammond said, indicating the lad who had appeared around a corner of the caravan.

"'Does thee, for what?'

"'As stable boy to The Fury, the colt owned by Colonel Ross.'

"The crone seemed much amused. "'Thee knows he be good wi' horses then?'

"The Colonel and I saw him handle the colt. The Colonel will pay a pound a week to the lad."

I nodded in reply to Ross's look at me. That was an excellent wage, twice, even three times what a stable lad could expect usually, but if the boy could handle a dangerous horse like that he'd have been worth every penny."

The old woman nodded. "Aye, then thee'll have him. But he comes home nights to me here else he don't go. I be too old to live alone an' I needs my grandson to help me evenings."

Colonel Ross's gaze met mine and he shrugged. "It was irregular, but if the boy could do what was required then it was worth meeting that condition. Hammond agreed, and the boy arrived the following morning at five. By the time Hammond was out there the lad had The Fury back in a stall, fed, watered, groomed, and standing quiet.

"In the next few weeks the horse was a changed animal. He would do anything the lad asked of him, and his training was easy. Hammond supervised but the boy, we were told his name was Joe Farr, did all the work. In a few more months Hammond's lad, Matthew, was riding The Fury in training—and so long as Joe was present The Fury was completely tractable. It was like a miracle and I thanked God for it."

"It is not so greatly uncommon," I said. "I have known of other cases. You are a horseman and will know of Lady Jane's Son. He would not race without his stable cat being present at the track. When she had kittens they played about his hooves and he was always careful never to harm one. The cat died, but her daughter took over and went with the horse when he was retired to stud."

"That is true, and I have known cases where the horse was rendered tractable with a stable companion that was a donkey, a pony, or even a goat. As you say, it is not unknown, but in my case it is now most inconvenient."

"So what happened?"

"Nothing for a long time. All appeared amicability. The lad was courteous when I visited and appeared utterly devoted to The Fury. Why, when some tout sneaked into the stables and attempted to bribe the boy to drug The Fury, he shouted for Hammond and my man says the lad was in a complete passion so that he had to pull him from the tout's throat. When The Fury was once ill the boy remained with him day and night until the horse was well again. I queried that he had been permitted to do so, and he said that he had spoken with his grandam and she had agreed since he loved the horse so greatly. The colt ran five times in his second year with Matthew Hammond riding him, and won four of the races. A great future looked likely for him."

"What then?"

"That is what I do not know!" cried Colonel Ross in exasperation. "There appeared to be some small tiff with another of the stable-boys. Hammond says he found them struggling one evening. He pulled them apart and asked what the trouble was; neither would say what had begun the quarrel, so he sent Joe home and the other lad to his bed. In the morning Joe did not return. Hammond sought out the caravan but it was gone—and from that day to this he has seen and heard nothing of Joe or his grandmother."

Here he wrenched his collar. "If I do not have the boy back, The Fury will not race. I can use him for breeding, but his best years for racing are now and as yet his reputation on the track is not all it could be. The fees I could charge are yet low. Find Joe Farr for me, Mr. Holmes, and I will pay and pay well. Can you do this thing?"

"What if the boy will not return, or asks for certain conditions?"

"I will meet almost any condition he may ask if only he will return. I will double his wage, sack the lad with whom he quarreled, allow his grandmother to have her caravan on my land so none may move her on, only persuade him back."

Holmes smiled briefly. "You are not a completely conventional man, are you, Colonel Ross?"

The Colonel stared. "I suppose I am not, Mr. Holmes. I'm a hard man perhaps, but a just one, I believe. If you are suggesting that Joe has been dishonest in some way and fled to avoid retribution, tell him that I know of no harm he has done me. If he has harmed another, I will stand for him. You know, Holmes, I liked the lad. He was a hard worker, never shirked his duty, and cared for The Fury as if he were his own. He had courage too.

I've seen The Fury panic, kicking and rearing, and Joe went in under flying hooves cool as you please to soothe the colt and bring him down. He's the sort of lad I'd have taken as many of as I could enlist for my old cavalry unit."

"Then I shall do my best." Holmes answered him. "Call here again in three days and I may have news for you. Meanwhile, please write a note for Hammond instructing him to allow me every access to the stables and his staff."

"At once, sir." I provided paper, pen and ink and Colonel Ross dashed off a brief note, dusted the ink dry, folded and sealed the sheet of paper and handed it to Holmes. "Here you are, sir. And I shall wait on you again in three days."

He strode out energetically and I turned to my old friend. "You have some idea already, do you not?"

He nodded. "The name of Farr is a gypsy name, but not as the Colonel believes it to be. The name is Faa; spelled as F A A and those of the line of Johnny Faa, who was a king amongst them a century ago, carry it. Years back I heard a scandal about a branch of the Faa family. The daughter wed a man who wasn't of their blood in any way; he was a blacksmith however, so the marriage was tolerated—but only the girl's mother remained in touch with her."

"And you wonder if Joe Farr is not the daughter's son, the old woman being the girl's mother?" I asked.

"Precisely. I must discover where the Boswell tribe has their *vardos* currently and speak to them. They may be able to tell me a considerable amount." As he was speaking Holmes vanished into his room and I heard his voice through the half-shut door.

"*Vardos*, Holmes?" I queried, "And will they talk to one who is not a gypsy?"

"A *vardo* is a caravan, Watson. And the gypsies will talk to me, I am known to them as an old friend under more than one name."

He then emerged and I stared. In every way he was a gypsy down to the small gold rings on his ears and the lurid-colored scarf about his neck. His face was swarthy, and even his hands and wrists were weathered to a deep brown.

"Holmes, it is wonderful!"

"It is convincing, that is more important." Holmes said dryly. "Meet Jack Smith of the Devonshire branch of the Smith tribe."

He pulled his scarf straighter and clattered down the stair in boots which I now saw, were old and slightly broken, with knotted laces. He did not return that day or night. But as I was brewing a pot of tea next morning he reappeared, looking tired.

"I was right, Watson. The old woman is Margaret Faa whose daughter, Leah, wed a blacksmith. He died twelve years later and his family cheated Leah of her inheritance and drove her and the child out. She returned to her people, but they demanded she remarry from amongst them and she refused since it would have meant that her child would have been forced to conform to Romany laws. In some altercation Leah was killed, and her mother then took her caravan and the child and left to wander alone."

"How long ago was that?" I queried.

"Almost four years."

I raised my brow in some surprise. "But Joe Farr has been working for more than a year for Colonel Ross. From what you say the lad must now be seventeen and Ross was convinced he was only twelve or thereabouts when he was hired."

"Gypsying can be a hard life," was all Holmes said to that.

"Where will you go now?"

"To Ross's stables. I would question Hammond, his family, and the lad with whom Joe Faa was quarrelling."

"And afterwards?"

"Afterwards I think I may have news for the Colonel."

"You have found the lad then?"

"I know where the caravan is, but it remains to be seen if I can convince them to return to King's Pyland. The old woman may not wish to bring the lad back, and he may not wish to come. There were reasons I suspect, for their departure, which reasons still apply."

That afternoon we departed for the moor. The journey is

arduous and it was not until the next day that we were able to seek out Hammond and question him.

Holmes began. "The lad, Joe Farr as you knew him, did he stand his watch one night in three as is your custom here?"

"He did, sir. He would return after the evening meal to his grandmother's caravan to see all safe there, then he would walk back after dark to stand his watch. By the time I was up in the morning he would have all shipshape with The Fury and would nap in the hay for a few hours. Several times after he first arrived I woke up in the early hours to check and see that he was watching according to his duty. Always, sir, he was awake and alert."

"What of his person, was he clean and tidy?"

"Indeed, sir. He washed regular and told me he took a bath each week at the caravan. I believed him, and his clothes were always well washed and neatly mended. I have to admit, sir, when first the Colonel insisted we hire the boy I was reluctant. But he stole nothing, and when a man attempted to bribe him to harm The Fury he attacked the man with such anger I must pull him away lest he commit bloody murder. I gave him his wages each week, fifteen shillings and two half crowns, and I believe he gave it all to his grandmother. He did not smoke or drink, and he was always quiet-spoken and polite. If all stable lads were like him, sir, the lot of a trainer would be much easier."

Holmes nodded slowly. "Colonel Ross said much the same. Now I would speak to your good wife." The lady was summoned, but could add nothing to her man's information—although I believed she knew something she was withholding. Yet, to my surprise, Holmes questioned her no further but allowed her to depart. After that her son appeared looking worried.

"I'm Matthew Hammond, sir, I understand you wish to question me?"

"I do," Holmes said.

I was looking the lad over as Holmes asked his questions and the boy replied, still with a concerned look upon his face. He was a good-looking boy of some five feet, eight inches, dressed in the country style. He was lean and small-boned, but fresh-faced, hard-muscled, and with an air of competence about him. I judged his age to be around twenty or so, and he had an honest, decent look about him that I liked immediately.

"What do you know of the missing lad?"

"Little enough, sir. He was a little shy for he seldom chattered, but he did his work very well, and all the horses would do more for him than for anyone else."

"Which perhaps caused resentment?" Holmes said quietly. The lad nodded. "The lad with whom he was quarrelling, is he one who might have resented Joe's abilities?" Again there came the wordless agreement. "Would you be pleased to see Joe back again?"

"I would that, sir. I miss him and so does The Fury. Joe and me always got on real well, and I gave Bob a beating after Dad told me about him quarrelling with Joe and trying to knock him about. Weren't no use though, Joe was gone and he mayn't come back."

"If he does, would you be glad of it?"

Matthew Hammond's face lit with hope. "You know where he is, sir? You'll get him to come home? Tell him if you find him as Matt says he should come back to us and there'll always be a place here."

Holmes dismissed the young man with a smile and turned to me. "The last piece of the puzzle, my dear Watson. Now we have only to seek out Margaret Faa and convince her and Joe that they should return to King's Pyland."

* * * * * * *

The dogcart we had used to reach the stables was waiting. Holmes took the reins and we returned in haste, a train took us to Poole in Dorset where we hired another vehicle and made our way to Morden heath. I was weary, but Holmes seemed tireless.

"Cheer up, Watson, we are almost there."

"Almost where?" I asked.

"Almost to where some of the Boswells are camped, and Margaret Faa with them." He flicked the pony lightly with the whip and we rattled over the rough heath track towards a clump of caravans surrounded by a ring of suspicious dogs, bored horses, and swarthy people who awaited our coming without signs of welcome.

Holmes halted the pony and looked at them. "I wish to see Margaret Faa, tell her Kooshto Bok is here." At that there was a burst of laughter and one of the men swaggered forward.

"Good luck is it?" Who are you to call himself that for a Romi?"

"Perhaps the *beng*," Holmes said. "Give her the word."

The man nodded and vanished among the caravans to return in minutes. "She'll speak to you. *Jal palla.*" We followed as ordered, winding through the vans until we walked down a long dip and around bracken clumps to emerge by a single caravan. Beside it grazed a skewbald pony, a plump and well cared for beast that looked us over and nickered hopefully. The man had left us here and I wondered what we should do now. Holmes produced a sugar lump from his pocket and fed the pony, then turned to the caravan and spoke quietly.

"Avel, joovel, dukker and roker."

An old woman peered at him from the window and snorted. "Who are you to bid me come out to talk and tell your fortune, *gaujo*?"

"No foreigner to your people, the Boswells have known me before."

"How do they call you then?"

"Jinomengro."

She nodded, "I know of you. I will come out and talk—but your fortune is your own."

"Maybe I'll tell you yours instead." She laughed an amazing laugh like that of a girl and disappeared back into the caravan to emerge seconds later to sit on the steps and survey us.

"So, why are you here, man who knows, and what is it that you know?"

Holmes seated himself comfortably on the grass. I followed suit more awkwardly, and he lit his pipe, blew out a cloud of smoke and started.

"Once there was a woman who loved a man of *sastera*." Here the old woman laughed appreciatively, and later Holmes explained that the word meant iron as was a pun on the man's trade as a blacksmith as well as a compliment on his physical abilities. "She wed him and it was not expressly forbidden since those who work as *komlomeskro* have magic. She bore him a child, but in time he died and his kinfolk drove her out saying that she was not of their breed and should inherit nothing."

"They were wrong."

"They paid," Holmes said quietly, "Did they not?"

"They paid," the old woman agreed. "Our curse on them— and all they had was gone over the years. But it did my daughter little good. She died, so I took the child and came away to live apart."

"Because you did not wish the child to be as the Romany, despised, apart, wed and bred too early and oft ill-used?"

"*Aava*," she nodded once, a short powerful downward jerk of her chin.

"Then a man offered the child employment. He would be well-paid, well-treated and valued and he would be let do the work he wished to do for he loves horses and can speak to them?"

"*Aava*."

"Until one he worked with uncovered the secret and would have used him ill, so that the child fled back to you and you took him on the road again. But behind him lies one who will die without him, one who loves with all his heart. Will you keep them apart?"

The door flung open and a slender girl in an explosion of skirts hurtled down the steps. "The Fury, he is ill, pining for me, or is it Matthew you mean? Tell me! Who is it you mean?"

I must admit that I sat on the grass almost too stunned to regain my feet. Holmes uncoiled his lean frame and stood to take her hand.

"It is The Fury firstly that I mean. He will neither eat nor work without you, but Matthew said if I found you that I should say this to you from him. 'Tell him if you find him as Matt says he should come back to us and there'll always be a place here' Those were his words and you yourself will know the truth to them."

The girl nodded. "His truth, but what of Mr. Hammond and his wife? What will they say when they know? What will the Colonel say who will not be so quick to take on a girl to groom The Fury?"

Holmes smiled at her. "I think the Colonel would take on the devil himself for a stable lad did the devil handle horses as you can. What is your name?"

"My father was Joseph therefore I used that name at the stables. My own name now is Ruth, a name from the Bible for my mother said I was Ruth to her Naomi. My father's people would have allowed me to stay with them if she was gone, but I would not. Before that I was called Leah after my mother."

"Ruth, then. Will you come back to London with us to meet Colonel Ross and after that to King's Pyland if he accepts you?"

Ruth Faa nodded slowly. "I will come. My grandmother will follow and meet me at the stables—if I do not rejoin her before she is there."

* * * * * * *

So we went back to London, stared at by fellow passengers as we traveled, watched half-contemptuously, half-suspiciously by those who wondered why we traveled with a young gypsy girl at our heels. On our arrival Holmes delivered the girl to Mrs. Hudson's hands, and she, good woman that she was, let the girl bathe and gave her the clothes to wear which Holmes had arranged.

Ruth rejoined us looking like the boy she had been at the stables. Holmes had provided breeches, a checked shirt, a neck scarf, and scissors for the girl to trim her hair again and that she had done. I could see how it was that she had been mistaken for a boy all that time. Her figure was very slender and her features aquiline so that with a boy's loose garb she looked to be no more than a young lad. I could see too how it was that Ross had mistaken her age, for she looked in her lad's clothing to be around thirteen or fourteen.

Holmes must have sent a messenger to the Colonel immediately upon our return, for we had no sooner eaten than the man was on our doorstep. He strode in, seized the boy by the shoulders and shook him gently.

"Joe, Joe, why did you run away? The Fury is pining, he won't eat, won't be saddled, won't be ridden and he's kicked young Jackson so that the boy is limping like a spavined horse."

"Good," Ruth snapped.

Colonel Ross stared down at her. "What? Good! Why?" His gaze on her sharpened, "What did he try on you, lad?"

Holmes drew him back from the girl. "I think before anything, Colonel, you should know who Joe really is."

"I don't care about any of that," said Ross impatiently. "So the lad got into some small trouble and fled, I can make it right whatever it may be."

"Possibly, Colonel, but you may find it more difficult to change the boy's sex. This is Ruth Faa who met The Fury. They loved each other at first sight and yes, she is a whisperer as you surmised. She wanted to work with the horse, but knew no stables would give a girl work as a stable lad."

Colonel Ross stared down, and gradually—I could see the transition in his face—he discerned the female beneath the boy's disguise. Ruth stood motionless before him, waiting. At last his jaw clenched in decision.

"I do not care. Let her keep to her costume, let others believe what they will. She is The Fury's groom so long as he races. If there is scandal over it I will face it out, so long as the horse keeps winning I will know it for sour grapes when men sneer."

Holmes nodded. "I expected no less from you, Colonel Ross.

But I would venture to say that you might have any problem resolved shortly. Let us go down to your stables in the morning. One thing I will tell you which Ruth—or Joe—will not. Bob Jackson discovered her secret and attempted to blackmail her of all her wages. When she refused that demand he said she could pay in another way and laid hands upon her. That time your trainer intervened, not knowing what the quarrel meant—but it was this which drove Ruth from the stables since she feared what next Bob would do."

Ross's eyes burned with a cold rage. "He will be gone the moment I set foot on my land there. And he will go with a warning on what may happen to lads who talk too freely."

"Just so," said Holmes. "I knew Joe could rely on you."

Still, I wondered, it was a makeshift solution at best. The boy would not keep silent forever, and how long would Ross hold up under the sneers of those who deem a young girl too fragile to handle a high-spirited colt? Holmes reassured me later on.

"Do not worry, my dear Watson." His eyes had the ghost of a twinkle as we approached the stables. "I think all will be resolved very well."

Matthew Hammond came out at the sound of our wheels and cried out as Ruth waved from the letdown window. I opened the door and they were in each other's arms. For minutes he held her, before he turned to face his parents who were standing at the door, his father agape, but his mother smiling, and I saw she too had guessed Ruth's secret.

"Mother, Father, this is the girl I'll wed. This is—" He grinned down at her and she supplied her female name with a tiny, joyous smile.

"Ruth."

"This is Ruth. She'll be lad for The Fury, I'll be his jockey, he'll make a fortune for the Colonel and nobody better say anything about her ever."

The Colonel went off into a great shout of laughter, I found I was following suit and even Holmes had something that could almost be described as a grin about his lips.

* * * * * * *

So that was the way of it. Ruth was stable lad for The Fury throughout the animal's career and that was long and illustrious. But well before it ended Ruth and Matthew had married and she bore him two sons and a daughter. The Fury bred fine foals and Colonel Ross became a rich man.

And Silver Blaze? He bred great fillies and many other fine colts, but there was never another one as brilliant or as dangerous as The Fury. Nor, I think, one who was so cared for and so greatly loved by his stable-lad—but then, I doubt that any other of his colts had a Ruth.

NOTE FROM THE AUTHOR: Acquaintances of mine in the United States who specialize in Sherlock Holmes, Caroline and Joel Senter, queried the Romany words used by Sherlock Holmes when I was writing this story. I was able to assure them (and you) that the words are correct for the country (England) and the time period for my stories (1890-1910). I also own a brief—and very rare—Romany dictionary put out by the English Folklore Society of that period.

DEATH AND NO CONSEQUENCES

BY RICHARD K. TOBIN

Having known my friend Sherlock Holmes for some years, I could tell by the sounds coming from upstairs that he was shaving. He was more alert than ever these past eight months. However his pipe was less active. In fact, until recently, he would still be abed at this hour. As for his pipe, while he had decreased its usage, he had increased his cigarette consumption this last fall till now, the Christmas season.

I could barely believe we had someone at the door, for it was only 7:30 in the morning. I went to tell the person to call at a more suitable hour. The person was not the usual trades person, but turned out to be the lovely Sarah MacGuillicudy. She was a personal secretary to Lord Hotchkiss, he being the nobleman who was the charge d'affaires of the Peerage Society Association. He was the watchdog to reckon with if a royal person misbehaved or a person other than royalty besmirched a titled member of British society. He contributed in other ways as well to make the lives of British crowned heads more amenable and trouble-free.

What use, pray tell, could she or Lord Hotchkiss, have for my friend of longstanding, Sherlock Holmes. On looking at young Miss MacGuillicudy, I saw a healthy young woman. She was well-washed and-dressed, with a spectacular head of blonde hair.

The fire was springing to life just as Sherlock Holmes walked into our room, thankfully covered decently, except for his argyle, fleece-lined slippers. I performed the introductions. All hope of a quiet breakfast was soon postponed.

Holmes asked, "What moved you, Miss MacGuillicudy, to come to me?"

The woman looked over at me and asked, "Is it safe to talk, you both knowing that what I now tell you, must never be repeated?"

Holmes remarked, "Of course, and I'm sure I speak for the doctor as well."

"Indeed," I murmured.

Our lovely female guest gave me a piercing stare and asked, "Is that so, Doctor Watson? The reason I must be sure is, it is something that has blemished our Queen's royal court and also a relative of hers is deeply involved."

Holmes, smiling, said, "Please tell us more."

We both sat there for twenty minutes and were told how Prince Henry had murdered a waitress late last night. He was a nephew of Queen Victoria and it was all being hushed up. We were told only what we needed to know.

Miss MacGuillicudy told us her given name was Eliza, and then informed us that this rather atrocious prince was a favorite of our Queen.

Sherlock Holmes, whose fame had spread over most of Britain, was being asked to investigate the murder, find out the reason or reasons, for the murder, and whatever made Prince Henry get mixed up with a waitress whose immediate family were Irish immigrants. However, the girl, Nellie Malone, was born in England and her father was a trained elementary school teacher. Her mother was a nurse before they immigrated.

My own feelings were that something was amiss here. I had no idea what. It didn't change anything when Miss Eliza informed us that this Malone female was very attractive.

This seemed an easy case and one that would pay well. Not that Holmes was practical about money matters.

After Miss Eliza MacGuillicudy departed, Holmes remarked, "I'm quite ravenous, Watson."

I replied, "No time for a fit breakfast. Speed is of the essence."

"What a time for my housekeeper to become sick."

I replied, "I looked in on Mrs. Hudson. It's not pneumonia but a bad case of the flu."

"So be it, Watson."

* * * * * * *

We soon were in a hansom and on our way. We were informed by young Eliza of the location of the victim, in the only decent Irish neighborhood in London, where she was employed in her uncle's restaurant temporarily. It was in that restaurant where her remains had been found. After the investigation, Holmes was to submit a report but we did not yet know to whom.

Holmes still looked rather fit. Any attempt at sartorial success had been completely lost on him. His dark hair had thinned but a mere trifle. His necktie couldn't be more pitiful. His thin facial features, however, drew most peoples' attention. Not that I had much to boast about. Less, since I received my second letter from the London Medical Society concerning my careless manner of managing my medical practice.

I asked my friend of many years, "Is there any way Prince Henry can be censured for his behavior?"

Holmes replied, "Not from his own kind. If the press were to discover Prince Henry's foul play, it may result in an unpleasant situation. People from many walks of life have long memories and a strong sense of propriety. The press is the only real threat."

I remarked, "One supposes the Prince is well aware there could be trouble but of such a minor nature, considering the deed, it must only be far from intimidating."

Holmes gazed on me benignly. Then he said, "I now understand the case fully and we shall no doubt do our part." Then he put his head back as if in a trance, and still no pipe. There were packaged cigarettes in his shirt pocket, however. On the positive side, I rarely had to escort him up the stairs to his bedroom anymore because of his foggy faculties.

Both Miss Eliza and Holmes fully understood the importance of hushing up the murder of Nellie Malone by the royal rake, just as I did. There was a bad seed in that young man. This Miss Malone was an attractive young woman, with beautiful blue eyes. She worked as a legal office clerk for a barrister, who, once retired, chose to close his office rather than sell it. She was filling time until some more suitable means of employment surfaced.

Despite Holmes' behavior, the case was made that much simpler; today being Sunday. The newspapers didn't publish on Sunday. Instead, other than a skeleton crew, even their printing presses were shut down. Our Christmas blessing, bah, humbug.

I buttoned up the top of my overcoat, as the raw, damp, cold settled in. We had travelled through a slum area but now were in a better district. The houses were an improvement and the passersby were better dressed and cleaner. That and fewer stray dogs and cats. Also, hardly any litter strewn about.

Once inside the restaurant, even with decent enough accoutrements, I could tell there was no heat on. It was cool but no dampness. There was a tall, slim, blond London bobby on the premises keeping a close watch . We introduced ourselves and when we asked, he said, "No disturbances and even less bother, sirs."

I asked, "Any reporters?"

The bobby replied, "None, sir."

Holmes asked, "The remains then?"

The bobby, Randolph Grover, replied, "It's down in the basement, and well, very grotesque."

I asked, "In what way?"

"The remains were found to be dismembered, sir."

"So I have been informed. Awful," was my reply.

Holmes asked, "Can you lead us down?"

"If you would, sir, certainly."

Grover lit an oil lantern and led the way. I followed behind

Holmes making note of his barely pressed, brown trousers. My years as a doctor, I felt certain, had prepared me for what was to come next.

We went into the stores room. Then Holmes uttered, "Oh, my God."

I took a look and started to gag. Even in a hospital setting I had never seen anything as macabre or horrifying.

Something caught my eye a short moment later. I asked, "What is that, Constable Grover or would you...well, of all...."

He replied, "I can answer you, sir, but because you are a man of medicine, you've likely digested it by now."

"Damn it!"

"What is it, Watson?" asked Holmes, "And at what month?"

"I believe it's time to brush up on my medical techniques." What I had just been looking at was a fetus.

In reply to Holmes' earlier question I said, "The embryo is approaching its third month. Possibly eleven weeks in the womb."

"Then, as you can see, we have a beast on our hands. The law is powerless."

I replied, "Barbarism, Holmes. And the Prince was obviously aware of the pregnancy."

Grover looked uncomfortable.

Holmes declared, "No murder weapon or other implements of brutality left behind. An act done by criminals of the most hard-core kind. An open-and-shut case with the scales of justice gone awry."

I replied, "There appears to be no redemption in sight. There is only evil here. Nellie will be mourned but nothing more."

Young Grover asked of Holmes, "Is there at least an attempt at justice to be done? What is your plan?"

Holmes replied, "No plan. This case is unsolvable and I shall say just that in my report."

"But why?" I asked.

Holmes replied, "This brutal act was inspired by the devil and I'm not one to lock horns with the supernatural." The Great

Detective's eyes were glittering with anger.

We then walked back up to the restaurant accompanied on our way by the sound of small scratchy feet on their way in to sample whatever they might.

* * * * * *

Back in the restaurant, an establishment called Morrissey's of Dingle Road, Holmes and I each found a chair. We sat at one of the tables and I soon adjusted my position to Holmes' long legs. Grover said, "I'm just going to nose about the kitchen for a bit. I'm not expecting trouble and still no reporters that I was told to stay clear of. A most favorable omen."

Holmes said, "We shall await your nose."

Grover replied, "Yes, sir. I should inform you, late this afternoon, three men will be arriving to remove the remains of Miss Malone. That corpse I predict will never be seen again. Then two men will come here shortly after. They are not police and I am told not to interfere. The next part is the good one. They will pay you both a generous fee, in cash only."

Holmes replied, "We also were told what to expect."

"But why cash, Constable?" I asked.

Grover smiled and said, "Harder to trace, sir."

Holmes snorted and said, "Were you expecting him to say something else, Watson?"

"Come to think of it, not really."

"And what's the good news?" Holmes asked.

"Well, generous pay, I presume."

"You presume not enough. The good news is Grover has gone into the kitchen and don't offer to do the cleanup."

"Indeed, no. However, I have been dreaming of a bowl of oatmeal all morning."

"First, here comes tea and sweet rolls."

Not long after, I did get my oatmeal and Holmes was served eggs sunny side up with fried potatoes and an unbelievable four fat German sausages. We ate and felt much better.

Nellie's parents, apparently Catholic, would be thinking, likely as not, to hold a memorial service for her. Her life ended tragically and no one would ever know why.

Time, however, was heavy on our hands. I walked up near the glass-front window. The window itself was unusual because it was divided into twenty twelve-inch-long panes of glass and just as wide. Each twelve-inch-long sheet of glass had its own frame, made out of what could be either walnut or mahogany brought up from the Caribbean. It was a nice effect as were the green-and-black place mats. As for Holmes, he seemed to be satisfied just to sit there.

Suddenly a booming voice bellowed, "Hear that Watson?"

"Other than your voice, nothing, Holmes."

"Listen closely."

It took a few minutes and then I did hear something. I asked, "What do you make it to be?"

Holmes replied, "We are being approached by a carriage and the prince in question may be a passenger."

"How is that so evident? I see no indication of that."

Holmes declared, "There are four horses, all of them trotting in unison and hauling a luxurious coach behind them."

"I could see trotting to perfection, but the coach, how do you surmise it to be luxurious?" I questioned Holmes.

Holmes remarked, "The horses are bearing a heavy load, not like a two-wheeled hansom. This coach has four wheels and is of the sturdiest construction."

I replied, "Therefore heavier and more expensive, which means high society may be approaching and noisily so, as you claim."

"Well done, Watson. Soon I shall be able to write the rest of my report and then doze silently."

I asked, "A tea first, Holmes?"

"Yes, we must have tea and a chat and hopefully the young miscreant doesn't barge in to see us."

The carriage arrived, a most handsome rig. It was made of varnished wood with many layers of varnish well appliqued.

The four horses were all black in color and were big and strong with excellent, well-trained behavior. All four of them were mares.

Then a man's head leaned forward and looked out the window. It was not just any face we saw. I had steeled myself for this moment. Holmes, however, wasn't at all flustered. Looking out the carriage window at us was the murderer of the pretty, well-turned Nellie Malone.

He leered at us, then smiled in a most brazen manner. He was obviously a young man with no conscience and his soul had departed already and rested comfortably in hell. Looks-wise, his teeth had an abundance of enamel and were a brilliant white, in front of which were well-formed lips. A crown of luxuriant charcoal-colored hair topped off a strangely handsome face. His features, all were well-sculpted and one melded with the other. He was ensconced in a black silk cloak with a bright red lining. One supposes the cloak was to fend off the chilly afternoon air. I did wonder about the gaudy lining. I didn't quite fear for my life and my friend Sherlock Holmes' life just then, but I was sure he'd kill the both of us if we caused him any grief whatsoever. It was a frightening prospect, especially allowing for the remains of Miss Malone. Then he reached under his cloak and pulled out a gun!

Holmes said, "Don't flinch. Stay where you are."

The prince fondled the gun briefly. He stared at it intently and then put it away. It made for a nervous few minutes. However, we recovered from the threat.

I asked, "Since he didn't aim his revolver at us, Holmes, would it be a favorable portent?"

Holmes replied, "Perchance, but what is more likely is he may have signified to us what is to be his next instrument of death."

"Then he's on a mad, hate-filled rage?" I asked.

Holmes adroitly remarked, "He's engulfed in himself. His faulty mind tells him his actions are perfectly appropriate."

"You are suggesting he doesn't understand the difference

between right and wrong?"

Holmes declared, "You are approximately correct. There was no guidance in his life and he became a shallow young man, one with no empathy or feelings. Whatever his emotional range, they are all disturbed."

Calmly seated next to him was a brunette young woman, slim and of some elegance and carefully attired in the best dress that London had to offer. Her shoes alone would cost me what I would make in a week practicing medicine.

I observed that the woman was having trouble turning her head, followed by a bad cough. Her eyes were clouded, perhaps from insomnia.

Holmes declared, "Mark that woman, Watson. I am sure within all reasonable doubt that is Lucy Waters, the contralto whose fame has spread near and wide."

"I see. Quite the impossible gentleman friend, I must say. But she is coping nicely."

Now the Prince and his contralto friend of the day, became engaged in a conversation. With one last look at Holmes and I and Constable Randolph Grover, the carriage departed. Miss Waters was coughing at the time and did seem to spit something up.

But the deed was done. Holmes took his seat, and I across from him, in-between his long slim legs. I was snug up against the table, my waistline was snug against my green tweed jacket, it having spread a couple of inches from my expanding girth. I made note not to fill my plate so much.

Holmes started a short but heartfelt tirade. That was his way. Myself, I felt lonely somehow, and depressed. Holmes finished by saying, "If I could be allowed to interrogate that horrid man, I'd tell him a few things about human decency. No doubt this was all his way of stating that our waitress, pretty and buxom as she was, with lovely blonde hair and blue eyes, beautiful even in death, was unfit to bear his child. Perchance he should have considered that matter earlier. Certainly he had his sport but did it have to end like this? Undoubtedly she was attracted to him but she soon found out about his second face. One could conjecture that she may have been deeply in love with him. Too late she realized he had a beastly streak in him."

Mercifully our tea arrived and a scone for each of us with a dish of marmalade.

Finally, and I wasn't surprised, my companion lit up his first pipe of the day.

Holmes closed his eyes and for but a brief second, I thought I saw a tear. He then finished off the scone and talked about the painful breaking apart of his home. His mother committed adultery and it was final. Holmes' father told him he could still wear his father's name. In another conversation during an investigation of a member of parliament representing the Leeds area, he had mentioned Sherlock was not his original first name. He then began to haul on his pipe furiously until the bowl was as red as the setting sun. I was now hearing his account of what started him on drugs. That story stayed the same from years previously when I had first heard it.

A misdiagnosis by a doctor when Holmes was a young adult left Holmes in much pain. The doctor prescribed morphine for over a month and my friend developed a lifelong craving, one that seemed to be ending over the last ten months.

I looked out at the sky just before dark and saw the clouds, one on top of the other spread thinly and in long parallel lines. On asking my learned friend, he told me it was a sign of a mild winter and early spring.

I asked, "Would you like more good news?"

"I have little use for good news, Watson, but let's have it. Out with it, now."

I said, "I'm sure you remember the rather striking young contralto."

"Actually, I'm trying to forget."

"Then put this in your pipe and puff away."

"Oh, this I must hear," spoke Holmes.

I sat upright and fixed my pale blue eyes exclusively on my friend of many years. I launched my commentary. "You see,

Holmes, Miss Waters had trouble turning her head in our direction. That could mean she's recently been inflicted with meningitis and either doesn't know, or she's not talking. Then came the bad cough and much spitting up. That is a sure sign of bacterial tuberculosis. Those tuberculosis germs are spread through the air. Both diseases are quite contagious. Now, one wonders if a small heaping lump of good old-fashioned justice is now about to happen."

"Amazing, Watson. However, both diseases can be treated. You will find that on page four of your official medical practice journal."

I shrugged and said, "Oh, well, but let us not forget he will go through a period of poor health. I should add the treatment isn't necessarily successful for either disease."

Holmes' face was more relaxed and he was about to say something when our fine friend, young Grover, came by and said, "It isn't much, but supper shan't be long."

I asked, "To what do we owe all this?"

Grover replied, "I've long wanted a soft, yet interesting shift."

Holmes declared, "Good man."

Then the three of us were caught by surprise. In walked three men, two carrying boxes and a few sheets of canvas. The other man carried a bucket and an array of cleaning supplies and a disinfectant. It was late enough in the day for darkness to have descended, in part.

I couldn't help but smile. This ordeal was coming to the only conclusion possible.

One of the men (all three were dressed in typical ruffian's garb) said, "We're here to spirit something away to a place where she'll never be found. Those are our orders, no matter what."

I asked, "You know your work then?"

"So Scotland Yard now tells us. Not that I ever considered me to be on such good terms with 'em."

Holmes asked, "And the other reason then?"

"Nifty packet, sor. The three of us."

They went down to the basement having received directions to the corpse's location from our bobby friend. They came up with the remains carefully packed up and discreetly loaded it on a wagon that had first transported them here. All done in a half an hour. Nellie Malone's history had just ended.

When supper was over, I asked Grover, "What now?"

"Your pay should come soon, ever so discreetly."

I stated, "No matter what, Holmes. I'll try to negotiate more."

"Hardly necessary, Doctor, I'm sure."

A few minutes later, a young man wearing a Tyrolean hat, with a short plume, came up the street aiming for the front door of the Morrissey. Another man with a cutthroat look about him jumped out from somewhere nearby at the young man. The young man in the meantime had pulled out a writing pad and pencil. Damn it, a reporter! Still, no corpse, no story, we hoped. He may have followed the Prince here. When he refused to leave, another man of anthropoid proportions added his weight to the discussion and the reporter left after the added threat. No wonder. The huge man had shoulders almost four-feet wide. I turned towards Holmes and said, "Please, no more reporters. It would ruin things irreparably."

Finally, in came two middle-aged, portly, well-dressed men, although the fellow with the green-and-white tie and light slacks was a little off center. The taller of the two with an impressive full-length beige overcoat said in a most excellent speaking voice, "Mr. Sherlock Holmes and Doctor Watson, one presumes?"

"You have us and in our usual state," spoke Holmes.

Then he gave me a most stern look. That was just as well. Not only were our fees most generous but there was a carriage at our disposal and we were free to go. Holmes did spend ten minutes passing on his take on this case. When Holmes commented on the gun, the improperly dressed officer remarked, "That sounds like an accurate facet of the Prince's personality."

Myself, I was most satisfied that the press had been successfully avoided.

Once out the door, Holmes suggested we had just been contacted by the British Secret Service. Then he asked, "Did I ever tell you how I chanced to become a private detective?"

"You did mutter something on the subject. As I recall, it was after we shook hands for the first time."

"What must I have said?" asked Holmes.

"As I recall, you were twenty-years old and through officially with your studies. It was just before your mother sent you a generous bank draft for four thousand pounds. But to the point, a woman asked you if you'd try to find her lost dog for her. She informed you that she would add just a bit to your pay if you found her missing husband as well."

"Then what?" Holmes asked snappishly.

I replied, "It's been a long day. However, you found the husband sleeping it off on the floor of a nearby grog house. No real money in the husband but as you tried to sober him up, the dog came out of hiding. You went on to say it was the only job you had ever done, and you felt shortly after, since you were experienced at it, you would make it your chosen path. A one-day advertisement in a London daily newspaper announcing your new chosen path was all you needed to get your start. The quality of your sleuthing to this day has left you never short of clients."

"You know too much, Watson."

I replied, "There is no such thing as knowing too much."

"I should tell you, I still have most of my mother's money. It paid my first two months' rent on Baker Street. Father paid for my education and nothing more."

"As for me, Holmes, my family life wasn't even as decent as yours."

"I've long suspected as much. A least I talk of mine," Holmes added. "To conclude, Watson, you and I were but a crown-owned insurance policy in this case. If this matter were to leak out, imagine the embarrassing headlines, the enormous gossip mill, also it would spread internationally. Then and only then would my investigation be of some use. The Queen's spokesman could easily and truly claim that I was hired to help the police to get to the bottom of this matter, no stone left unturned, as it were. It would have helped, but only if needed."

"Indeed," I replied. "I couldn't help but feel early on that the facts in this undertaking didn't quite add up. Nor does your one pipe for the entire day."

"Ah, thank you for the reminder. Perhaps I could offer you more payment?" Holmes said with a wry grin.

I shook my head and replied, "If my medical license is suspended, I may need it."

"Ah, in that case, Watson, you can perhaps write this matter up under the title of 'The Case of the Indolent Doctor.'"

MURDER AT THE DIOGENES CLUB

BY JOHN L. FRENCH

Sherlock Homes stood alone in the room. The bodies had been removed but their presence was not needed. Standing in the center of the crime scene, he let it speak to him.

The first to die had been prone on his bed when the heavy weight crushed his skull. One blow was all it had taken. Two for the second man who had risen slightly before being struck. This one may have moaned or otherwise cried out for the third had been fully awake and sitting up when he met his end. It had taken at least three blows, no more than five, to put him down.

It was the blood patterns that told the story. Holmes surveyed the scene, taking in the stains on the walls and ceiling. Slight upward spatters over the first bed. Against the opposite wall, high over bed two, was blood cast off from the weapon as the murderer swung around. More upward-traveling spatter, this time at a slight angle. Holmes's eyes traced the trajectory determining at where the rising head would have been struck. Six inches, no more, off the thick pillow, on the side of the skull. It would have stunned him, no more. Cast off from the first blow above the pillow. Low angle spatter, some on the wall, most on the pillow, shows evidence of the second blow and final blow.

The third bed was against the far, outer wall, between two windows, one of which was broken. Holmes saw the action in his mind as if shown by Charles Jenkins's Phantoscope. The third man rising, awakened by the attack on his roommates. He pushes off his wool blanket, swings around, his feet on the floor, perhaps groggy from his awakening. The only light on this, the second story, comes from the moon through the window. Maybe he sees his killer, maybe not, before the weapon comes down on top of his skull.

Pausing his thoughts, Holmes checked his conclusion. Yes, spatter on the ceiling and some on the far wall. He went on.

The third man slumps. One, possibly two blows to the back of the head. Blood on the floor shows where he fell, face up, before one last strike finished him.

Satisfied, Holmes nodded to himself then set about searching for what else the room could tell him, his keen eyes picking out tiny slivers of glass on the first bed and the pillow of the third. "Curious," he said aloud, and walked over to the broken window, careful not to step on too many glass shards.

Both windows looked out onto an adjacent first floor roof, an easy entry point for a cracksman. There was little glass from the broken one on the roof. Most of it was on the floor inside. Using his magnifier, Holmes examined the stress marks caused by the breakage of the glass. As he expected, they indicated that the window had been broken from the outside.

A spot of what was very probably blood on the wall near the window drew Holmes's attention. With magnifier still in hand, he bent to the floor to search for a mark that may or may not be there.

That's where he was when Dr. John Watson came into the room. "Like a bloodhound on a scent," Watson thought, not for the first time. He knew enough not to interrupt Holmes while he was thus engaged, so he waited patiently until his friend was finished.

Satisfied with his examination of the floor, Holmes straightened. "Good afternoon, Watson. You've been to the morgue? You've viewed the bodies?"

"As you requested, Holmes. After examination, it is my professional opinion that they were all killed with the same weapon, possibly a...."

"Leaded walking stick," Holmes interrupted, "wielded by a powerfully built left-handed man."

"Really, Holmes," Watson bristled. "If you already knew, why send me to the morgue?"

The detective smiled at his friend. "I did not know this, Watson, when I asked you to assist me. It was not until I came here that the room told me most of what I need to know."

"And what it that, Holmes?"

Stepping to the doorway where Watson was still standing, Holmes waved his hand in invitation. "Ask it yourself. You know my methods. Apply them."

Watson had grown used to these challenges from Holmes. He welcomed the opportunity to put his observational skills to the test. Although he seldom was able to match his friend's deductions, he believed that what he had learned from Holmes over the years had made him a better physician.

Like Holmes had before him, Watson took a long, close look around the crime scene. "The round red stain on the wall by the window," he said when he finished, "you were looking for a mark on the floor when I came in. You found it and the two together suggested not only the type of weapon used but, from the length of the supposed cane, the height of its wielder."

Holmes smiled. "Very good, Watson. You are progressing. The length of, as you say, 'the supposed cane' suggests a man about five feet, nine inches tall. My retirement to Sussex now seems closer. What else?"

"From the victims' injuries I could tell that their killer was left-handed. As for what told you...you did write that monograph on the analysis of blood stain patterns."

"One of the few of mine you have read," Holmes chided.

"I have little interest in bees, tattoos or polyphonic whatevers. But getting back to this crime, it would take someone powerful to kill three men with so few blows in so little time. The window?"

"Definitely broken from the outside."

"Then what happened is, as you would say, elementary. A sneak thief out to burgle the building, broke a window on entry. On finding the room occupied, he panicked, killed the three of them and fled the room."

"Is that all, Watson?"

"All that I can see, Holmes. Although I will allow that there may some small details that I missed that will lead you straight to the killer's lair."

"One or two, Watson, one or two. May I suggest that you look out the broken window."

Watson did so, then turned to his friend. "Shoemarks on the roof leading away from the window, consistent with the theory that that was the murderer's point of exit."

"You see nothing else?"

"No I don't. Why, is there something else to see?"

Holmes joined the doctor at the window. "No, there is not. Now if you'll excuse me," Holmes easily raised the lower sash, "I wish to measure those shoemarks. I'll join you downstairs in the Strangers' Room when I have finished."

"As you wish. But really, Holmes, I do think the only mystery here is why the Diogenes Club would need your services for the simple murder of servants by a burglar, no matter how brutal."

Holmes let out a sigh, one unheard by Watson, who had already left the room. "Murder," he said softly to himself, "is never simple. As for the victims being servants, I think not." Then as he climbed through the open sash, he sighed again. "Sussex, I'm afraid, is still many years off."

No sooner had Watson seated himself in the Strangers' Room than he heard, "He's in here, Mr. Holmes."

Odd, the doctor thought, there were several shoemarks on the roof and Holmes would have measured them all. He could not have finished that fast.

Then the light from the entrance hall was eclipsed by a large shape and Mycroft Holmes entered the room.

"Easily a seventh of a ton," Watson observed to himself, as he viewed the elder Holmes with his professional eye. Making his way across the room. Mycroft sat next to Watson, allowed a minute as if to make sure the chair would not collapse beneath him and greeted Watson with,

"I assure you, Doctor, that despite my size I am in near perfect health."

Unperturbed by Mycroft's seeming to have read his thoughts, Holmes did it all the time, Watson countered, "Except for a touch of gout, some shortness of breath and hypertension I would agree with you, Mr. Holmes. I'd suggest a change in diet, some exercise and a complete examination, but you are too much like your brother to take my advice."

Mycroft chuckled. Had he not been within the confines of his club he might have laughed out loud. "Bravo, Doctor. Your association with my brother has done you good. If I ever decide to place my fate in the hands of medical science, you will be my first choice. And speaking of my brother, how did he come to be called into this situation?"

"I had assumed you called him."

"Now why would I need Sherlock when I am every bit as... ah, it is your fault he is here."

"Mine, how is that, Mr. Holmes?"

"Elementary. When the murders were discovered someone no doubt suggested sending for 'Mr. Holmes.' Thanks to your writings, it was my brother who was first thought of, despite this being more home to me than my own dwelling. Now then, tell me, if you can, what did Sherlock find?"

"Just what I was meant to, Mycroft." Looking up, Watson saw his friend standing in the doorway. His pants were dirty, his coat dusty, his face scratched and his hair very much uncombed. Somewhere between the roof and the club's front door, Holmes had lost his hat. "Is there someplace private we can talk? Possibly your first floor office?"

"How did you know that I had...no matter, now that I think of it, it is obvious. Very well, come along, Sherlock." And after some hesitation added, "You as well, Doctor, but let it be understood, this is not a matter for *The Strand*."

An Otis lift deprived Watson of a sight he had always wanted to see, Mycroft Holmes ascending a staircase. Once in his office, seated behind his desk in a chair that had to have been specially built for his comfort, Mycroft began by saying,

"You were not meant to find anything, Sherlock. The Yard was. Some of the brighter ones have begun employing your methods. It was, as I explained to Dr. Watson, mere chance that you were called in."

"And so the police viewed your staged scene and came to the same erroneous conclusion that Watson did?"

"Precisely, brother. As we speak they are scouring the city for a murderous burglar. "

Watson sighed and asked, "What did I miss this time?"

"You missed nothing, Watson. Rather, you saw everything you were meant to see—the bloodstains, broken window, shoe-marks leading from the window, even the artfully placed signs of a possible weapon—a distinct touch, that, Mycroft."

"Thank you, Sherlock."

"What you saw, Watson, but did not note was the glass in the bed of the first murdered man and on the pillow of the third. If the window was broken before the killings, it should not have been there. In addition, the noise from the breaking of the window would have been enough to awaken at least one of the three."

"But Holmes," Watson protested, "you yourself stated that the window was broken from the outside."

"Indeed it was, Watson, by whomever my brother had exit the room through that portal, break the window then leave behind traces of his descent to the alley. Really, Mycroft, you should have had your man leave shoemarks in both directions. And by the way, the shoemarks on the roof indicated a taller man than did the marks from the cane."

"Some of us are not as familiar with scenes of crime as you are, brother. It was enough to fool Scotland Yard."

"Especially with you there to confirm their conclusions, brother."

Watson spoke up. "It's a pity then that someone called in the wrong Holmes, isn't it?" To his friend Watson added an aside, "That's what your brother conveyed to me." Then to both brothers, "So if entry or exit was not by way of the roof, the murderer must be part of the Diogenes Club, either a member or servant. What is being done to find him?"

The brothers looked at one another. "Is he really that blind, Sherlock?"

"Watson no doubt assumes that my appearance is from falling off the roof, or tripping in the alley."

"You have been known to do so, Holmes, when sufficiently distracted."

"Once only, Watson. Twice if you count the cataract."

"Three times. The last time was in that stable. You had to throw your cape away. So those dark stains on your trousers are...."

"Blood, Watson, but not mine, I assure you." Addressing both the doctor and his brother Holmes went on. "With Mycroft, then the police then me on the scene, it would have been foolhardy for the bludger to try and leave the building. He would only have drawn attention to himself. But I hope I am not being immodest by saying that with the both of us present he must have known that it was only a matter of time before he was exposed. It was his singular ill fortune to leave by the rear door as I was descending from the roof."

"I would think, Holmes, that his bad luck was in not realizing that you had no doubt surmised his continued presence in the Club and were prepared to wait all afternoon for his departure."

Nodding at Watson's compliment, which he did not bother to deny, Holmes continued. "I saw right away that the man was of the proper height to have delivered the fatal blows. I approached, and even in the dim light of the alley I could see his bloodstained clothing. I threw him my hat, which he caught in his left hand. His game was up, mine had begun. After a brief but ultimately ineffective resistance," Holmes rubbed the scratches on his face, "I subdued him. I left him bound in the alley with several of the kitchen help to watch him. No doubt the police, summoned on my order, have him by now."

"And on leaving here you will, of course, go straight to the Yard where you will explain that you used your great powers of observation to track the burglar from his own descent from the roof to his nearby hiding place, leaving out any mention of his being in the Diogenes Club."

"An order, brother?" Holmes asked with one eyebrow raised.

Mycroft's hand raised in supplication. "Let's call it a request."

"Why should Holmes lie to the police?"

"It would not be the first time, Watson," the detective told his friend. "And in this case a plausible lie is better than the truth."

"Which is, Holmes?"

Holmes looked at his brother, who nodded in permission, then replied. "That an agent working for a foreign power gained access to the Club as a servant, waited his chance then assassinated three covert members of Her Majesty's overseas service."

"My word, Holmes! How did you...?"

"The murder room, Watson. There were sparse furnishings, no personal effects and the bedclothes were of a higher quality than one gives to servants. Given my brother's elaborate charade and what we know of his true activities, what other conclusion could there be?"

A satisfied smile briefly crept over Mycroft's face. "Well done, Sherlock. I trust that when you talk to the Yard you will do the right thing."

Returning the smile, Holmes said, "As always, brother."

"But what of the man Holmes took into custody?" Watson asked. "Will he not talk?"

"That man, Doctor, plays the same game as do I. He will not talk, not to the police. Later, when agents of her Majesty's take custody of him, he will then be—persuaded—to talk. Then we will find out all he knows."

Watson felt a sudden chill, one he knew came not from the temperature in the room but from within him. He arose, the proper English gentleman believing in justice, fair play and all that was right. He then asked the question he did not want to ask, hoping not to hear the answer he feared the most.

"I trust, Mr. Holmes, that you did not sacrifice three good men just to trap a foreign agent who may have vital information?"

If Mycroft took offense at this query he did not show it. "I assure you, Doctor, that I would never sacrifice good men for any reason."

Was there a slight emphasis on the word "good?" Before Watson could decide Holmes had taken him by the arm. "Come Watson, we've taken up enough of Mycroft's time."

Once on the streets of Pall Mall, Holmes said, "It's me to the Yard and you, well, you must have patients."

As if letting other matters drop, Watson quipped, "With you, Holmes, I need all the patience I can muster."

It was a few days later in their Baker Street lodgings that Watson said to Holmes, "You never asked me why I thought the murdered men at the Diogenes Club were servants."

"I had not thought to ask," Holmes said calmly. He then smiled and in a close approximation of his friend's voice added, "What did I miss this time?"

"I saw the bodies, you did not. Their clothing had been removed but it was there, in a heap by the examination tables. It was of poor quality, servants' wear, not what the government would provide to trusted agents about to embark to the continent."

Watson paused to give Holmes time to absorb this, then went on.

"As a matter of course, in my examination I noted lividity on all three bodies. While it was consistent with the position in which they would have been found, your description of events leaves little time for it to have occurred. And on reflection, I could not swear that the wounds I observed had not been made post-mortem."

Their roles somehow reversed, Holmes sat listening to Watson in surprise, thinking, "So this is how it feels." He barely heard Watson as the doctor asked,

"Tell me, Holmes, were I to test the blood samples that I know you routinely take from scenes such as these, would they prove to be human? Or was the whole thing an even bigger charade than we have been led to believe?"

For a time the detective sat silently, his fingers forming a tent in front of him. Just when Watson thought his friend was not going to answer, Holmes said,

"Pig's blood in bladders, I suspect. Easily obtained from the kitchen. Mycroft reads all my monographs and would have known what to do to achieve the desired results. The bodies he would have obtained from a charity hospital. Or from a burke, he would not be beyond that. Beaten, as you said, post-mortem. Had I been there to see the wounds Mycroft's scheme would have fallen through before it was hatched. Still, it was enough to fool the police. But not you, my friend, and for that you have my congratulations."

"But to what ends, Holmes?"

"Wheels within wheels, Watson. Do you really think that a foreign agent could infiltrate the Diogenes Club without my brother being aware of his presence? A double agent, most likely. One of Mycroft's men seeming to work for the other side. Mycroft's position being mostly secret but not entirely unknown in certain circles, it is likely that the club was being watched by this foreign power. So we have three murders—the police are called, bodies removed, 'The Great Sherlock Holmes' summoned." Holmes said this last with no little self-mockery. "The so-called assassin arrested. His bona fides now in place, he can now be released to the other side in trade for one of ours. One of our agents freed and another in what is hoped a position of trust and confidence."

"And how can Mycroft be sure he can trust the man who is returned?"

"Not for nothing is it called 'The Great Game,' one with deadly consequences and more moves than chess. Makes me glad I am but a simple consulting detective, one who deals with the more honest crimes of theft and murder."

THE ADVENTURE OF THE NIGHT HUNTER

BY RALPH E. VAUGHAN

Sherlock Holmes leaned back against the cool damp wall, hands shoved deep into the pockets of a shabby dark coat, chin resting upon his chest, eyes half-closed, a dirty merchantman's cap pulled low over his forehead.

A thick yellowish fog swirled through the narrow, cobbled street, obscuring most of its gritty length. Holmes, however, did not rely on vision alone.

Somewhere a gas lamp burned, but only its fitful sputtering and hissing gave it away, not its feeble illumination.

No footfalls broke the silence, for the inhabitants of London were cowering in their dwellings, whether those abodes were mean or palatial. Terror made all men equal.

For the past several nights, a killer had prowled the chartered streets of London, more wide-ranging than had been the Ripper of three decades back (though that creature was still fresh as new-spilt blood in Holmes' memory), and certainly more ferocious in his cutting, in his taking of trophies from the kill. This new terror that had come to the capitol of the world was of a nature never seen before, no respecter of place or position.

Both the titled and the untitled had fallen: the tradesman and laborer; the merchant and the moneyed wastrel; the lady returning from a West End theater and the grimy doxie wandering the East End's foul and lust-stained alleys—none were safe from the predations of the faceless killer christened the "Night Hunter" by the fevered imaginations of the scribes of Fleet Street.

None were safe from his....

No, not a knife, Holmes thought. He had examined the wounds and the remains of the dead, and those cuts, those slashes that sliced through bone as easily as soft flesh had not been made by any blade he had ever seen; no knife had ever filleted skin from muscle so cleanly and effortlessly. Heads were usually taken, sometimes hands, sometimes suits of skin—the detectives of New Scotland Yard still resisted what Holmes knew to be the truth, that those parts which had been taken had been taken as trophies, and that the appellation awarded by the gentlemen of Fleet Street was more correct than they knew.

The Home Secretary had dismissed Holmes' speculations, not because he did not believe, but because he refused to believe.

Once more, as was not unusual, Sherlock Holmes found himself on a solitary quest, separated from the other guardians of law and order by an intellect unfettered by the restraints of ignorance and banality.

Once again, Sherlock Holmes hunted a hunter.

And this time the hunter was a hunter indeed.

Maps were still strewn across his rooms on Baker Street, much to the continued consternation of Mrs. Hudson, the most put-upon and aggrieved landlady in all of London, maps marked not only with locations of murders, but with notations about each locale, analyses of such things as would never concern the regular police—the air temperature and humidity, reports of unknown lights and sounds, the archaeological remains found beneath the current habitations, and the nature of each area's local geology, particularly the presence of "lost" rivers.

Yes, the hidden rivers of London which wound their ways through caverns and chambers unknown even to the city's sewer rats, two-legged as well as four.

Holmes could hear the soft murmuring of one of London's lost rivers now, where he stood, an almost inaudible whisper in the wall he leaned against, a persistent ripple beneath his feet.

"I don't see what you are getting at, Holmes," Professor Edward Challenger had remarked after examining the results of Holmes' research three days earlier. "Are you tracking a man or an animal?"

"Neither, I think," Holmes had replied. "The basic mistake made by the great minds at Scotland Yard and the Home Office is that they are looking at this outbreak of violence and murder as nothing more than another expression of rage and frustration by someone of the lower classes."

"Preposterous!" Professor Challenger exclaimed. "I examined many victims myself; those wounds were no more made by a man's hand than they were by an animal's tooth or claw."

"Obviously not an animal," Holmes agreed, "else I might have asked for the temporary release of Colonel Moran."

"But I thought he was...."

"No, not hanged, quite unfortunately," Holmes replied grimly. "Despite my best efforts, and the testimonies of both Doctor Watson and Inspector Lestrade, the Crown Prosecutor declined to seek the rope." Holmes shook his head. "Too many nervous people in high places want his silence held; evidently, when Professor Moriarty vanished from the scene, Colonel Sebastian Moran became heir to much valuable information, and thus the Colonel retains a grip on life."

"Big game hunter, was he?"

"The best of the lot when it came to the animal kingdom, and most of the human realm." Holmes uttered a rare soft chuckle. "But not all."

"So," Challenger asked, "if not a man and not a beast, then what?"

"So-called common sense gives no answer, and must yield to logical deduction," Holmes replied. "When you have eliminated all possible answers, whatever remains, however outlandish it may seem, must be the answer."

"Not a man, not a beast?"

"Exactly," Holmes declared, "and nothing of the spirit world, for we need not enter the realm of djinnes and demons, ghosts and ghouls to account for these murders."

"But still not of this world? Are you mad, Holmes?"

Holmes smiled. "Not at all, my dear Challenger. The Earth is one world in the heavens. Astronomy may not be one of my strengths, but if one world exists, then others must as well, for nothing in nature exists as a singularity...present company excepted, of course. And if life exists here, logic dictates it must exist elsewhere, some at levels much more primitive than known on Earth; by the same reasoning, however, it stands there must also be worlds unknown where there exist cultures that are as far in advance of our own as we are to the savages of the Pacific islands or the aboriginals of Australia."

"And, as we know all too well, Holmes, the more advanced the civilization—"

"The more efficient the methods of killing."

"It appears a very efficient and ruthless hunter has come to London Town," Challenger remarked.

In the three days that elapsed since that meeting of the minds, Holmes and Challenger had searched for patterns in violence; additionally, since they now had a working theory, albeit unconventional, they also considered reports and events which the police would never connect to the murder spree. And that investigation had led the two of them to the East End of London, not far from the River Thames, quite near a blood-stenched slaughterhouse, and the murmur of waters which had flowed atop during the time of the Roman legionnaires.

A bell tolled through the night, its leaden tones muffled by distance and blinding fog. There was no certainty the Night Hunter would come this way tonight, but in the absence of certitude even Sherlock Holmes, whose mind functioned as coldly and keenly as a mathematical engine, could grasp at probabilities.

When the last tone faded to silence, Holmes realized another sound had joined the soft background noises, but this was not the murmuring of rivers lost or found, not the whisper of breezes in the city canyons. Something moved in the darkness, cloaked by the choking London fog, something not far away.

It was not Challenger, Holmes knew, for he was stationed a bit closer to the slaughterhouse.

"Up to a night of fun, dearie?"

The voice was soft, sibilant and close by, but no form could be attached to the words. Another unfortunate abroad in the haunted night, forced to travel the mean streets of the metropolis by a desperation that trumped fear.

Another lady of negotiable affection.

Holmes started to speak to the voice in the darkness, but held silent. There was something very odd about the intonation, about the cadence, about the timbre. Sherlock Holmes knew more about human speech than any man in London, except, perhaps, old Higgens, of course, and there was something about the voice in the fog that did not sit right with him.

It appeared the be the voice of a woman, and yet it was not. Holmes was a consummate actor and adept at disguise; in his time, there had been a few occasions when he had not only disguised his features and nationality, as he did this night, but his gender as well. It was easy to play the part of a woman, as long as one did not speak. It was one thing for a woman to pretend to manhood and confidently say, "Good evening, Mr. Holmes," in passing, but it was quite another thing entirely for a man to attempt the same, much less to carry it off. And this did not seem to be a man voicing a woman...more what Holmes would expect from a high-quality wax cylinder, an approximation of fidelity, but no more than a facsimile.

Something paused in the night, as if sizing up Holmes despite the fog cover, as if the eyes of the intruder could pierce the night.

Holmes stealthily raised the muzzle of his weapon in his coat pocket, aiming by every sense except sight.

Some predator sought prey under the cover of night, something that was neither man nor beast. Its predations, though, had not brought it to prey, but to another hunter, a hunter who also sought the most cunning quarry, a hunter old in the most dangerous game.

"Are you looking for me?" Sherlock Holmes murmured.

"Are you looking for me?" hissed the night.

Holmes' eyes narrowed and he lifted his sharp chin from his chest, his height revealing itself as his muscles tensed like iron cords. As he emerged from the persona of a drunken Lascar, he noted three red dots of light precisely over his heart. Instantly, without pausing for thought or analysis, Holmes dropped and rolled across the hard filthy cobbles, his revolver appearing with the suddenness of an Indian cobra.

As Holmes moved, reddish pellets of light burst from a height just over six feet above the ground, but it was such a light as the detective had never before seen, unlike any ever produced by lantern or even the artificer's electric coil. Where the unearthly beam struck, the wall exploded outward, silence shattered, molten fragments erupted, dust roiled, and the force of the explosion for a moment pushed back the wall of yellowish London fog.

In that moment, Sherlock Holmes fired his weapon three times, guided by a glimpse of a vague shape shimmering in the mist, as if the mist itself had tried to congeal into a form, not man-shaped, but one that was a travesty, a mockery of that image which was created to be crowned with honor and glory; no, this had the seeming of a being of diabolical proportions.

Two of the rounds from Holmes' revolver struck mid-mass, thunking with the solidity of lead slugs slamming against a beef carcass.

The third bullet hit somewhat higher, about the same place where the strange pellets of light had emanated. Immediately, something exploded, flares of energy arced upward and out; flames burst to life. In the glare, the vague shape shimmered into firmness. Sherlock Holmes, who had seen so many strange things in his life that he at times considered himself totally jaded to the grotesque, at times considered returning to the sublime oblivion of the seven-per-cent solution, was actually startled.

The being was neither human nor animal, but seemed a

parody of both.

It was huge, nearly seven feet in height, massively muscled, more that thirty stone in weight, wearing some sort of metallic armor and mask, with oily coils of hair flowing from under the helm like black venomous serpents. The breastplate was covered with a kind of netting, and affixed to it were skulls of various sizes and types, including one that could have been a chimpanzee or small human. Trophies. Arcs of silvery lightning rippled across the body armor, and for a long moment the creature seemed to shift between visibility and invisibility.

Sherlock Holmes smiled thinly.

The being, this predator that hunted through nighttime London, was neither god nor demon; obviously it was better armed than would have been its human counterpart, and the industry of mechanical genius had given it fearsome tools of destruction and subterfuge, but it was subject to the same sort of technological failures that cost the lives of men in sport and upon the field of battle.

Its clawed hands ripped the blazing weapon from its shoulder and flung it in Holmes' direction, deflecting a fourth shot from his revolver.

Holmes aimed at the onrushing beast.

The revolver jammed.

The hunter surged toward Holmes, taloned hands ready to flay flesh from bone, to add the skull of a certain consulting detective to its trophy room.

Sherlock Holmes did not avert his gaze.

He stared at the black polished eyes behind the mask.

Thunder shattered the night.

The hunter staggered back, armor pealed open to reveal tattered flesh and spouting streams of phosphorescent green blood.

A strong hand grabbed Holmes' arm and helped him scramble up; he cleared his weapon and out the corners of his eyes saw the hunter fall to its knees.

"Challenger!"

"What is it, Holmes?"

Professor Edward Challenger could not take his gaze from the beast. Cradled in his arms was the .577 Nitro Express rifle he had insisted upon bringing, upon keeping in the urban blind he and Holmes had prepared before the fall of darkness.

"Our Night Hunter," Holmes replied.

"Where on earth—?"

"Not of this Earth," Holmes murmured, unable to keep a measure of satisfaction from his voice.

"Holmes!" Challenger cried, pointing.

The creature started to rise, then fell forward, rolling onto its back. The two men approached the carcass, Challenger with his elephant rifle at the ready.

Holmes kneeled, pulled several small connections from the mask, each releasing a hiss of foetid pressurized gas, then slipped the long fingers of his left hand beneath the edge of the mask; his other hand held the revolver point blank to what should have been the creature's throat. The mask unlocked with a solid click, then came away.

"Good God!" Challenger exclaimed. "What a monster!"

A monster it was indeed, with a face straight from an opium nightmare, less flesh and more like the carapace of a crab, having a mouth gorged with fangs but hinged to open from side-to-side, opposite the motion of a human mouth.

"It breathes still," Holmes said.

Challenger brought the elephant rifle to bear.

"We must bind it so—"

Holmes' sentiment remained unstated. The beast erupted into motion. It pushed Holmes away but not before Holmes discharged his revolver. The aim was spoiled, however, and what should have been a killing shot became a deep graze; the greenish ichor that passed for the hunter's blood spouted across the cobbles. The roar of Challenger's Nitro Express shattered the night, but the huge shell went wide, and by the time the explorer had chambered another, the hunter was fleeing into the night.

Holmes and Challenger gave chase.

A clang sounded hollowly.

"Into the sewers," Challenger muttered grimly.

"To the underground river that empties into the Thames," Holmes explained.

Challenger merely nodded.

They found a ragged opening in a narrow alley between two buildings where an iron grate had been frenziedly ripped away.

Holmes and Challenger dropped into the darkness without hesitation, following thudding footfalls and a trail of glowing green blood.

A break in the brick sewer wall led to unknown regions, and the men followed.

In its time, this strange being had hunted the citizens of London, taking trophies as a man might take a tiger's skin for a rug or a head to adorn a space above a mantle, but now it was the hunted. In hunting man, it had not possessed the advantage that man has over the beasts of the jungle, for man was a thinking animal, a reasoning beast; lacking claws and fangs and speed, man had bested the primordial creatures that would have devoured him by reason of his cunning mind, and history had repeated itself here in the capitol of the world.

Suddenly, in that stygian world where a river now flowed unknown, a strange noise sounded, a whining sound that betoke raw power and yet was unlike any sound of propulsion made by the machines of humanity. Simultaneously a bluish illumination flooded the underground chambers. As they entered a cavern very close to the river they saw a machine resting in a large expanse of muddy water, the source of the light and sound, reflected in the water's surface.

A hatchway closed, but not before Holmes and Challenger saw the outlandish form of the hunter, had one last chance to fire their weapons. The hunter fell within, the hatch slid into place, and the engines of the convoluted craft flared to life.

Holmes dove downward into the mud and water, taking Challenger with him. They felt heat blast over them, heard the shattering of brick and mortar.

They leaped to their feet when the heat vanished and ran to the opening created by the craft ramming through.

For an instant, they saw a manta-like ship nearly skimming the black river's surface, its blue flames reflected by obsidian waters. Then it soared abruptly upward, vanishing into the murky, misty night. Silence surged softly back and soon they heard nothing but the lapping of water against quays and men involved in ancient maritime enterprises.

"Damn," Challenger muttered after a few moments.

"What is it, Challenger?"

"Damn, but that head would have made a good trophy above my fireplace," he explained, tilting his head and giving his friend a wry smile. "I doubt I shall ever have a chance to take that again."

"On the contrary, Challenger," Sherlock Holmes countered as they turned and started away. "I have every confidence that you will."

THE ADVENTURE OF THE DEVIL'S FATHER

BY MORRIS HERSHMAN

Fame, as my friend Mr. Sherlock Holmes occasionally insisted, is the destroyer of function. Let a man be recognized among the general public, Holmes might add pensively, and it promptly becomes impossible to proceed about his business, particularly that of pursuing the craft of detection, a fate which for his part he claimed he owned entirely to the accounts which I had indicated about certain of his cases.

Holmes happened to be holding forth in this vein on a chill pre-Christmas afternoon at our quarters in Baker Street when he suddenly halted himself almost in mid-sentence.

"I can relieve your mind, Watson, by informing you that the man you expect to join us will be arriving very shortly."

"Holmes, is this black magic on your part? How could you possibly know what is on my mind?"

"It is absurdly elementary, my dear fellow. You are continually looking at the door and then examining the face of the turnip watch you wear."

"Could I not be expecting a woman to join us?"

"In that case, you would be dressed far more like a bird showing off its plumage."

"And how do you know that the man will arrive 'very shortly'?"

"Because a glance out the window shows a florid-faced and

worried looking gentleman (with much military experience in his past, I'll be bound!) halting before our premises and looking at the exterior. Someday I must compose a monograph about the effects of anticipation on the reasoning processes."

Before I could apologize for not having spoken about the impending visitation, Mrs. Hudson, our landlady, was ushering a new arrival into our premises.

I said, "This is Colonel Phineas Warburton, late of Her Majesty's Service, whom I knew in Afghanistan." Indeed, he had been among the first to reach me when that infernal Jezail bullet I still carry had penetrated my flesh. "We recently encountered each other in the Strand, and he asked to consult you."

"Let us hope that your problem is of interest, Colonel Warburton. Pray be seated and make your statement."

"I'll get right to the point. I have a son, Mr. Holmes, adopted as a baby by my late wife and myself shortly before a fever carried her off. I was left to raise Trevor, but my duty so occupied me that I couldn't be the best of fathers. Trevor, in a sense, raised himself."

"An elder's duty has warped more children than the basest of crimes," Holmes observed. "Please continue, Colonel."

"Trevor married and was soon in need of funds. No part of my pension would have sufficed to help sufficiently. Not long after his marriage to Violet. I was horrified to learn that my son had illegally invaded the premises of a jeweler in Hatton Gardens to commit theft. With his revolver he fired at a drawer containing valuables and opened it."

"Mr. Trevor Warburton's impatience could dispose him toward further violence."

"It is that possibility, Mr. Holmes, which brings me to ask for help. You see, Trevor was captured and convicted for his crime. He is to be released from Dartmoor on a day not yet determined, but within the week, and has written me that he intends returning to Surrey."

"Where, I presume, he has lived with his wife."

"They rent a cottage in the village of Casshire."

"And you feel that he may be tempted once again into the commission of a crime."

"Tempted into violence is how I must put it. Trevor has previously written that he feels strongly about an extravagant wife having argued him into taking draconian measures to support her. It grieves and shames me to say that I greatly fear possible consequences of his anger at Violet, whether or not justified. He might perpetrate an even greater—ah, indiscretion, than in the past."

"Hm! I must tell you, sir, that I appreciate the difficulty but am not aware of any way in which I must help."

"I dreaded as much, Mr. Holmes, but there may be one solution to this hellish difficulty. If my son is told by so famous a man as Mr. Sherlock Holmes that he will be watched as closely as a dealer in a gambling hell to prevent any misstep, it may be enough to keep Trevor law-abiding from then on."

Holmes looked displeased. "It is not gratifying to confront a commission in which my façade as pictured by Watson, is wanted rather than my hard-won skills as a consulting investigator. You will be aware, though, Colonel, that I can be strongly moved by the task of preventing crime."

"You will not find me ungrateful for your help, Holmes."

"Our good landlady, Mrs. Hudson, will certainly be pleased to hear as much," Holmes said dryly, rising. "I take it that you remain in London at least till the matter can be apparently resolved. Where can you be reached? The Albany? Capital?"

* * * * * * *

Holmes spent the balance of the daylight hours wrapped in thick coils of silence, rather than bestirring himself to arrange a prison interview with Warburton's devil of a son. He sat staring wordlessly at our bullet-pocked walls, his eyes half-shut, an unlighted meerschaum planted between his lips.

I said peevishly, "Sitting immobile for hours will not prevent a woman's being battered, or worse, murdered."

"Without evidence or the means to procure it, I do not yet know how to proceed."

Aware that I was on the threshold of an argument at a difficult time, I descended instead to the street to take the wintry London evening air. Returning not long after, I was surprised to see Mrs. Hudson near the stairs, evidently awaiting me.

"Mr. Holmes told me to let you know that he has left until tomorrow midday, Doctor."

At least Holmes was about to give that wicked young Warburton the sort of talking to that had been richly earned. Holmes was not too late to prevent a horrid crime.

* * * * * *

Holmes did not reappear into the breakfast hour. A telegram from Warburton was delivered, inquiring about the current status of the matter he had placed before us. After some thought I wrote out a telegram to the effect that all was proceeding satisfactorily. Having signed my friend's name to the concoction. I requested our page-boy to drop it off at the appropriate location.

As for the remainder of that morning and into the early afternoon, I hardly recall it. The fire was burning in our grate, adding warmth to the winter day, and I very much fear I dozed off. Suffice it to say that I knew nothing more until my ears made out a sound nearby and I forced both eyes open.

"Just a moment, my good man," I snapped to the scruffy stranger who had invaded our quarters. "Did you receive an appointment to meet with Mr. Holmes at this time?"

Whereupon I was astonished to hear a familiar chuckle issuing from that intruder's parched lips.

"You are ever loyal, Watson, the blessed British bulldog of the life," said Sherlock Holmes. "The blame for my *outré* wardrobe lies at your door, you having published such accounts of my work as to make it far more difficult for me to accomplish in everyday clothes, as I have often explained."

"Spare me, Holmes."

"To business, then. I was unable to visit Dartmoor, the trains to the area not running because of the recent snow and the current icy weather."

"What have you been doing?"

"I hiked myself to Surrey and the village of Casshire, where I repaired to the Pipe and Shag, as the local pub is rather felicitously named."

"Ah! You wanted to question various residents without seeming to do so."

"Bravo, Watson! Your capacity for logical deduction grows apace, I am happy to hear. Yes, in my disguise, it seemed to me that the natives would talk easily about young Warburton. I found several who were happy to indulge in that supposedly feminine sport of gossip. It seems that the young Warburton— had fared badly as far as obtaining the needful was concerned. The young man attempted to find means of honest employment in London and elsewhere, but was thwarted at every turn. He had made application to serve in Her Majesty's forces when the crime took place with its grim aftermath."

"How has Mrs. Warburton lived while her husband was detained at Her Majesty's pleasure?"

"There, Watson, you have put an unerring finger on a point of great interest. It would appear that Mrs. Warburton has inherited money from her late mother's will. An adequate stipend for two will shortly be arriving on the first of the month and into the foreseeable future."

"One hopes it will be enough to save her from possible unpleasantness at her husband's hands," I said. "He has been imprisoned while she, at liberty, has a newly gained income. Is it possible he feels no regrets? That he can persuade himself she was not to blame? Is it possible? Is it likely?"

"I have taken a step to prevent the worst, if only a small step," Holmes responded. "After an overnight stay in Surrey, I met with Violet Warburton, introducing myself correctly. She understood the necessity for my garish costume without referring to it, a young woman who thinks before speaking. Cautious, obviously, with no bent for risk, which may be quite fortunate in the situation that confronts us."

"Did you tell her of the possible difficulty?"

"I did indeed. Violet Warburton loyally refuses to believe that her husband committed the crime for which he was detained, or that he might do her some mischief. She was familiar with my reputation, so she gave me her word that she would be cautious in dealing with her husband and to allow no stranger into her home for the near future. She promised to inform the local constabulary with no delay if any difficulty occurs along those lines. As the trait of caution is part of the young woman's disposition. I accept her word."

"In other words," I said, suddenly triumphant despite the current strains, "she was familiar with your reputation which enabled you to gain her consent, because of the 'sensational' accounts I have caused to be published about your many achievements."

"A touch, Watson, distinctly a touch!" My friend's hearty chuckle was lost in the search for a stubby pen and paper on his cluttered desk. "I am writing to the principal warder of Dartmoor, a bit belatedly, asking when Trevor Warburton is to be released. Then, my dear Watson, you and I will take a hand in the game."

* * * * * * *

In the next hours Holmes beguiled himself by adding cuttings from the newspapers to his various volumes about criminal cases in the length and breadth of Empire. This chore concluded, he favored me with several sentimental German Christmas *lieder* skillfully rendered on his violin. I was breathing deeply in pleasure when a reply came to his recent telegram. Holmes was suddenly galvanized.

"Trevor Warburton was released from Dartmoor early this morning."

"He will have returned to his wife before you can warn him

to restrain from further violent impulses!"

"An immediate trip must be made to Casshire. It is dark now and dirty deeds blend invisibly into the sheath of darkness." He reached for a timetable. "Dress quickly, Watson! Your company will keep strangers from noticing my undisguised presence."

"Shall I take a revolver?"

"There is less chance of mishap if we bring sticks, and I expect further assistance from the full moon."

* * * * * * *

Our train was approaching the snow-tipped chalk downs of Surrey before it occurred to me to regret that my army friend had not been asked to join us. I said as much.

"There is no reason to think that the colonel would like what he might have to witness, Watson. In this matter, even if in no other, circumstances may have conspired for the best."

My further desultory efforts at conversation were met with silence. Holmes was straining to see through the once spotless windows at our sides. He jumped to his feet shortly after we saw the ice-tipped River Way looking like a blue knife in a *blanc-mange*. I joined him as the train let us off in the appropriate village, which was no different in external appearance from many others I had seen.

"The local will serve as a rough compass needle pointing north." So saying, he set off down the High Street, stick at the ready, eyes squinting straight ahead. I found myself several steps behind no matter how hard I struggled to catch up.

Despite my having been of assistance to him—or perhaps I flatter myself—in a number of cases. I never did become used to the lightning quickness with which my friend could act. When he whirled about to urge me by a gesture to walk more silently, I was so taken by surprise that several seconds passed before I was able to do his bidding. I was at my usual two-three paces behind when he halted and raised one hand to keep me from moving straight ahead.

"Behind that tree," he whispered.

Holmes' face was hard, as if contemplating an enemy, eyes narrowed, lips taut against each other. Most surprising of all he had gripped his stick so tightly that the moon's light gave those taut knuckles a semblance of fury.

"Do you think that Trevor Warburton has arrived?" I asked, careful to keep my voice low.

"No," Holmes returned. "Every room but the parlor is dark, and those who live alone are proverbially sparing of light."

The full moon shortly enabled me to see a male approaching the Warburton door, his back toward us. Warburton's devil of an adopted son, I felt sure, was walking along grounds he knew. A sturdy devil, he looked.

I turned to Holmes for guidance and received a shock when he pointed firmly back to the unfolding drama before us. A woman's footsteps eagerly approached the other side of the door as the new arrival knocked imperiously.

There was a pause, and then along the brisk night air, it was possible to hear a slurred and almost gravelly voice.

"It is I, Trevor."

No movement could be heard from the other side of the door.

Holmes, already in motion, called back to me, "Now, Watson!"

Even as Holmes raced to the door, myself only a step back, Trevor Warburton's body thundered against it, striking at the correct angle to force it open. He had shown a devastating lack of caution by not hearing or paying attention to Holmes. The full moon let a cone of light over his broad back into the large room.

Holmes had raised the stick and connected solidly with the man's form. The man grunted and showed a revolver which was promptly knocked out of his nerveless hand. He suddenly staggered, having taken a total of ten steps into the room, then fell back to the floor.

Only now that Holmes had prevailed did I turn to the woman. Blood marked a cheek where she had surely been struck in the seconds that the villain had been able to do what he wished. She was pluckily recovering her balance before I started to attend her.

That done, I looked down at the monster writhing at our feet and received one of the most profound shocks of my life. For I was staring not at the youthful Trevor Warburton, but at Trevor's adopted father, my army friend, Colonel Phineas Warburton.

* * * * * * *

"The criminal himself made me suspicious of his villainy," Holmes observed on the morning train back to London. "In speaking to us at Baker Street, he offered a jarring simile about a dealer in a gambling hell, you recall, while discussing a matter in which the prime factor was a lack of money. It caused me to view other aspects of his story in a different light, and to wonder whether he himself was afflicted with a shortage of the necessary."

"And he was?"

"Indeed, yes. I was able to learn the truth in the briefest time by making contact with my brother, whose acquaintance you have made over the years. To a far greater extent than myself, Mycroft knows everything about potential scandals of any interest. Truly, he is the *Debrett's* of the disreputable. He provided me with the information that Warburton had been on the ropes, financially, for quite awhile, and staving off discovery by the skin of his teeth."

"I can hardly believe that Phineas Warburton acquired gambling debts that drove him to steal his son's revolver some years ago and commit a robbery, then say nothing when Trevor was sent to prison in his stead."

"The colonel's confession freely given, even boastfully given for some reason, must force you to accept those facts, Watson, as well as the horror that followed. Learning that his daughter-in-law had inherited enough to solve his difficulty he decided to take that money for himself by lying, cheating, and committing a base murder which could involve exposing another human being to a judicial sentence of hanging."

I nodded sadly, well aware from his jaunty confession that Phineas Warburton had lied, among other things, about Trevor's feelings for his young wife. Later, he had urged Trevor to spend a few restful hours in London upon his release from imprisonment, promising to telegraph Violet Warburton with the good news that her husband was free. Of course he had done nothing of the sort.

When the young man finally rested, the colonel felt able to wreak fatal mischief that would be laid at the door of the luckless younger man. If Mrs. Warburton hadn't failed to accept the colonel's claim of identity as Trevor in those last moments, he would have been entirely successful, inheriting the dead daughter-in-law's money from Trevor's estate after the latter had been hanged.

"Couldn't he have thrown himself at the mercy of the young people and borrowed a considerable portion of the money that he needed?"

"He lacked enough judgment to consider doing so," Holmes tapped his own forehead as if to say that the man's faculties had been impaired by greed.

"I fear, after having seen him, that the matter may be more tragic than you believe, Holmes. Warburton's reason may have been shaken to the foundations by his many reverses, and he may never leave an institution for the—the insane."

"Your apprehensions could be wholly justified, Watson, but Warburton's stay cannot be without an end. Everything in this span of our lives is *pro tempore*, old fellow, for we begin afresh after we leave this first plane of existence."

I introduced to this notice the problem of Colonel Warburton's madness.

—A. Conan Doyle,
"The Adventure of the Engineer's Thumb"

A MEMO FROM
INSPECTOR LESTRADE

BY MARVIN KAYE

Those who have faithfully read Dr. Watson's many accounts of Mr. Holmes' adventures and exploits may wonder that I begin this piece with a reference to Dr. Watson as my old friend. My appearances, of course, in various of his compositions are restricted to the details of those investigations. But in my ongoing involvement with Holmes, I swiftly apperceived Dr. Watson as one of the kindest gentlemen I have ever met. In the earlier years, we had no occasion to interact socially, but when I learned that Sherlock Holmes had supposedly died at Reichenbach Falls, I paid Dr. Watson a visit to offer my condolences. Both touched and grateful, he poured us two generous measures of brandy and proposed a toast. I lifted my glass and with heart-felt sympathy drank to Holmes' memory.

It is true that Holmes was a trial to me at times, but for all his unorthodox modes of investigation, his ratiocinative abilities were formidable, and I freely acknowledge (at least now) that it was a privilege to work with him. But work, you see, always defined our relationship, whereas Dr. Watson's affability, humor, and his skill as a raconteur made him a splendid companion to sit by a fireside and share a wee dram with.

I saw less of the doctor after the astonishing return of Sherlock Holmes, but on one occasion, all three of us were brought together when I sought assistance on a purely personal matter. I am grateful to have this opportunity to tell about it, and to thank Mr. Holmes through the aegis of this public forum.

* * * * * * *

The year prior to my retirement was less demanding than I was accustomed to; I was relegated to a desk job, and a younger officer was assigned to duties that I suspected were now considered too taxing for my accumulated years. My wife, at least, was pleased, and for two reasons: first, I was less at risk; second, my hours were now much more regular, which resulted in my being able to spend more time at home.

It was this second reason that prompted me to seek membership in the Nonpareil Club. This was a gentleman's establishment a short distance from Holmes' Baker Street quarters. The geographic proximity proved fortuitous, though that never would have occurred to me had not the club extended its hospitality to one Colonel Barton P. Upwood, a person who soon earned the disfavor of the rest of the members, myself included, though I had not sought to cultivate his acquaintance. But his presence in our sacrosanct "quiet chamber" swiftly disturbed all of its denizens.

Do not be misled; what I refer to as the "quiet chamber" was the Nonpareil's main room. Our club is not very large. It has a few private parlors devoted to whatever business might prompt members to reserve their use for a designated time, and the upstairs floor offers a few modest suites designed for overnight stays.

The central chamber of the venue holds a number of over-stuffed armchairs that I generally lounge upon whilst sipping brandy, reading daily news-sheets, and perhaps puffing upon a Havana cigar. There are also tables and upright chairs for those who wish to play at whist, *vingt-et-un*, and other card games. At one time the addition of a billiard table was considered, but the idea of all that clicking of cue-sticks against the balls did not appeal to most of the membership, and the notion was, shall we say, tabled.

The main room, you see, always was intended to be a quiet place—not to the extent that I have been told pervades a certain chamber at The Diogenes Club, to which Sherlock Holmes's formidable brother Mycroft belongs. But all actions and events pursued within the Nonpareil, whether they be for business or pleasure, are expected to be done with gentlemanly discretion and an irreducible minimum of sound as is humanly possible. A long array of potables arranged along one wall, paralleled by a counter with several high stools for imbibers to perch, is presided over by a bar-tender who carries on his duties without producing anything louder than an occasional chink of an ice-cube. As for the gentleman's gentleman who serves drinks, empties the ash-trays and dusts the furniture, the Executive Committee even went to the extent of hiring a deaf-mute named Richmond.

* * * * * * *

Now try to imagine the consternation that was wrought when Colonel Upwood joined our club! Dr. Watson once made passing reference in print to the man's "atrocious conduct" as well as that card scandal which the Nonpareil Executive Committee vainly tried to hush up, a circumstance that I regret, though that body of worthies perhaps deserved what they got for accepting Upwood as a member in the first place.

To begin with, the man was incapable of addressing anyone in soft tones; his customary mode of utterance was precious close to a shout. He even spoke loudly to Richmond, though the Colonel was told more than once that our butler was not only incapable of speech, but also suffered from a hearing deficiency. This would have been bad enough, but Upwood was responsible for a variety of coarse nonverbal noises: snorts, burps, ear-shattering sneezes and equally loud nose-blowing, as well as other sounds I prefer not to name.

The elder club members naturally began to complain, but it

soon became general knowledge that the Executive Committee, which for some time had been troubled by difficulties in balancing the club's budget, had voted in favor of membership for the Colonel because of the generous gratuity he elected to pay over and above the usual initiation fee and annual dues assessment.

This so thoroughly exasperated one Admiral Norrington Miles, one of the club's founding members (and chief complainant against Colonel Upwood), that he took it upon himself to confront him. In a frosty tone that I imagine once chilled the Admiral's nautical subordinates, he said, "Sir, from now on you will desist from disturbing the Nonpareil with your loud voice and catalogue of abominable noises."

Colonel Upwood's response was raucous laughter. He banged a large pistol on the card table where he sat. "This thing," he declared, "makes a *lot* more noise."

I half expected Admiral Miles to seize the weapon and pistol-whip the man, but after several seconds of tense silence, he pivoted smartly, and left the club. As soon as he was gone, Upwood pocketed his firing-piece and riffle-shuffled his deck of cards three times, declaring, "Is anyone in the mood to play bridge-whist?" After it was clear that no one intended to answer him, he snorted, "Hardly surprising. Obviously, none of you have the *cojones* to challenge me, not even at cards."

This was more than I could tolerate; I stepped up to his table and demanded to know what the stakes were. Two other Nonpareil members followed my example, and for the next few hours I sacrificed much of the currency in my billfold, but my suspicions were confirmed: Colonel Upwood was not only a bounder, he was also a cheat.

* * * * * * *

"How curious!" Dr. Watson exclaimed. "This is the second time that we have heard that name this evening."

"Tut, Watson, tut, we must not disclose the identity of our

previous caller."

"Of course not, Holmes! You know me better than that." The good doctor offered me a snifter of excellent brandy and we all took seats in the front chamber of 221B Baker Street, where a cheerfully crackling fire warmed us.

Sherlock Holmes regarded me thoughtfully, "Inspector, assuming you are correct and Upwood is a devious gambler, why come to me about it? After all, you have the resources of the London police force available to pursue the matter."

"I am loath to subject the Nonpareil to the distress and negative publicity that might entail. Furthermore, as yet I have no evidence to support my belief that he is cheating. I know a few things on the topic, but it is not my area of expertise. I could speak with someone in the vice squad, of course, but even that might have negative results. Thus I have come to you, for I know I may rely upon your, and Dr, Watson's, discretion."

They both thanked me. "As Watson has revealed, we have already been visited tonight about Colonel Upwood."

"Has someone else complained that he cheats at cards?"

Holmes shook his head. "I am not at liberty to discuss the nature of the commission I accepted, but I have already consulted both my library and my brother and you may he interested to know that Upwood is not a British colonel."

"I wondered about that. His raucous speech patterns are decidedly unfamiliar."

Dr. Watson chuckled. "I should think so. Holmes has placed him as an Australian who migrated to Canada."

"So he only pretends to be a military man!"

"Not so, Inspector," Holmes replied. "He's also been in America and took an army commission there, though Mycroft says Upwood has seen no significant action. Watson, another round, if you will?"

Our friend, replenishing our brandy, asked me, "Why do you think Colonel Upwood is rigging his card games?"

"I have two reasons. The first is the manner in which he holds the deck."

"Describe it for me," said Holmes.

"He lets it nestle in his palm with his thumb on top. His pinky, ring and middle finger press the edges against the heel of his hand."

"And," Holmes added, "his forefinger curls round the deck's top edge?"

"Precisely. A magician I know holds cards in the same manner."

Holmes smiled. "I learned about it the same way, Inspector. It's what is sometimes called the engineer's clutch, or the mechanic's grip. It allows for considerable control of the deck should the manipulator wish to deal from the bottom, execute a false shuffle, or a variety of other stealthy maneuvers. In itself, of course, it constitutes no proof that Upwood is doing any such thing. But you said you have another reason to be suspicious?"

"Yes. The man almost never loses."

"That," Holmes nodded, finishing his brandy, "is indeed a telltale. I think a visit to your club, Inspector, is, shall we say, in the cards? Could Watson and I accompany you there in a few days?"

I said I would arrange it. Holmes then had me describe the Nonpareil Club to him in considerable detail, from the physical arrangement of the main chamber, its shape, size, furniture and related appurtenances, to the customary club members and staff; he even had me describe the design of the club's card decks.

* * * * * * *

Three days later we met in the early evening at the club's front entrance. Holmes outlined his plan of action in the most general of terms, for, I suspect, his sense of the dramatic, which Dr. Watson has mentioned on several occasions, compelled Holmes to reserve the particulars of the evening's intended program, except to the extent that he found it necessary to instruct me and his friend in what he wished us to do.

Our chief role, he explained, was to play cards with him and "our mark," as Holmes put it, and we were told to play like the veriest amateurs.

"Do not be concerned about your losses, gentlemen. Our costs tonight are amply underwritten." With that he produced three large rolls of currency, two of which he gave us, keeping the third bundle for himself. This circumstance reinforced my suspicion of the identity, though not the mission, of Holmes's secret client.

As we entered the club's main chamber, the first person I saw was Upwood, who was seated in the middle of the room at a green baize card table. He faced the bar where several members sat nursing drinks, their backs turned (necessarily, due to the angle, yet also deliberately, I supposed) to the abrasive Colonel who was playing some variety of solitaire, cursing quite audibly from time to time at the turn of the cards.

"Richmond!" he shouted suddenly. "Fetch me some rum!"

This, of course, produced no immediate result from the subject of his demand, inasmuch as that worthy was occupied emptying ashtrays with no idea that he had been summoned.

The bartender, however, certainly heard. He proceeded to fill a glass whilst Peter Farringwell, assuredly the most amiable denizen of the Nonpareil, tapped Richmond's shoulder. When he had the butler's attention, Farringwell explained what was wanted in that fidgety finger-talk which Richmond was proficient in, though only a few other club members, and certainly not myself, were able to manage for his behest. Thus did the man hie himself to the bar and in such wise the disruptive interloper finally got his rum.

Holmes nodded to me, and then murmured something to Dr. Watson, who, I was surprised to see, immediately quitted the room we had just entered. Still, as thespians say, it was my cue, so I crossed to Colonel Upwood and said that I sought an opportunity to recompense the losses I had incurred the last time I played cards with him.

A raucous laugh. Adjusting his garish neck-tie, he loudly riffled the cards and declared, "The more fool, you! But if you propose to play bridge-whist, we shall both be disappointed. No one else is likely to join us."

"Never fear," I said, "I've brought two friends along for the purpose."

"You mean, sir, that you've rounded up a pair of ringers?" He belched, and did not apologize for his solecism. "Very well, bring 'em on."

Holmes stepped forward. I introduced him as Mr. Sherringford Vernet (a family name, he'd told me earlier).

"Have a seat," said the Colonel. "I've met your companion the other night, but I never learned his monicker."

"Vernet," introduced me as Mr. Gregson. He had not prepared me for that, and I almost protested, but bit my tongue (literally, unfortunately).

Upwood took a sip of rum, then wiped his mouth with the back of his hand. "We're still one player short."

At that fortuitous instant, Dr. Watson reappeared. As he approached our table, Holmes-Vernet introduced him as one "Ormond Sacker." (Later I asked Holmes where he'd come up with such an odd name. Dr. Watson, with a chuckle, informed me that Sacker was another client of his Scottish literary agent.)

* * * * * * *

Before proceeding with my tale, it strikes me that contemporary readers will not be familiar with the game of bridge-whist, which, at the time of the Upwood scandal, enjoyed a brief period of popularity in London.

Whist, of course, is a fairly venerable trick-taking game, one which bridge eventually supplanted in most gaming circles, both in England and America. The two, however, are more similar than different. Each consists of a series of tricks, that is, rounds of play in which each contestant sets upon the table one of the cards he or she has been dealt. The highest card wins the trick, thus contributing or detracting from each player's final score for the hand.

Bridge is distinguished by the declaration of a "trump" suit, which is determined nowadays by players bidding for the advantage of naming it. For those of you who are not conversant with the term, a trump suit is one of the four card denominations—clubs, diamonds, hearts, spades—that for the duration of the hand is declared higher in value than the other three suits. Thus, let us say that a player sets down a seven of diamonds. His first opponent produces the queen of diamonds, but the next player, in partnership with the one who played the seven, sets down the king of the same suit. The second opponent, however, plays the two of spades and since that is the trump suit, he or she wins the trick.

In terms of years, bridge-whist was an ephemeral pastime. Its play was distinct from the hyphenated halves of its name inasmuch as the dealer of every hand, after reviewing the cards he'd gotten, named the trump suit for that round of play. This, of course, was a major advantage, but every player got to deal and thus enjoyed the same privilege.

* * * * * * *

To report alphabetically (and pseudonymously), Gregson, Sacker, Upwood, and Vernet played bridge-whist for a few hours. During that time, Upwood and Holmes both smoked incessantly, cigarettes for Holmes, whilst the other puffed pungent cigars, one of which I accepted. Poor Watson coughed pointedly, whilst Richmond had frequent occasion to hover about us and empty our oft-filled ash-trays. As the game progressed, the store of cash bet upon each successive hand slowly dwindled for Messrs. Gregson, Sacker and Vernet, though not for the Colonel.

At length, our ears and sensibilities were assaulted by an ungentlemanly eructation (in other words, a rude burp!), but for once said unpleasant noise was not committed by Upwood, but rather by Mr. "Vernet."

It was meant as a signal to me and Dr. Watson. I'd been waiting for this moment, but when it came, I confess to being concerned by the great quantity of alcohol that Holmes had imbibed. I knew it was part of the general plan to demonstrate to our opponent what easy "marks" we all were, but I feared Holmes had thrown himself into the part much too heartily, to our potential disadvantage. (When I expressed my doubts after the evening's business had been accomplished, Holmes said, "O, ye of little faith!" and Dr. Watson assured me that Holmes' capacity, though seldom put to the test, was enormous).

"I have to go home soon," Holmes-Vernet slurringly declared. "Before I go, though, I'd like to play just one more hand."

Upwood's laugh was reminiscent of the bark of some large sea-mammal. "In other words, buster, you've got more money you want to throw away?"

"Vernet" smiled. "Possibly, Colonel—but I have a proposition that might amuse you."

Upwood grunted. "Go on. Make me laugh."

"These are the stakes—" said Holmes (I attribute this remark to him, not his alter ego, because his tone was suddenly coldly sober)—"If you win, you get all of the remaining money in my possession, as well as that of my companions."

The Colonel's eyes narrowed. It was clear he'd noticed the change in his opponent's demeanour. "Well, Vernet, those are handsome stakes—but how do I know that you chaps have anything left to gamble?"

We were prepared for this possibility. We all displayed what was left in our wallets, which, in the aggregate, still comprised a fair sum of lucre. This, of course, made Upwood even more suspicious, but Holmes had also anticipated that.

"Those are stakes worth playing for," our opponent admitted, "but I've already won a considerable amount this evening, and I have the distinct feeling that I am now being, as they say, hustled. Do you expect me to risk everything I've got on the outcome of a single hand?"

"By no means, Colonel," Holmes demurred. "I trust that the counter-stakes I am about to suggest will appear quite modest to you."

"All right, name them."

"I only ask you to risk two things: nine guineas to be paid to my friend Gregson here, plus the granting of a single favor to me."

The sum, which was certainly modest compared to what we'd already gambled, was the precise amount I'd lost to the Colonel a few nights earlier.

"How generous, Mr. Vernet. But what's your favor?"

"You will only find that out if you lose the hand. But I promise that it will be well within your power to grant, and it will neither be dishonorable, immoral, nor will it compromise you in any fashion, fiscally, legally, nor spiritually."

"I confess that, against my better judgment, you have me hooked. Shall I shuffle the cards?"

"Not just yet," Holmes replied. "There is one further condition. I don't want to continue with bridge-whist, at which you are obviously an expert. I propose to play another game."

"What? Poker?"

Holmes shook his head. "A game called Niagara Falls bridge-whist."

Upwood slammed the table with the flat of his hands. "Damn it, sir! There's no such game!"

"Indeed there is. It's played all the time—in Canada."

That made the Colonel stop and think. He'd lived in Canada, of course, but did he want to declare that in public? Before he could think of what to say, Dr. Watson suddenly slumped over the table, slipped off his chair and landed on the floor. He had apparently fainted.

"Douse him with cold water," Holmes-Vernet suggested heartlessly.

I strode to the bar, grasped a pitcher and dashed its contents in poor Watson's face. He sputtered, toweled himself with a handkerchief, and apologized profusely. Upwood, with uncharacteristic concern, suggested we forgo our game and take our inebriated friend home. Sacker-Watson wouldn't hear of it, though, so we all resumed our seats at the table and commenced to play "Niagara Falls bridge-whist."

Along the green surface, Holmes spread the cards face-down so that they described an arc. "This pattern," he said, "is where the game derives its name. It's meant to look like Niagara Falls—the American side, I do believe."

"Very pretty," said Upwood. "Now what?"

"Since I am this hand's dealer," Holmes said, "the first thing I must do is to select my cards at random, without looking at their faces." He proceeded to fish out thirteen cards from the "waterfall" and arranged them, still face-down, in front of him. "Now each of you does the same, one at a time, eldest hand first."

Eldest hand meant the player to his left, and that was the Colonel. He chose his cards, assembling them in a row without turning them over. It was Dr. Watson's turn next, and I picked up the rest.

"Now, I suppose," the Colonel said, "we pick up our cards and you declare trumps?"

Vernet-Holmes shook his head. "Not in this game I don't. I must name the trump suit *before* I examine my cards."

This idea vastly amused our "mark." As for myself, I was half-convinced that Holmes was both drunk and slightly mad. Certainly I saw no way short of Divine Accident that he could win.

"Well, sir," Upwood prompted, "what suit do you choose?"

Holmes shrugged, imbibed more brandy, shrugged again, then finally selected spades as trumps.

After the Colonel had studied his cards, he played the Ace of Hearts. Dr. Watson set down a four of the same suit and I sloughed off a ten. Holmes won the trick with the two of spades.

"Well, that was lucky, wasn't it?" the Colonel grumbled. "Now try to beat this!" He played the Ace of Diamonds. Holmes beat it with the three of spades.

Upwood did not laugh again. Holmes won the eleven remaining tricks. His hand consisted solely of the entire trump suit.

* * * * * * *

"I confess," our foe growled, counting off nine guineas from his billfold and shoving them onto the table in front of me, "I admire your ruse. However you brought it off, it was brilliantly executed."

Holmes regarded him with a cold smile. "Do you mean to imply that I cheated you, sir?"

"Of course you did! There has never been such a hand as yours in the entire history of whist, bridge, or any of their variants."

"Perhaps I was merely lucky."

"Perhaps tomorrow the moon and sun will suddenly change places." He waved it away. "I suspected you were up to something, but I chose to play, anyway, and I am glad I did. It's not often one witnesses such entertaining flummery. Had I spent the night dining and taking in a play, it surely would have cost me more. I do not know how you brought it off—"

"That, Colonel, is your weakness."

"If you are trying to insult me, calling me weak is an excellent way to do so. But I will let it pass. I am curious to know what favor I must do for you now that I've lost the hand."

"Effective immediately," Holmes answered, "you will resign from the Nonpareil Club and never attempt to renew your membership."

Upwood plunked his pistol down on the table. "I'd like to see you make me do that."

Holmes sighed. "I was sure this is how you would respond— not as a gentleman. Since you have decided to welsh on your bet, I shall resort to other means. First, I will tell you the real names of the players you have spent the night with. I am Sherlock Holmes, the man on your left is my friend Dr. John H. Watson, and this other gentleman is Inspector Lestrade of Scotland Yard."

The bounder's face turned beet-red. "I don't give a damn who any of you are! You've got nothing on me!"

"Colonel," Holmes continued, "I prefaced the introductions I just made with the word 'First.' My second point is that your partner in crime, one Toddy Armbruster, is at this moment in the custody of the London police."

Upwood looked round wildly, then shot to his feet, but before he could lay hold of his weapon, Holmes seized the Colonel's wrist. "If I release you, sir, will you leave here quietly?"

"Holmes, you are—" Here the man uttered a great number of obscenities, but once he'd vented his anger, all the fight went out of him. "Yes, damn you, yes."

Holmes permitted him to pocket his pistol. Colonel Upwood quit the Nonpareil Club, never to return.

* * * * * * *

Back at 221B, Holmes, Dr. Watson and I were pleased to discover that Mrs. Hudson had set out a snack consisting of cold beef, aromatic cheese, hot biscuits, condiments, and mugs of amber ale.

As we heartily tucked in, I remarked to Holmes that I was by now not only certain of the identity of his secret client, but also the nature of the task he'd set him. "Admiral Norrington Miles wanted you to find a way to oust Colonel Upwood from the club, am I correct?"

My host smiled, "Excellent, Lestrade. You *might* be right." Then his smile disappeared. "Inspector, I'm afraid that I owe you an apology."

"For what?"

"As soon as we entered the Nonpareil, I recognized Toddy Armbruster, though fortunately he had never met me.

I understand now why he was apologizing. We had hoped to conduct the night's adventure without incurring curiosity and unwanted publicity, but once Holmes told Dr, Watson to inform the police about Armbruster, there was no going back, and the press soon reported the Upwood card scandal.

"It was the one circumstance I had not anticipated," said

Holmes.

At that moment, Mrs. Hudson came in to clear the empty plates and brush crumbs off the table. Holmes gestured; Dr. Watson and I joined him in the sitting room where strong coffee and brandy awaited us. After a few sips of each, Holmes went to a low table covered with newspapers and periodicals, which he bundled into a pile in order to make room to spread out the deck of cards he produced from one of his pockets.

"I say, Holmes," Dr. Watson exclaimed, "have you taken up petty thievery?"

"What on earth do you mean? Ah, I see—you're referring to my cards!"

"But they're not yours...they belong to the Nonpareil Club!"

"Calm yourself, Watson. I got these from the bar-tender. He has an ample supply for anyone who wishes to purchase a deck."

"When did you have the opportunity?"

"I went to the club the day before."

That surprised me. "How did you gain entry without being a member?"

"Mycroft arranged it."

"But, Holmes," his companion said, "you've never shown much interest in card games."

"True, Watson, but you may recall that I asked the Inspector to describe the design of the club's cards. When he did so, I knew that I must arm myself with a spare deck before we met Colonel Upwood."

"Why?"

Holmes spread the cards out on the table in the same curved arc he'd made at the outset of our hand of Niagara Falls bridge-whist. He indicated the array and asked us to tell him whether we noticed anything (other than the curved shape of the display) that we might deem worthy of comment.

We examined them. The back of each card bore a simple gray-and-white design with the words "The Nonpareil Club" in the middle of it, and the club's address on a line below the name in smaller type-face.

Permit me now to state that cinema and theatrical actors who depict Dr. Watson as a sort of bumbling Colonel Blimp do the man considerable disservice. In fact, he's quite an intelligent chap. Not on Holmes's level, of course, but then, other than brother Mycroft, who is?

I make this observation prefatory to revealing that it was Dr. Watson who first realized what Holmes meant us to see concerning the Nonpareil card deck.

"Though I cannot tell what denomination any of these cards may be, since they are all face-down," Dr. Watson said, "yet I do notice that, in a manner of speaking, several of these cards call attention to themselves."

"Excellent, Watson." He turned to me. "Do you see how they differ?"

"Yes, Holmes, now that I study them, I do." Several of the cards, perhaps when they had been shuffled, were turned around so that the club's name and address were upside down.

"Conjurers would call this a one-way deck," Holmes told us. "If all the cards are arranged in the same orientation, the backs look identical, but the trained eye will easily locate a card that has been turned around, especially if the deck is ribbon-spread in a manner similar to what I have done."

"So is this the way Colonel Upwood cheats?" I asked.

"I doubt it, Inspector, not altogether. I am sure that the man noticed this peculiarity, but even armed with such knowledge, a crooked gambler would not be likely to tip fortune by more than a few admittedly telling degrees. Now the manner in which Upwood gripped his cards, as we already discussed, is a sign that he knows how to execute false shuffles, deal from the bottom, and employ other sly methods to stack hands in his favor. As a matter of fact, as we played, I caught him a few times using such techniques. But still, the man rarely loses. That suggested to me that he also had an accomplice feeding him information."

"Aha!" Dr. Watson suddenly exclaimed. "I see how you won that game!" He then appeared unsure of himself, an attitude I suppose is integral to sharing quarters with Sherlock Holmes.

"Well, I *believe* I do...."

"Tell us what you think, dear fellow."

"You told me, Holmes, that there would come a time when you would need me to create a diversion to distract the Colonel. That's when I pretended to faint."

"Yes, Watson, and one of your better performances, I may say. Continue."

"While the others were helping me off the floor, you switched the deck we'd been using with the one you bought earlier."

Holmes nodded. "Go on."

"The deck you'd bought had all of the spades reversed so that you'd recognize them when you assembled your hand."

"Precisely."

I broke into the conversation with the observation that it was fortunate Holmes was acquainted with a game such as Niagara Falls bridge-whist with its odd variation whereby the dealer names the trump suit before being permitted to examine the cards he'd chosen blindly.

"Oh, dear Inspector!" Holmes exclaimed. "There's no such game. I invented it!" He took a moment to pour more coffee for us and also refilled our snifters. I was beginning to worry at the growing lateness of the hour, and hoped my dear wife was not in a pet, but before I left, there was one more thing I positively needed to know, and dear Dr. Watson surely shared my curiosity.

"Holmes," I said, "who was the Colonel's accomplice?"

"Why, Toddy Armbruster, of course."

"But there's no such member in the club!"

"I never said there was. Toddy Armbruster is the confidence trickster who was involved in an attempted securities swindle last summer in Manchester. He's the only member of the gang who got away. I've seen his face on the wall of nearly every police station I've visited during the past few months. I'm surprised you don't know about him, Inspector."

I sighed. "Since they relegated me to a desk job, I've not been able to stay current with the day-to-day, so to speak."

"Another bit of luck for us," said Holmes. "He'd never met either of us, so he had no idea what was ahead for him. But during Watson's pretended fainting spell, I not only switched decks, I also managed to whisper to him, "Hello, Toddy." That's when he tried to bolt."

Now I understood! "Great Heavens! You mean that Armbruster—"

"Yes, Lestrade," said Holmes, "Toddy Armbruster was pretending to be none other than the Nonpareil Club's speechless employee, Richmond."

"Damn him!" I swore. "So while he fussed about emptying our ashtrays, he peeked at our hands and told what he'd learned to Colonel Upwood in the sign language of the deafmute!"

"Yes, gentlemen. It is, you see, a case in which the silent butler did it."

"Ooh, Holmes," Dr. Watson groaned. "How *could* you?!"

THE BUTTON-BOX

BY LYN MCCONCHIE

It was the year of '96 in which the following case occurred. Like so many of Holmes' cases it began with the trivial and ended with a more serious crime. And the trivial in this case was so bewilderingly trivial that initially I could see no rhyme or reason in it.

Holmes had been busy investigating the case of the Bermondsy abductions and at the end of that depraved and vicious series of events we were taking our leisure for a time while I attended to personal matters and Holmes, despite his pipe and his violin, had already become bored. So that it was all to the good when it appeared that a new case was presenting itself hopefully for our inspection.

It started with the arrival in our rooms of Mr. Hilton Soames, tutor and lecturer at the College of St. Luke. We had aided him in an earlier mystery when one of his students had attempted to gain an unfair advantage in pursuing a scholarship, and now he was again on our doorstep begging for our assistance.

"For," he said, as he accepted a cup of tea. "My grandmother is so enraged by this insolent theft that I fear for her health."

I looked at him in surprise. I had believed Soames to be in his mid-forties and I would have supposed his grandmother to be long since dead. He caught my look and understood it at once.

"No, I fear it is my appearance which deceives you, Doctor. I am but thirty-six although I know I appear some years older, also the women of my family have always been healthy and long-lived. My grandmother is eighty-seven and in her energy you would think her near a score of years the younger."

Holmes intervened. "Tell us why the lady is so agitated and why it is that you require my aid?"

Soames shivered. "It is terrible, that a lady of her age cannot walk abroad without being flung to the ground and having her property seized from her."

"What property?" I questioned him. "Her handbag, I assume?"

"No, that is the foolish thing. It was her button-box that was stolen."

I stared at him. "Her button-box? What is that, and why should your grandmother be carrying it about with her?"

Holmes broke in quietly. "A button-box is a box that contains buttons, Watson. Many women build up quite a collection; since buttons can cost quite large sums it is not uncommon for the woman of the house to select a container and place in it any loose or spare buttons she obtain. Then if a button is required she may search within the box and use one from her store. Into the box go also complete sets of buttons from garments which are otherwise too worn out to continue to give service."

I nodded. "Now that you mention it, I do recall my mother had such a container."

Soames sighed. "My grandmother's button-box was old. It was, so far as any of us know, passed down to her from her grandmother who had it from hers. The container is referred to as a box, but in reality it is more of a tiny chest. One apparently made in imitation of a sailor's chest—and family legend has it that it was given to some long ago Soames as a gift from someone for whom he had done a favor."

"Is there a curse?" I asked frivolously.

Soames groaned. "No, there is not, although I shall think there is if Holmes cannot retrieve the item. My grandmother is a woman of strong character and we are not like to ever hear the last of it if her button-box is not returned to her."

I eyed the lecturer as he paced in his agitation. Soames was a tall, spare man of a nervous and excitable temperament at the best of times—which these were not. I imagined his grand-mother to be a tall lady, gaunt of features, nervous, excitable, and with a penetrating and shrill voice, which would drive Soames to distraction.

Besides, Holmes needed a trivial case to occupy his mind, and one of such pleasantly bewildering and minor importance should occupy him splendidly. I could see he was considering the proposition and I hastened to endorse the idea.

"Are you sure you wish to use your time in seeking out a lost button-box, Holmes?"

My friend eyed me with amusement, while Soames' look as he stood up was one of reproach. Holmes turned to the lecturer. "No, no, Mr. Soames. Watson is merely using reverse psychology. He hopes that by stressing the unimportance of the case that I may be moved to investigate."

He waved Soames to a seat again. "Tell me how your grand-mother came to lose her button-box—and I foresee," he added, "That we shall all become very tired of hearing those two words before this case is concluded. But to begin your tale, how is it that she was carrying the item about the town?"

"My family, Mr. Holmes, have lived near the University for some generations. My grandmother has a small house near the University and is often about visiting friends and doing good works in connection either with the church or with the University. A week ago yesterday she was calling on an old friend who has a small granddaughter staying with her, and my grandmother took her button-box to amuse the child while her elders were in converse.

"She had taken a cab to her friend's home which is in a short close. This backs onto the University and the close is too narrow for a cab to enter. My grandmother therefore paid the driver off at the entrance to the street and it was shortly after she alighted and began to walk down towards her friend's house that she was seized from behind. The button-box was wrenched from the crook of her arm and she was thrust to the ground. Whoever did this clearly had no intention of her seeing him since, as he did this, he also dragged her shawl over her head and by the time she was able to clear her vision and rise to her feet again, there was no one to be seen.

"It may be noteworthy that her handbag was untouched and she is positive that there was no attempt to take it from her. My grandmother is a woman of resolution. Bruised and shaken though she was she returned to the main road, hailed a cab and had herself driven at once to the police station where she laid an official complaint. However, she says it was clear to her that the police would take no interest in the case. As one man said to her, it would be some child, no doubt, and what fence will pay out for buttons?"

"I have known buttons which were worth a considerable sum," Holmes observed.

"That may have been true had some of her buttons been ornamented with precious stones. But, Mr. Holmes, they were not. Oh, here and there she may have had a set with paste stones. But mostly they were merely attractive buttons or the more workaday items from family shirts. But they are the collection of her life, passed down from her own grandmother and she feels, I think, that in some way they were a trust. She is distraught and angry. Please help her, Mr. Holmes!"

Holmes rose in a leisurely fashion. "Well, Watson, are you game to go in pursuit of Mr. Soames' grandmother's button-box?" I nodded. "Then let us firstly interview the lady, and after that we shall seek out the scene of the crime and discover what we can find there. Where shall we find your grandmother, Mr. Soames?"

"Back in her home, sir. I will guide you there and introduce you, if indeed you wish to go at once."

"We do." was Holmes' rejoinder and he swept us out to halt momentarily while a cab was hailed, and we were ushered into the vehicle. Soames gave the address and we were off, bowling down the street in pursuit of a button-box.

Hilton Soames' grandmother was not at all as I had expected

her to be. She was short, dumpy and stout, with a low voice—
which I thought would usually be pleasant but which just now
had a note of real rancor contained within its tones—and something of the look of Queen Victoria about her. Certain it was
that she was not amused.

"It is a disgrace, gentlemen! My button-box, stolen, and what
possible use could it be to any save myself? And the police who
tell me that they have no time to search for lost button-boxes.
It was not lost; it was violently stolen from me. The police are
dunderheads."

Holmes nodded. "It is indeed an outrage and if the police do
not take it seriously, than I assure you, Mrs. Soames, my friend
Watson and I do."

"Then you will endeavor to restore it to me?"

"I will, Mrs. Soames. Now, to that end, tell me everything
that occurred, omit no detail." We settled to listen.

"I was intending to visit my friend, Marjorie Fuller, in
Garnet's Close. She had her little granddaughter staying, the
child is only six and children of that age can become easily
bored if they have nothing to do while their elders' talk goes
above their heads. Thus I did as I often do in such a case. I took
with me my button-box so that the girl might have something to
amuse her while Marjorie and I discussed the flower roster for
the Church's Saints' Days.

"I took a cab—I know the driver, a most respectable man
named Brown who treats his horse very kindly—and as Garnet's
Close is too narrow for a cab, I alighted at the entrance around
ten in the morning, paid Brown and began to walk up the close."

"Did you see anyone walking towards you, or near the close
entrance?" I asked.

"No, the close was empty of people and the street when I
alighted appeared to be so as well." Holmes nodded for her to
continue.

"I passed the first three houses and was opposite the fourth—
the houses are on one side of the close only, the other side is
the wall of the University—when I was seized and held. At the

same moment my shawl was flung over my head, my button-box was torn from my arm, and I was pushed to the ground. For perhaps so much as three or four minutes I was stunned by the unexpected assault, but then I thrust my shawl back, struggled to my feet and discovered that I was unharmed. I hurried to the main street and looked to either side, but could see no one who might have been my assailant."

"Assailants," said Holmes.

The old lady bridled. "Two of them? I have been attacked by two ruffians?"

"Think back, madam. Were you not already being held while at the same time your shawl was used to blind you and your button-box was seized?"

"By heavens, yes, it was so. You are right, Mr. Holmes. There must have been two men. I distinctly remember the grip one of them had upon my arms even while my button-box was wrenched from me. Then that same grip which held me was transferred to a thrust that saw me measure my length on the ground."

"Now, madam, I am sure you are still shaken and bruised. But if you will allow, I would like to perform an experiment?"

"I am in your hands, sir."

Then please stand and turn your back to me." The old lady obeyed. "Indicate whereabouts upon your arms you were gripped." Her fingers touched the upper level of her left arm, and then the other hand came up and matched the gesture to the right.

"Here, Mr. Holmes."

"Thank you. Now, If I place my hands in the same position, does it seem to you as if the man who seized you could have been of my height?"

"It feels as if you loom over me, sir. I think he was not so tall."

"Mr. Soames?" Her grandson took up the position while the old lady considered again.

"He still feels too tall."

"Your turn, Watson." I took up my position and it seemed I was too short. Holmes looked pleased.

"Then we have two assailants, one of whom is around five feet eight inches to five feet ten inches in height."

Mrs. Soames, who had sat down by now, stared up at my friend. "But, that is no child."

"Indeed so, and as you will realize this changes things. Now, let us venture further. You say you were level with the fourth house when you were attacked. We will go to examine this close shortly, but what can you tell me of the fourth house and its occupants?"

"There are none, Mr. Holmes. The family that used to live there has gone. The father had, I believe a position as head clerk at a large firm of merchants. However, they have moved the factory further from the town and he packed up his family and moved to live in the village near the new building. The house is to let, but however, and to my knowledge, no tenant has as yet taken up residence."

I saw understanding dawn on her face. "I see, sir. The police think that I was pushed over and robbed by some child attracted by the appearance of my button-box. You can already show I was robbed by two men acting in concert who carefully chose the location of their attack."

Holmes made a slight bow. "Wonderful, madam. You have summed up all our discoveries. There is one final point thus far. This act was surely premeditated, with your button-box as their deliberate objective. Nor could they have come upon you by accident. Ordinary thieves would have taken your handbag. These men wanted your button-box and your button-box only. I think we must go immediately to study this Garnet's Close."

Mrs. Soames would by no means be left behind so that there were four of us who presently studied the short secluded close. It was a pleasant aspect. Down one ride ran a line of twelve houses, each in its own grounds with ample shrubbery. The road was wide enough for a dogcart but the wider cab would not have been able to negotiate it nor to turn without intruding on private property.

The houses were of a reasonable size, most two-storied, and with a drive leading to a stable behind. On the other side of the close a high wide brick wall arose, which I understood from Soames to be the back wall of the University, with a number of storage sheds and stables for visiting vehicles on the University side. The wall was a good ten feet and I feel it unlikely any thief would have found it possible to scale without ropes or a ladder which Mrs. Soames would have seen as she approached down the close.

Holmes agreed. "No, Watson. I think the thieves had another escape in mind." He turned to the old lady who was watching him with interest. "Do you recall any sound of footsteps after you were flung aside?"

Her reply was unequivocal. "No, sir."

"Ah, that may be useful." With that he walked along the line of houses, halting outside the fourth and studying the driveway keenly. He twisted and turned, surveying the surface then walking cautiously up and down the lawn while stooped over. He then came towards us and I saw satisfaction in his face.

"We were right, madam. There were two men. One was of medium height, powerfully built and originally athletic. He wears a size ten shoe and weighs about twelve stone. The other was smaller, slight in build and wearing shoes that are narrow in the foot. He wears a size six shoe and weighs around nine stone or perhaps a little less."

"The old lady peered up at him. "So they ran in here before I could drag the shawl from my eyes?"

"They also waited here for you to pass. Do you see the significance of that, madam?"

Mrs. Soames snorted vigorously. "I'd thank you, sir, not to assume me a fool. If they waited for me they must have known I was visiting my friend that day, and how could they have known that? You will wish to know whom I told, and whom they may have told in turn." She turned to her grandson. "You knew, for I called on you the day before and said that I would be visiting

Marjorie on the following day. I also mentioned Marjorie's granddaughter and said I would take my button-box to amuse the child."

Soames appeared horrified. "I told no one, why should I speak of such small family matters?"

"No," I said thoughtfully. "But in which of your sets of rooms were you while this visit was discussed? Your personal rooms or the ones allocated by the University?"

"Why my rooms at the University, the two where I receive pupils and have my teaching materials."

Holmes nodded. "Yes, and where you seldom close any door to the outer corridor, where anyone who loiters may hear your conversation. Your grandmother has a clear voice. But you see where this evidence too leads? Only those with business within the University could have overhead what was said."

Soames threw up his hands. "But why, Mr. Holmes? Here we have two men, possibly students at the University, they set out to commit the premeditated crime of stealing an old lady's button-box. How is it they know of the item, what can they want with it, and why have they gone to such trouble to obtain it?"

Mrs. Soames glanced at my friend. "I think that Mr. Holmes will discover the answers to those questions, my dear. He appears to be a most intelligent and energetic young man. I leave the matter in his hands with the utmost confidence." And with that, she marched to the main road, hailed a cab, and was driven away while we stared after her.

"Well, Watson," Holmes said, "We must deserve that lady's belief in us. You go with Soames. I want a list of everyone at the University who might know anything at all of his grandmother's movements in the ordinary way. Then speak to the porter of Soames' building. I would know if any of those on the first list appear on his list as visiting the building the day Mrs. Soames was speaking to her grandson of her planned engagements."

"And you, Holmes, what will you be doing?"

"I would have a few words with the police. Meet me at the Grand Hotel where I will have taken rooms once I have completed that errand."

It was a long and tedious discussion. I wrote while Soames endlessly racked his brains for his colleagues and pupils who might know of his family. With the list in hand we met Holmes at the hotel, went upstairs to where a good meal had been laid for us in our suite, and ate heartily. Once the wine was passed I spoke to my friend.

"What did the police have to say to your new information?"

"It seems they are of the same opinion still, that it was high-spirited children and that I am wasting my time. But they did give me some other valuable information that we shall use later tonight. We have a few calls to make."

"Where do we go?"

"To a number of the pawn shops in the area about the close, Watson, a discovery in one of them or even the lack of findings may confirm an hypothesis I am developing."

* * * * * * *

I followed Holmes over the course of the evening to a number of grimy establishments and it was in one of the most cluttered shops I have ever seen that we came upon a small chest that seemed to fit the description of the stolen button-box. Holmes picked it up and opened the lid carefully.

"The contents appear to be intact, Watson. Now I wonder what the proprietor will tell us of his purchase of this." He turned to the man who was hovering anxiously behind him. "This is stolen property," Holmes said sternly. "How did you come by it?"

The pawnbroker gaped at us. "Gentlemen, who would bother to steal a trumpery item? I thought I might sell it for a few shillings to someone who likes such things. It is a nice box with a good selection of buttons, but I gave the man who sold it to me only a florin. He told me it had been his wife's and with her dead now he had no use for it."

I handed him a florin. "I will take the box back to its owner and you shall lose nothing by your purchase. Come, tell my friend of the vendor."

"He was a not a gentleman. I took him for a laborer and I think I may have seen him about the streets near the old market." With further questioning we obtained quite a good description of the man, what the pawnbroker believed to be some of his usual haunts, and, with the button-box securely under my arm, we set off in search of the seller. We found him in a bar but not yet more than slightly drunk. Holmes approached him.

"What is your name?"

The man recognized authority when he heard it. He straightened up slightly and spoke with a strong country accent.

"I'm Isaac Tremain, who be you as asks?" Holmes and I recognized the accent, it was Cornish or South Devon—on the edge of the counties they overlap in places.

"My name is Sherlock Holmes and this is my good friend, Doctor Watson. Tremain, you say? What is your village?"

"Duloe, sir."

"I know it, a pleasant place. How is it you are so far from home?"

Isaac Tremain heaved a sigh. "I followed the work, sir. But I'll go home as soon as ever I can. My brother, he says there'll be a place on the squire's estate for me very soon. Let me once get back and I won't never be leaving again."

"I agree, a man wants to have his own friends and family about him. Those people and places he has always known."

"Aye, sir. That he do."

"Would it not help if you had a train ticket back?"

"Aye, it would. But 'tis six a' one an' half a dozen a' the other, sir. I be homesick so I drink, then I ain't got the money for a ticket, then I drink a'cos I be homesick and can't afford to go home." It was with difficulty I repressed a smile at that. Holmes, however, remained unmoved.

"What if you received a ticket? One you could not turn into coin."

"Why, I reckon I'd go to home right now, on the very next

train as ever was. My brother, he'd give me a bed 'til this job wi' t' squire be ready."

"I will give you a ticket, and there will be no policeman asking you questions after me if you do as you say. I want to know about the button-box you sold to the pawnbroker. Where got you it?"

Isaac Tremain looked at him and of a sudden any drink was out of him. "I heard of you, you'm a man as has made the police look silly a time or two. All right, I'll tell you so long's I gets the ticket?"

Holmes nodded. "Right then. I were walking along the street an' ahead of me I sees a lad drop this li'l box over the wall into a garden. Guess that's something he don't want, I says to myself. Wonder what it is? He keeps walking like he's done nothing so I walks along quiet until he turns the corner then I trots back and picks up what he dropped.

"I find it's this li'l box and I'm mortal worried it'll have jewels or something inside. Police ask questions about a man like me having that sort o' thing about them. So I open it careful like and blow me down if'n it ain't filled wi' buttons. Just like a box me mother had when I was a boy. Knows no pawnbroker will ever think I stole that so I takes it to one and he gives me two shillin' for it."

"I believe you and you shall have your ticket. Now, describe the man, carefully now, I have some idea whom it might be and if you lie I shall know."

"I won't tell you no lies, sir. He was a little fella, mebbe five feet an' six or seven inches in height. I walked along behind him a ways and I saw that. He wore narrer shoes, fancy ones, and I'd say he'd strip to about nine stone or thereabouts. Not much muscle, least ways he didn't walk like it but he were well fed enough, he hadn't never starved. Good cloes, not like no lord, but good enough quality fer a shopkeeper in a good way 'o business." Oh, there's one way you'll know him for certain sure, sir, ain't many of his kind in town." He added the final detail and I saw Holmes' jaw set. "Have I done well for you, sir?"

Holmes clapped him gently on the shoulder. "You have, sir, very well, and you shall have your ticket. Come with us now and I will obtain it for you."

* * * * * * *

We left Isaac Tremain at the station, he to go to his room and pack his meagre possessions before using his ticket, we to our hotel to sleep. I spoke quietly as we rocked along the road in our cab.

"You know who the thieves were, do you not?"

"I believe so, but I have been more fortunate in this matter than you, Watson. I know one thing you never learned. If I am right then Mr. Hilton Soames and his grandmother will receive a most pleasant surprise quite apart from the button-box you will be able to return to her tomorrow. But before we do so, I wish to make an examination of the button-box. I think there may be more to it than is easily visible."

And with that he took up the box, emptied it of its contents, and began to poke and pry gently at all aspects of the pieces where they joined. There was no sound, but of a sudden a portion of the inner lid came open and Holmes muttered in satisfaction.

"I thought so. Look here, Watson. A secret cavity, there is nothing within, but I think there once was. It was the contents of this cavity the thieves sought."

"How did they know it was there, do you know?"

"I believe so. All we have to do is ask a last question or two of Mr. Hilton Soames, and I must check some papers at the University library. I saw them when I was researching some early English charters there last. With a sight of that to refresh my memory, and the answers I seek, all the threads shall be in my hands."

We departed the hotel mid-morning the next day, and took a cab to the University where Holmes paused at the library to ask for certain documents that he perused carefully. We then gathered up Soames and went thence to his grandmother's small house. Her joy when I produced her button-box was extreme.

"I knew you could do it, Mr. Holmes. I was sure a man like you would succeed where the police would not even look. But who stole it from me and why?"

Holmes spoke to her grandson. "When I was here some months ago you had three pupils each working towards the Fortescue Scholarship. One attempted to cheat and then in a fit of conscience resigned from the attempt. Tell me of the two who remained, which of them gained the valuable scholarship?"

Soames shook his head. "Both and neither, sir. In the end they were so closely marked on all their work that it was decided to share the scholarship between them."

"How is it that neither can afford the University without the Fortescue?"

"Miles McLaren is a brilliant scholar, he has vast amounts of knowledge in many areas, some quite exotic, but he is completely undisciplined and will not work. Nor are his family wealthy since I fear that the family trait of gambling has lost them most of their estates over the generations."

"What are the exotic areas of which you speak?"

"He loves antiques and knows something about many periods; he also enjoys history and has often spent time when he should have been working in looking up obscure and rare papers at the University library."

"What of your other scholar?"

"Daulat Ras is Indian of the highest caste. His father was once a ruler and a fanatic, or so I am told, on the family's history, but through a rebellion of his subjects he was cast down. The family has some money but not enough to keep the lad at St. Luke's for the time required for him to qualify. Both had sufficient money to pay their first year, the Fortescue will allow them to complete their second year and a half of their third. Both however, wish to continue for the third and fourth years."

Mrs. Soames piped up. "Now, sir, we have answered your questions. Do you answer mine. Who stole my button-box and why?"

Holmes reached for the box and manipulated it so that the hiding place opened within the lid. "Your box was stolen for the buttons it held, not in the body of the box, but within this hiding place." Both Soames were staring at the box incredulously. "I believe that your family's name for the box arose, not because you used it for buttons after you were given it, but because it was given to your family first to hold safe and secret a very special set of buttons.

"If there is one thing I have learned over and over, it is that family legends hold truth in them, but equally, that that truth may be confused and obscure even to the family who tell the story. This button-box is not English to begin with. Some noble in this land would never have given it to a Soames. It is of Indian work and no more than two hundred years old. It appears English because the maker copied an English sailor's sea chest.

"Now. Much further back in history there was a Soames who was valet to King Charles the First. I cannot prove this sequence of events, but it is my belief that the valet passed letters between his imprisoned king and the king's son. In gratitude for the kindness, and before King Charles was taken out to die, he cut a set of buttons from the clothing he would leave behind him and gave them to the valet. These were retained in the family as a treasure.

"Some generations later a Soames visiting India came into possession of the button-box, being shown its secret and deciding that it should be used for the keeping in secret of the set of buttons. I think it was for that that it was named the button-box. Since using it for other buttons would hide its other purpose, it was so used and that usage continued.

"Tell me, was not your great-grandfather slain when he was only a young man?" Soames and his grandmother both nodded. "So, the secret was lost. This box became just the family button-box and no more. However, there is another secret. In the University library there lies an early English Charter covering all Universities that existed at that time. In that the second Charles has written a brief paragraph which is obscure to any who do not know the reason."

Holmes took from his pocket a piece of paper and read slowly. "And further to scholarships listed, if any shall come with a set of the buttons once owned by my dear father and present them to any University, then shall that man or any other he shall designate, be free of whichever University he please for the period of five years in total. Such a time he being free also to break or change at his own choosing."

He looked at Soames. "As I understand it, that can be construed to mean that the man who produces this set of buttons is free to attend any University of his choosing for five years and all expenses must be borne by that University. He may also as it says, 'break or change the period.' In other words, that five years may be split between two or even three persons. Your pupils apart did not know enough to utilize the information, but I believe one spoke to the other and together they decided to steal the button-box."

Mrs. Soames glared. "You mean the Indian knew about the hiding place in my box, that it was possibly from his family when mine received it? And that other man read about King Charles and then about the charter, so they decided to steal my button-box to make sure they could stay at St. Luke's?" Holmes nodded. "What will you do to them, and—" in something of a wail, "what about the buttons?"

"Do not fear for them. What would it profit Ras and McLaren to flee? No, they will stay waiting for the right time to produce their plunder and buy themselves time to study without cost. We have only to approach them correctly and they will yield up their loot tamely I believe, so long as there will be no prosecution."

And the thieves did so once it was put to them what they had done and a search of their rooms uncovered the priceless buttons. I saw them once before they were taken to the Soames' family bank and deposited there. Upon that sight I realized why they had been kept secret originally. The set of twelve was of fine gold, each centered with the monarch's crest, and that centered again with a fine diamond. The edge of each button was outlined with a ring of small sapphires.

To be found in possession of those before the Second Charles ascended the throne would have been death for valet Soames. Afterwards he may simply have cherished the last memento he had of his fallen King. None of us can be sure; it was all too long ago.

* * * * * * *

Ras and McLaren were not charged with the robbery of Mrs. Soames. However, their scholarship was stripped from them and where they went after that I do not know. It was Holmes who had the last word on them some weeks after we had returned to his rooms in London.

"The true folly on their part was the open robbery of Mrs. Soames and that they would have used the King Charles buttons to fulfil the charter. How could they explain their possession of them? Whereas had they stolen the button-box quietly from the Soames' house, abstracted the buttons, returned the box and made arrangements to sell the King Charles buttons privately to some American millionaire who would remain silent, they would have obtained sufficient money to have paid their required time at the University twice over—and would have been most unlikely to have been caught—or even suspected."

With which conclusion, and needless to say, I agreed. Holmes was right in another thing as well. Neither of us ever wishes to hear the words 'button-box' again, nor have I any wish to see one. The Soames' button-box has been sufficient to last us our remaining years.

SHERLOCK HOLMES— *STYMIED!*

BY GARY LOVISI

"I see you have been unable to resist the allure of the links once again," my friend Sherlock Holmes said to me one afternoon upon my visit to our old digs at 221B Baker Street. He was running his eyes over my attire with disdain, having obviously surmised that I had come over straight from playing a round of golf.

I nodded my acknowledgement. Since my marriage and the sometimes heavy workload at St. Barts I'd seen Holmes only sparingly during the last year, so these occasional visits were moments of great joy for me to see my old friend again and catch up on his cases. My only spare time of late had been taken up with my new guilty indulgence; that fascinating creation called golf.

"A most stimulating and enjoyable exercise," I told my friend.

"Hah!" Holmes huffed sarcastically, "a gross and unmitigated waste of time. Adult men chasing around a little ball in a game of simple and utter luck. I'm afraid *that* is not for me."

"It is a sport, Holmes, not merely a game," I countered inexplicably upset by his words, feeling it was somehow my duty to defend the sport. "I have found it an enjoyable pursuit over the last few months and have been invited to play at some of the most prestigious courses in England and Scotland, including the very home of golf, the Royal and Ancient Golf Club at Saint

Andrews. I have even become friends with Tom Morris himself, Old Tom Morris as he is called, a legend of the game. I tell you it is not a game of luck, it is fraught with hazards and challenges which require a high level of skill."

Holmes brushed all this aside with a casual wave of his hand. If it was not criminal in nature, nor fell within the narrow scope of his interests, he was rarely engaged.

"You know, Holmes," I told him allowing a hint of annoyance to enter my voice, "We are now four years into the 20th Century, a time for new beginnings and newer things—such as golfing. The game has lately set up strict rules of play affecting every contingency. I would think this is one aspect of it that you would find appealing and even approve of."

"Rubbish! You mentioned rules as in a sport, yet you yourself just called it a game. Checkers would be more stimulating."

"Oh, come now, Holmes!" I retorted peevishly.

"You yourself called it a game," he countered with a wry grin.

"That was merely a figure of speech."

Holmes looked at me shaking his head in mock despair, "Watson, poor, poor Watson, I am saddened to hear that you have succumbed to the frippery of such a game of chance. Far better it would be to spend your time and your meager funds on the roulette wheel. Better odds, eh?"

"I beg to disagree. I have found there is great skill involved in every aspect of golfing, from the opening drive down the fairway, to the chipping, and of course putting on the green. It can be most stimulating and challenging. You of all people should not be so quick to disparage a game—or dare I say sport—which you have never once tried yourself."

Sherlock Holmes looked thoughtful and then gave me a wry grin, "You have me there, old fellow. You may be correct. Perhaps some day we shall have a go at it."

"I would be most delighted to do so, Holmes. Perhaps when you are not so heavily engaged with cases?"

"Well, Watson, you have come at the perfect time. Cases have been few and far between lately. It seems the criminal classes have gone on holiday. Most disappointing."

I laughed at his dilemma, "Well, I am sure something of merit will turn up soon."

"Obviously it shall, but tell me more of this golfing mania you have contracted like a bad London cold. I see that there is something that evidently disturbs you about it."

I looked at Sherlock Holmes closely. The man was remarkable. So far I had been quite careful, through neither word nor gesture, to let on to him the true nature of my visit. "You are as perceptive as ever. How did you guess?"

"Guess! Did you say 'guess'?"

"I meant.... What I meant to say...," I fumbled quickly.

"Never mind, old boy," Holmes smiled indulgently at my discomfort. "Put it down to my knowledge of your person through our long association. I can see there is something bothering you, and yet you are loathe to bring it up, but it picks at you nevertheless. It is about this game of yours, is it not?"

I sighed, "Yes, Holmes, it is a most depressing problem, but surely it does not rise to the level where your magnificent talents need to be employed."

"Why not let me be the judge of that. As I told you, interesting cases are scant right now so if you have something of merit I should be happy to hear the details."

I nodded with relief that my friend was concerned, collected my thoughts and then began my narrative as I sat down in my old chair across from his own. "You are correct that it has to do with golfing. I have already mentioned that I have made the acquaintance of Old Tom Morris. He is a most decent and gentlemanly fellow. These days he is the greenskeeper at the R&A, the Royal and Ancient Golf Club at Saint Andrews, in Scotland."

"Yes, where they play the British Open. I believe Old Morris even won the championship four times in the '60s?" Holmes stated.

"Why, yes," I smiled. "So you know something of the game?"

"A niggling bit here and there. I heard about the fellow primarily through the mystery that befell his son, Young Tom Morris."

"Young Tom?" I asked casually, but curious. "I had not heard."

"A most tragic affair, Watson. Old Tom's son, Tommy—these days known as Young Tom—was a golfing prodigy. He was a legend in his own time who followed his father into golfing history by winning four British Opens. He was young, barely 24 years of age when his wife and child died in childbirth. Young Tom died three months later on Christmas Day in 1875 of unknown causes. It was all quite mysterious, but most people at the time blamed it on a broken heart."

"A sad tale," I said softly.

"Sadder still was the loving father's reply when asked if such a death could be possible."

"What did he say, Holmes?"

"It is said Old Tom replied that if it were possible for a person to die from a broken heart, then he would surely have died himself at the time."

I sighed, "That is sad. I had no idea."

"Old Tom has outlived his son by a quarter of a century. By all accounts he is a man of unique and outstanding character and talents. I should very much like to meet him some day." Holmes stated, then he looked directly at me and asked, "So, now Watson, tell me what you came here for."

"Well, Holmes, the Open will be concluded tomorrow evening with the presentation of the Championship Cup to the winner—it is a large silver trophy more commonly known as the Claret Jug. The problem is, the Claret Jug has turned up missing."

"Is this jug valuable?" Holmes asked with more interest now.

"Yes, sterling silver, worth a considerable sum—but it is priceless to the club."

Sherlock Holmes nodded, looked at me from his seat and said calmly, "Tell me, has anyone at the club turned up missing?"

I looked at Holmes, shrugged, "No, not that I know of. However Old Tom mentioned to me that one of his boys, a caddy, has gone sick and not reported to work for the last two days. Old Tom says it is most unlike the lad not to be available for any match, much less a championship."

"And is this boy interested in the game?"

"Well, I assume so, most of the caddies are enthusiastic about golfing. Old Tom told me this boy is well-mannered but rather more fanatical than most about the game."

"I see," Holmes said thoughtfully. Finally he looked up at me with an inexplicable smile upon his face. "Well, Watson, you must know there is little I can do about this here in London."

"I understand, Holmes," I replied softly, apparently defeated, but grateful he had at least listened to my story. "It's just that Old Tom is very upset over the loss of the trophy. It will be a disaster for the Open, for the club, and for the game of golf itself."

Holmes suddenly stood up from his seat and looked at me sharply, "Well then, there is nothing else to do but set off for Scotland at once and remedy this situation. Come, Watson, the game—of golf this time—is afoot!"

* * * * * * *

Due to the efficiencies of the British railway system, Holmes and I reached Saint Andrews in no less than eight hours and once at the club I introduced the great detective to Morris. Old Tom had also been a winner of the British Open no less than four times, but these days he was a famous ballmaker, club-maker and course designer. For many years he had been the head greenskeeper at Saint Andrews.

Old Tom Morris certainly looked every one of his 83 years of age, sporting a long, flowing white beard that rested on the center of his broad chest. He was dressed in golfing attire, a sporting jacket and plaid cap on his gray head. His left hand often rested in his trouser pocket where he kept an ever-present pipe and he used an upside-down hickory-shafted mashie niblick as a cane. While he never seemed to smile, his piercing blue eyes exuded intense energy and gentle kindness.

I introduced the golfing legend to the detective legend.

"Ach, as I live and breathe, can it be none other than Mr. Sherlock Holmes come hither to Scotland to visit our lovely club?" Morris asked with a thick Scottish brogue and a joyful face that lit up with mirth. He proved a most hearty and cheerful fellow. While it appeared he never cracked a smile and was the epitome of the dour Scot, Old Tom was truly a kind and warm-hearted man. His eyes fairly twinkled as he spoke. "I am so honored to meet you, sir, and I welcome you to Saint Andrews. I assume Doctor Watson has told you about our little problem?"

"Yes, he has, that is why I am here, Mr. Morris."

"Well, I thank you, but please, just call me Old Tom, good sir."

Holmes allowed a warm smile, "Well, Old Tom, you have a missing trophy and I hear the presentation is later this evening?"

"Aye, the championship is just finishing up and we find ourselves in dire difficulty," Old Tom said sadly. "The Claret Jug, as it is called, has permanently resided at the R&A—as we call the Royal and Ancient Golf Club at Saint Andrews—since 1873. The trophy is presented to the winner of the British Open each year. The winner gets to keep it for a year before returning it to the R&A, thence to be passed on to the next champion. It has lately been returned to the club by last year's winner. Now the trophy has gone missing. I fear it may even have been stolen."

"The good doctor has told me that one of your boys has gone ill and not turned up for work."

"Why yes, that is true. Young Daniel Roberts, a caddy, a good boy."

"And where may we find young Mr. Roberts?" Holmes asked.

"In the village. He lives with his mum over her dressmakers shop."

Holmes nodded, "Then let us repair there immediately, for

we have no time to lose."

* * * * * * *

When we reached the home of the boy we found young Daniel Roberts upstairs in his room in bed with an apparent and dire illness of unknown origin. With the consent of his mother and under Holmes' instructions, I quickly attended to the boy, giving him a thorough medical examination. Finally I walked outside the room to confer privately with my friend.

"Well, doctor, what is your diagnosis?" Holmes asked me.

"There's nothing physically wrong with the boy at all. But he is terrified of something that he is desperately trying to hide. His heart is pounding fearfully from it."

Holmes just nodded, then walked back into the room with me. There we saw Old Tom and Mrs. Roberts looking sadly upon the boy laying so sickly in the bed. The boy saw us enter and coughed lightly.

Holmes grew grimly serious, "This will not do, Daniel. Doctor Watson has given you a full examination. There is nothing wrong with you. I know you are feigning illness. Time is wasting. You must tell me what you did with the Saint Andrews trophy."

The boy's face fell into despair, he was trapped and looked over to his mother.

"Daniel Roberts, now you tell these men the truth!" the boy's mother commanded.

Daniel looked shocked, fearful with despair, but he did not reply.

"I know you stole the trophy, young man," Holmes declared. "The game is up so you might as well make a clean breast of it now."

"Come on, lad, 'tis time to speak up," Old Tom prompted, looking dour and disappointed that one of his boys had actually stolen the famed trophy.

The boy began to cry.

"Come now, Danny," Old Tom added gently, "tell me what happened. Why did you steal the trophy? Who did you sell it to?"

"Oh no, that's not the way it was at all, Mr. Tom," the boy blurted through tears. "I took it when the previous winner retuned it to the club a few days ago. I just wanted to see me name on that trophy like all the great golfers of years before, because one day my name could be etched there too. So I used some ink to write me name there, right below Young Mr. Tom's last win from '72, I did."

"Danny Roberts, you didn't!" his mother shouted angrily.

Holmes motioned her to silence, "Go on, Danny. Where is the trophy now? Did you sell it?"

"Sell it? Of course not, sir! I would never think of such a thing," the boy stammered obviously upset at the very thought.

"Then what did you do with it?" Old Tom prompted.

Danny looked grim, wide eyes pleading with Old Tom, "I'm so sorry. I was scared, sir. I know I did wrong by putting me name there and was trying to remove it, but it just would not come off. I was terrified! Then I got the idea to take the trophy down to the stream to use the water to wash off the ink. To my relief my name came off, but then I dropped the trophy down into the stream. It went in deep."

"So why didn't you dive in after it?" I asked the boy.

Danny looked up sheepishly, "I cannot swim."

"I see," Holmes said, hiding a wry grin.

Danny went on to explain, "I was fearful of disappointing Mr. Tom. He been so good to me and all. He always told me how golf teaches responsibility and good sportsmanship, then I failed him. So I pretended to be ill so I would not have to face him. I am sorry, Mr. Tom."

Old Tom smiled gently, "Think no more of it, lad."

"Will I be going off to prison?" the boy asked nervously.

Old Tom laughed with gentle warmth, "Of course not, Danny."

"So where's the trophy now?" Holmes asked.

"Why, still at the bottom of the stream, where I left it," Danny replied.

Holmes nodded, "Very well then. Now Danny, get yourself out of that bed and let us go and fetch it immediately."

* * * * * * *

It was early the next morning when Sherlock Holmes and I played our first round of golf. The problem of the day before had been solved satisfactorily; the trophy had been retrieved and then presented in time to the championship winner with nary a hitch. Young Danny had been suitably chastised by Old Tom but was allowed to keep his position as a caddy at the club. Once again all was right and well at the R&A.

Still and all that next day offered us a lovely, brisk, Scottish morning, perfect for a round of golf at the Royal and Ancient Saint Andrews. Old Tom had made a gift of a favorable tee time to Holmes and I, in gratitude for our deed. So my companion reluctantly agreed to play a round. We decided to play a singles match, just him and I, stroke play. Old Tom and Danny even volunteered to act as our caddies, each giving us much needed and helpful instruction and information before we began play.

The course at the R&A was sandy in nature, with small hills that played havoc with even the most well-struck drive, frequently knocking the ball devilishly off-line and into an insidiously placed pot bunker that only the most diabolically warped mind could have created. It was a challenging course to play.

The first hole, known as the "Burn" hole, was a par four. With a good deal of luck, Holmes and I both bogied it with five. We were lucky to shoot only one stroke over par. I did better on the second hole actually making par, while Holmes did better than I on the third. By the fourth hole I began to realize that Holmes seemed to know a lot more about playing golf than he'd ever let on to me. We played a few more holes and we did well enough, mostly through the good advice of our caddies, both of us going over par of course, but not terribly so.

"Where did you learn to play so well?" I finally asked Holmes, astounded by his quality of play. I was no master of the game, nor was he, but I was surprised by the rapidity with which he had picked up the essentials.

Holmes only smiled, adjusted his deerstalker cap, and replied, "On the train to Saint Andrews, of course. While you slept the hours away, I studied up on the game reading the golfing books in your pack. I found Horace E. Hutchinson's volume most useful, while *The Art of Golf* by Simpson was highly informative. Did you know it even includes photographic plates of our friend Old Tom demonstrating the value of the swing? His advice is priceless. You may be correct in stating that once you understand this game it opens up a true appreciation of it."

"Posh, Holmes! Golf from books!" I snorted derisively, but I could not help but laud his improved attitude. "All right then, we'll see where this leads, we're off to the Tenth. So far we are even, so let's see what you can do on the back nine."

We moved on to the Tenth hole and played through. I went ahead by a stroke, but by the next hole Holmes had drawn even with me. He went ahead on the Thirteenth, but I caught up to him by the Fifteenth. At this point it was anyone's game. Holmes played with grim determination, scowling at bad shots but seemingly elated when he made a good one—in that way he proved no different from any other golfer.

It was on the approach to the last hole that Old Tom announced, "Gentlemen, the Eighteenth Hole. It is a par 4, at 360 yards in length, and you both be even up to this point."

"A close contest, Watson," Holmes said ruefully. "You are quite right, this pursuit can be most challenging. I think I shall win this hole and then put to bed once and for all your obsessive dreams concerning this game."

"I shall give you a good fight, Holmes," I warned.

Sherlock Holmes smiled, "I would expect nothing less, old man."

It had taken us each two strokes to get onto the green of the

Eighteenth. Holmes had a difficult 20 foot putt to make the hole. My putt was shorter, being almost 12 feet in distance. Being farthest from the hole, Holmes played first.

Holmes' putt went straight and true right towards the hole. It looked like it just might go in. My face grew grim with the bitter taste of impending doom. Surely his ball was heading straight for the hole and would fall in right away. I looked over at my friend and he appeared elated. Then I saw his ball suddenly stop dead, less than a foot from the cup. Holmes stared at the ball in utter shock and disbelief as if willing it to move on it's own accord and go into the cup. But it did not.

Now it was my turn. A grim smile came to my face as I prepared for my putt. Danny, acting as my caddy took out one of his favorite hickory-shafted putting cleeks and handed it to me. "Here, Doctor, try this one. You have a level shot, play it straight and it should go true."

I nodded, my face serious with the competitive spirit as I got into position and made my putt. It was a less forceful stroke than my opponent's. I intended a simple and straight stroke, but my ball immediately veered off curving in a wide arc. I shook my head with dark trepidation and took a deep breath. I saw that Holmes held his breath also.

All four of us watched intently as my ball rolled in a wide arc, slowly moving closer and closer to the cup with what appeared to be the sureness of inevitability. I let out a tense breath. It looked like I just might make the hole. Then the ball suddenly encountered a rough patch on the green and by some devilish action hooked in front of Holmes' ball and rolled to a dead stop. I tried to figure out what had just happened. My ball now lay between Holmes' ball and the cup by barely over six inches— effectively blocking him from the cup.

"That's the way, doctor!" Danny, shouted with glee.

Old Tom Morris just laughed with uproarious mirth, "Aye, well played, Doctor Watson, it appears you've stymied Mr. Holmes quite nicely!"

"Stymied?" Holmes blurted. He was obviously not aware of

this particular rule.

I was surprised myself by the turn of events but quickly realized it could be a potential game changer for me.

Old Tom explained, "Watson's ball blocks your own from the cup, Mr. Holmes. It's an old and valued rule of golf, called the Stymie. In golf you must hit your ball true to the hole. Hence, when another ball blocks your own, you are stymied. It's your play, Mr. Holmes."

"How can it be played, if Watson's ball blocks mine?" Holmes asked.

"Indeed," Old Tom said most sympathetically, "the balls be just over six inches apart—so Watson's ball canna' be lifted as per the rules. Your only option is to concede the hole, or negotiate the stymie. When a player be stymied he obviously can not putt straight for the hole, but if he strikes his ball so as to miss his opponent's ball and yet go into the hole, he is said to negotiate the stymie. Well, Mr. Holmes?"

The Great Detective carefully regarded his options. They were woefully limited. "You have placed me in quite the pickle, Watson. I shall not concede the hole to you, so you leave me no alternative but to attempt, as Old Tom says, to negotiate this... stymie."

"Bravo, Mr. Holmes!" Old Tom enthused warmly at my friend's obvious pluck. "Here now, use this Jigger, it will give you the loft you need to play your ball."

Holmes took the hickory-shafted Jigger and prepared to make his play. He took his time and hit the ball with a sudden and sharp lifting motion that lofted his ball into the air. I was shocked to see his ball ride over my own—a bare two inches in height and straight towards the hole. Then his ball kicked right *into* the hole—*and bounced right back out!*

Holmes' ball slowly rolled away to rest a few inches from the cup.

It was heartbreaking. Danny grimaced while Old Tom shook his head good-naturedly at the mystical vagaries of the game. I stood there amazed by what I had just seen. Holmes for his part said not one word, his face had become a solid mask of stone. I decided it was not the right time for me to make any comment about what had happened.

It was my turn now. I took my time. With the utmost care I took my putt, lightly tapping my ball so it fell squarely into the cup with a soft plop. I sighed with relief and looked over at my friend.

Sherlock Holmes seemed to hardly believe what had happened. A moment later he mechanically tapped his ball into the hole, officially ending the game, and then he walked away in a rather sullen funk.

I had beat Holmes by one stroke but my victory was bittersweet.

I thought I could hear my friend murmuring to himself as he walked off the green, something about how he had been right all along, that golf was a stupid game, a horrendous waste of time, and based solely upon luck rather than any true skill.

"You know, Watson, some day that damnable stymie rule will have to go," he commented to me sharply as the four of us walked off towards the clubhouse.

Old Tom Morris cut in before I could reply, "Never, Mr. Holmes! Not while I live! Aye, golfing tradition, it surely be. One of the most sacred rules of the game."

"Hah!" Holmes snorted derisively dismissing the entire affair. Then he looked at me and suddenly smiled with renewed good humor, "Well played, Watson. I must say, well played, indeed."

"Why thank you, Holmes, that is very gracious of you. It was a close contest. I am sure you will do better on our next outing," I said in an upbeat tone, trying to offer him some measure of support, but I knew the truth. I knew my friend. This was the first and *last* game of golf I or anyone else would ever play with Sherlock Holmes.

I shook my head in consternation as Holmes and I accompanied Old Tom towards his clubmaking shop off the 18th green. We had sent young Danny off, and now the three of us sat down enjoying a few pints, sharing stories about golf and life, and never once did we ever mention the stymie again.

* * * * * * *

HISTORICAL NOTE: Much of the background of this story is based on historical facts that deal with the Royal and Ancient Golf Club at Saint Andrews, in Scotland; the British Open trophy, better know as the Claret Jug; and the lives of Young Tom and Old Tom Morris. I also want to thank the real Dan Roberts, as well as the Gerritsen Beach Golf Museum Library for their assistance. The Stymie rule was finally taken out of golf in 1952. Before then, players could not lift their ball, but after 1952 they would use a marker on the green and then lift their ball so as not to obstruct an opponent's ball. There are many who wish the Stymie was still in effect.

BAD HABITS

BY MAGDA JOZSA

ONE

Imagine my surprise when I entered the sitting room of my comfortable abode at 221 Baker Street and could hear the plucking of Holmes's violin, but he was nowhere in sight. It sounded like he was picking at the violin like one would a guitar, running up and down the scales. I looked around the room in confusion. The sound appeared to be coming from behind the sofa. As I moved closer I spotted Holmes's ungainly rear sticking up as he backed up slowly. He was on all fours, plucking at the strings of his violin, and shuffling backward with his knees.

"Holmes?" I queried. "What on earth are you doing?" I moved closer.

"I'm trying to kill a spider, Watson."

I moved around to the front of the couch and looked down. Near Holmes, crawling along undisturbed by his efforts was a large gray huntsman.

"How will playing your violin kill it?" I asked—although there were times when his playing preyed on my nerves enough to be almost fatal.

"I'm trying to find the right note that will disable it," he explained. "Certain pitches can paralyze the nerves."

I shook my head in exasperation and stamped my foot down on the spider, flattening it.

Holmes sat back on his haunches. "Your way works, too," he

said mildly.

"You need a case, Holmes," I said. "If this is all you have to occupy your time, you must be desperate for something to do."

"I am. I'm beside myself with lethargy and mental tedium. There are no challenges in life. What's the point of being the world's best—the world's *only* consulting detective if I have nothing upon which to try my talents?"

I ignored his slight conceit. "Why don't you take up some research? Better still, file your old cases," I said pointing to a stack of papers in the corner, which Holmes insisted no one must touch but he.

He tossed his violin carelessly onto the sofa and stood up. "Nice try, Watson," he said without rancor. He knew I was curious about those old cases, as they occurred before I'd met him.

"Maybe I will. Perhaps I should tell you about the case in which I first met Lestrade—he was just a sergeant then...." He wandered over to the fireplace, selected a pipe from the rack on the mantle and filled it with tobacco from the Persian slipper. "Interesting case that," he mused. "First time I was ever shot."

I looked up with interest. "You've been shot? I'd be interested to hear about it," I said, also lighting up my pipe.

"It was in the summer of '79," began Holmes, only to be interrupted by Mrs. Hudson bringing up the afternoon mail. He flicked through the envelopes, tossed a couple to me and dropped the rest onto the floor, opening one. This he perused with great interest.

I glanced at my own mail, which was of little consequence.

"What do you make of this, Watson?" he asked, handing the letter over.

I read it aloud:

"Mr. Holmes, we fear for our lives. We are imprisoned by evil. Please help us. I will try to come to London by the evening train. Sr. Mary Ignatius."

"A nun?" I queried, looking at Holmes with surprise.

He smiled, obviously pleased to have something out of the ordinary.

"From the village of Sherbrook, Dartmoor," he said, studying the envelope. "Young woman. She wrote this hurriedly—note the strokes. Strong and clear but smudged as if she couldn't wait to blot the letter properly."

"Dartmoor eh? Well, I guess that's the place for demons and such. But what is this evil she talks about?"

"I have no idea. She uses the plural 'we'. No doubt she is from a convent and the danger that threatens her also threatens the other sisters." He rubbed his hands together. "I've never had a nun for a client before," he enthused. He checked the Bradshaw for train timetables. "Last train from Sherbrook is seven p.m."

His boredom was gone, and so was his inclination to share the details of his old case. Instead, he busied himself with studying his commonplace books. When eight o'clock came and went, he began to pace.

"She should have been here by now," he muttered over and over.

"Perhaps she couldn't make the train. She did say she would *try* to come. Maybe she couldn't make it," I suggested.

"Maybe she was prevented," Holmes replied gravely. He went to his desk and scribbled a telegram on one of his blank forms, then rang for Mrs. Hudson.

"Send the boy with this please, Mrs. Hudson—it's urgent," he instructed.

It was another two hours before he received a reply, and during that time he paced about our rooms restlessly.

He tore the telegram open. "Blast!" he cried.

"What?"

"I wired the Sherbrook station master to find out if a nun had boarded the train."

"Did she?"

"Yes." He grabbed his hat and coat. "Coming, Watson? I fear foul play."

I grabbed my own coat and hurried after him. We made our way to Paddington Station. At the station-master's office, he asked if the train from Dartmoor was still at the station.

"You're in luck, Mr. Holmes," said Mr. Phillips, the station-master. "The carriages have been moved to a siding for cleaning." He detailed one of the security men to take us to the train.

Holmes searched every carriage from third class to first. No sign of our errant nun. We returned to Mr. Phillips' office.

"Can you give me the route the train took?" asked Holmes.

The station-master obliged.

"You're not planning on going along the track now, are you, Holmes?" I queried. "It's pitch dark—even more so in the country. You won't see anything."

As much as he hated to admit it, I was right. "First light, Watson; but I fear we are too late."

We returned to Baker Street. I retired, knowing full well that he would not sleep this night.

TWO

It was still dark when I felt his hand upon my shoulder. "Wake up, Watson."

I grunted and grumbled my way to consciousness.

"I have made tea, but I'm afraid we will have to forgo breakfast."

I groaned and sat up. "It's still dark," I complained.

"It will be light by the time we get to Paddington. Now bestir yourself."

He left the room and I forced myself to get up. I was too bleary-eyed to risk shaving. I'd be more likely to slit my throat. Fifteen minutes later I joined Holmes and drank my tea. The clock showed the time to be four-thirty.

There was a hired buggy waiting for us out front and I was glad of my overcoat, scarf, and gloves when we went outside. It was bitterly cold in the pre-dawn gloom.

Holmes clambered up and took the reins.

"Up here, Watson," he said. ""When we get to the tracks. I will look to the right and you can search the left."

By the time we reached Paddington a pale sun made its appearance. Holmes drove through the rail yard and then picked out a rough bumpy track alongside the rails. Just as well I hadn't had breakfast, it would have been shaken out of me.

"Keep your eyes peeled," he instructed tersely. I didn't have to ask what for. I knew we were looking for the nun's body. He no doubt feared that she had fallen—or had been pushed—from the train.

We passed several villages, and as the sun rose higher, I was hopeful that Holmes would stop at one long enough to get some breakfast. A vain hope. He wasn't interested in food.

It was nearing eleven. We'd been travelling for some six hours and I was getting ready to insist that we stop long enough to get some lunch, when I noticed something black against a bush, down at the base of the railway embankment.

"There—Holmes!' I cried, standing up in the buggy for a better look and almost toppling out when he stopped abruptly.

"What did you see?" he demanded, also standing up.

"Down there!" I pointed.

Holmes leapt from the carriage and slithered down the steep embankment.

I followed, somewhat more cautiously. I stopped by Holmes, as he knelt beside the body of a young woman dressed in a nun's habit. She was bloody and battered from her fall from the train, but it wasn't the fall that killed her. The white front of her habit was stained red.

"She's been stabbed," he said soberly. "Stabbed, and then thrown from the train."

I glanced around at the barren landscape that surrounded us. "If we hadn't been looking for her, I doubt if anyone would have found her for weeks."

"Yes. That's why the body was dumped here. Her fear was genuine."

"I guess it's out of your hands now," I said. When he looked in askance at me, I added. "I mean, she can hardly retain you now."

"She already has. She became my client the minute she wrote that letter. I may be too late to help her, but she spoke in the plural—there are other lives at stake."

With effort, we managed to bring her body up the embankment. I wrapped her in a blanket and placed her in the back of the buggy. Holmes then drove to the nearest village where we reported the crime to the local constabulary.

The town constable was a bellicose bulldog of a man. "We can't handle this," he complained. "It's a job for Scotland Yard."

"Then it is your responsibility to notify them," said Holmes abruptly.

"Yeah, but if you're going back to London, you can do it. It's a London case anyway. It's not like she was killed here...you might as well take the body, too. I'd only have to send her up," said the constable, making excuses for not doing anything.

"No wonder you're stuck in this backwater. It's all you're good for," said Holmes, his temper rising.

"Come on, Holmes," I said pulling his sleeve. "He's not worth your wrath, and too stupid to be of use. We might as well go to Scotland Yard ourselves. It will be more worthwhile."

Holmes allowed me to lead him out and even agreed to stop long enough for a meal before starting our long journey back. We left the horse with the local blacksmith to feed and tend while we ate, then resumed our journey an hour later. The pace was much brisker and more comfortable, as we now travelled on the road. It only took four hours to return to London.

Holmes drove straight to Scotland Yard. The Inspector on duty turned out to be Stanley Hopkins. He greeted Holmes with enthusiasm, and Holmes in turn, was pleased to see him. He considered Hopkins one of the brightest the Yard had to offer.

The body was taken to the morgue. Hopkins expressed his shock at the murder of a nun. Holmes told him about her letter. She had no identification on her except for a silver cross around her neck with 'Mary' inscribed on its back.

"We'll do what we can to investigate this, Mr. Holmes, but if you want to follow up the Sherbrook side yourself...," began Hopkins.

"Most definitely. Do send the official police to the convent to inform them of her demise, and for proper identification. As to what it was that she feared—that is still to be determined."

Holmes looked grim. There was something base and heinous in the murder of a nun, far more so than the murder of an ordinary woman.

THREE

After leaving Scotland Yard, Holmes dropped off the buggy and we returned to Baker Street. We had missed the last train to Sherbrook. It concerned me that Holmes would spend another night pacing, but he surprised me by retiring at nine o'clock.

Just before going into his room, he advised me: "You should go to bed early too, Watson. First train leaves at eight in the morning and I want to be on it."

I nodded, finished my pipe and called it a night. I confess I was rather tired. Getting up before dawn has never been one of my favorite pastimes. It had been a long day.

* * * * * * *

We were both up and breakfasted by seven the next morning, and at the station before eight. Stanley Hopkins met us there.

"Thought I'd catch you here, Mr. Holmes," he said in greeting. "There is a convent about five miles from Sherbrook, called the Sisters of Mercy. They're an order of the Catholic Church that has taken a vow of silence. Only the Mother Superior is allowed to talk. They didn't report the nun missing, but apparently they have been looking for her themselves."

"Why didn't they report it?" I asked.

"It seems she's gone missing before. They usually find her and bring her back without anyone being any wiser."

"That implies that there is something odd about her," said Holmes thoughtfully.

"Well, yes...that letter of yours is a bit odd too, if you don't mind me saying. If it wasn't for the knife in her chest, I'd be inclined to think she fell from the train on her own."

"Perhaps that's what we are meant to think," replied Holmes.

"The local Sergeant's name is Reid—Robert Reid. I've telegraphed him to expect you. He will arrange accommodation for you. He'll also be able to fill you in on the local scene."

"What about you, Hopkins? How is your investigation proceeding?" asked Holmes.

"We've been trying to trace the people that were on the train, in the hope that someone might have seen something—or at least seen the nun in the company of someone else. I'm afraid we haven't had much luck so far. We've managed to trace a couple of people, but they boarded after the place where the body was found."

"The murderer was unable to return to Sherbrook after the deed, as it was the last train. It is unlikely he would disembark at a small town for where he is more likely to be noticed and remembered. Logically, he would have travelled on to London and become one of the crowd. He may already have returned to Sherbrook yesterday, or, for all we know, could even be on this train," said Holmes nodding towards the train that steamed up to the platform where we stood.

"What makes you think the murderer is from Sherbrook?" I asked.

"How else would he have known the nun was on board?" countered Holmes.

"He may not have known. It could be just some crazy fool with an aversion to nuns," said Hopkins.

"While that is always possible, it seems hardly likely in view of the fact that she was coming to see me. I believe she was killed to be silenced."

Hopkins nodded. "Well, if I come up with anything, I will let you know," he promised.

"As I will you," returned Holmes.

I waved good-bye as we boarded the train, and, instead of moving immediately to first class as we usually did, Holmes loitered in the passageway watching the travellers board.

"Excuse me, sirs," said a soft feminine voice. I turned and was rewarded with the sight of a very attractive young woman with the face of an angel surrounded by a halo of blonde hair.

"May I pass please?" she asked sweetly.

"Of course, my dear, of course," I said, stepping back hurriedly.

She smiled brightly at Holmes and me in passing.

Holmes also stepped back a pace to let her pass.

"Come on, let's find a carriage," he said ignoring the woman.

I stared after her, hoping to catch a final glimpse of that delightful countenance. With a wistful sigh I followed him as we moved on to the first-class carriage to our reserved compartment. We travelled in silence—Holmes lost in his thoughts. I was always loath to interrupt him at such times.

* * * * * * *

At Sherbrook, only seven people disembarked, including Holmes and myself. Four were men in various types of dress, and one was the angel-faced woman.

I noticed Holmes paying particular attention to the men.

"Mr. Holmes?"

Holmes turned. "I'm Holmes, this is Dr. Watson."

"How do you do, sir? I'm Sergeant Reid. Inspector Hopkins said you were coming."

We shook hands with the pleasant-faced young man. I liked the look of him; he had honest blue eyes, brown hair, and stood some six feet tall.

"Pleased to meet you," I said as we shook hands.

"I'm afraid there isn't a hotel in town, but I can put you up at my place. It's not extravagant but it's comfortable, and the missus is so excited at having the famous Sherlock Holmes in the house, that she's been cleaning and cooking all day."

"Er, thank you, but really she needn't trouble herself on our account. Our needs are simple," replied Holmes, a little disconcerted by Reid's enthusiasm. It was obvious he was yet another admirer of Holmes.

"No trouble, Mr. Holmes," replied the other cheerfully. "We can go to the house and drop your bags off first if you like."

"Actually, I would rather go to your office and learn more about the local situation here."

"Yes of course, anything you like. Inspector Hopkins said I was to give you every assistance." The sergeant was young and eager, and keen to watch a master in action. It was a pleasant change from that other country policeman we had encountered just two days ago.

We strolled leisurely through the village to the small police station, which was little more than a one-room shack with one corner fenced off by bars.

"We don't have much need for a jail here," explained Sergeant Reid at our curious glance. "Princeton Prison is only ten miles yonder. If we have any dangerous criminals that need to be kept overnight, I take them up there."

"I see. Tell me about the Sisters of Mercy Convent?" requested Holmes, sitting down in front of Reid's desk and taking out his cigarette case.

"It's been there for as long as I can remember and I've lived around these parts all my life. They do charity works; make preserves that they sell; help out the local doctor when a midwife is required, and visit the prison to comfort sick or dying inmates."

"How long has it been a silent order?"

Reid frowned. "Now that you mention it, not that long. I think it is something that came in with the new Mother Superior."

"New Mother Superior? How new?"

"She's been here for about a month. She and three nuns

arrived early last month. Mother Superior Capuano was pretty old and sick. This new one—Mother Superior Augustine came to take her place. Mother Superior Capuano was planning on going up to their main convent in London, but died two days after the new Mother Superior arrived. It seems that they've taken the vow of silence to honor the death of old Mother Superior Capuano. I think it is only a temporary thing. A mark of respect, like."

"Quite. The Mother Superior was willing to talk to you?"

"Sure. Someone has to be able to talk—especially when dealing with outsiders. She was quite helpful and pleasant."

"When you told her about the nun we found, how did she react?"

"Well, she was shocked of course, who wouldn't be? Said that it was something that Mother Superior Capuano feared would happen to Sr. Mary Ignatius."

"Why?"

"It seems that the sister was a bit odd. She'd be all right for months, and then would suddenly take it into her head that she was surrounded by monsters or demons or evil or what have you, and would escape from the convent to get away from them. The other nuns would search for her whenever she did that and fetch her back. Usually they would sedate her for a couple of days and then she'd be right as rain until the next time some fool notion got into her head."

"The Mother Superior told you this?"

"Uh huh."

"Why wasn't she in an asylum?" I asked.

"They look after their own, or at least that's what the Mother Superior told me. Said as how Sr. Mary wasn't dangerous and the delusional episodes only came out every now and again."

"Why were they expecting her to get killed one day?" asked Holmes.

"Well, it's not like they were expecting her to get murdered. They feared she would come to harm when she wandered off." The Sergeant frowned for a moment. "I mean; they were worried that she would meet someone crazier than her.... I guess she did."

"Did they know why she was going to London?"

"No. I mean, I didn't ask."

"How often do the sisters come to town?"

"Not often. They're pretty self-sufficient at the convent. Since taking the vow of silence, I've only seen one or two of them and the Mother Superior. Only the ones that are allowed to talk come in."

"Did anyone see Sr. Mary posting a letter on the weekend?"

"I don't know, but she wouldn't have to come into town to do it."

"What do you mean?"

"Well, the nuns have a deal going with the postman. They put their outgoing mail in the letter box and he collects it when dropping off their new mail."

"I see." Holmes butted his cigarette and stood up. "Now, Sergeant, I would like to visit the convent. Is that possible?"

"Yes, of course. We can go right now if you like. I've arranged to borrow Jim Pyke's buggy."

"Excellent."

The Sergeant beamed at Holmes's approbation and hurried out to fetch the carriage.

FOUR

An eight-foot high stone wall surrounded the convent. As we drove through the gates we could see nuns working in the vegetable plots. There was one nun that appeared to be super-vising the others—though what supervision they needed was beyond me. I also wondered how she gave orders if she wasn't allowed to speak.

We pulled up in front of the main building. As the horse came to a stop, the heavy oak front door opened and a tall, stately woman in the traditional black habit emerged to meet us at the steps. She nodded to the policeman.

"Sergeant Reid—back so soon?"

"Mother Superior," he greeted. "Sorry to disturb you, but these gentleman have just arrived from London and wished to see you about the dead woman."

She frowned. "What more can I tell you? We are all devastated by Sr. Mary's death, but she wasn't murdered here. Why aren't these gentleman looking for her killer elsewhere?"

"Because we need to find out why she was coming to London, and if she planned on meeting anyone there," said Holmes smoothly as he stepped forward.

Her eyes scoured Holmes, missing nothing.

His return scrutiny was just as thorough.

"Who might you be, sir?" she asked. If she weren't a nun, I would have described her tone as imperious. In fact, take away the habit and she would have been a good looking, well preserved woman in her early sixties. She matched Holmes's stare unflinchingly. It struck me that she had as strong a character as Holmes, and was plainly used to getting her own way.

"My apologies. I am Sherlock Holmes and this is my colleague, Dr. Watson."

"Sherlock Holmes!" If the name disconcerted her, she concealed it well. "I have heard of you of course, but you are not the official police. What has this to do with you?"

"Scotland Yard often utilizes my services on difficult or delicate cases," explained Holmes truthfully, if not accurately. Clearly he didn't want her to know about the letter.

"What can you tell me about Sr. Mary Ignatius?" asked Holmes, getting down to business.

The Mother Superior repeated what the sergeant had already told us. When she finished, Holmes glanced past her at the middle-aged nun who had come silently out the door to stand behind the Mother Superior as she spoke.

"Is that correct, Sister?" he asked.

The Mother Superior turned sharply and stared at the nun. The nun licked her lips, looked at the Mother Superior, and then nodded. It seemed to me that the rigidity of the Mother Superior's shoulders slackened at the response and she relaxed.

"Sr. Agnes has taken the vow of silence and must not speak. I am sure you will respect that, Mr. Holmes."

"Yes, of course," replied Holmes, with a slight bow in her direction.

The nun came down the steps and stood near us. She seemed nervous and fidgety and her feet kept scuffling the ground.

"Go join the others in the garden, Sr. Agnes," ordered the Mother Superior.

The nun nodded, but before leaving she touched Holmes's sleeve and fingered the silver cross at her neck. Her eyes seemed to plead with him.

The Mother Superior glared at her. "Go—now!" she said sharply, then as an aside to Holmes, added: "What she is trying to tell you is that we are all praying that you find the villain who murdered Sr. Mary."

"Mm," murmured Holmes in assent as he took out his pipe. It slipped from his fingers. "Clumsy of me," he said, bending to pick it up, and only succeeding in sending it slithering away. He followed it and finally managed to capture it. He stopped near where the nun had stood and picked up his pipe, scuffling the dirt in the process. He looked up at the Mother Superior and smiled: "Now where was I?"

"There is no smoking here," she said sternly.

"Ah—yes. My apologies." Holmes returned the pipe to his pocket. "Do you know why Sr. Mary was going to London?"

"No. She did not confide in anyone. She just left."

"What time did you notice her missing?"

"Around six o'clock Monday night. She never showed up for evening prayer. Naturally we began to search for her immediately."

"Naturally. May I look at Sr. Mary's room please?"

The Mother Superior frowned. "What will that avail you?"

"You say that normally she just runs away from the convent but has always stayed in this neighborhood. She has never boarded a train before, has she?"

"Not to my knowledge."

"Exactly. Therefore there was something different about her psychosis this time. I may be able to discover a reason for her behavior. Murder does not just happen—there is usually grounds."

"I see. I hadn't thought of that."

At that moment, another nun emerged. This one was a rather striking looking woman with coal black eyes, her hair hidden by her veil.

Holmes studied the newcomer with interest. "That's interesting," he said casually. "I didn't think Catholic nuns were allowed to get married."

"Pardon?" asked the Mother Superior coldly.

Holmes nodded to the dark-eyed nun's left hand. "She's wearing a wedding ring."

"Oh that." The Mother Superior smiled. "It is a small affectation that some of the sisters wear. It symbolizes their marriage to God. It is the practice of some convents, as is the giving of a silver cross when one moves from novice to sister. Each order has their individual way of marking the transition. I also used to wear a ring," she added, waving her hand in Holmes's face. Now that she brought it to my attention, I noticed the pale line of a ring mark against her finger.

Holmes smiled and had a rather curious expression on his face. "I see. I stand corrected."

"Will there be anything else, Mr. Holmes?" she asked blandly.

"Just Sr. Mary's room. I haven't any more questions for you at this time."

At that moment, a commotion broke out in the garden. "Goodness gracious, I hope they haven't seen another snake," murmured the Mother Superior. "Sr. Julius will take you to Sr. Mary's room. Bear in mind that she also has taken the vow of silence."

We nodded as she hurried off toward the garden. Sr. Julius of the dark eyes motioned for us to follow her.

While we walked, Holmes said, "Sr. Julius, are you one of the nuns that accompanied Mother Superior Augustine here a month ago?"

Sr. Julius put a finger to her lips indicating that she couldn't answer.

"A nod will suffice," said Holmes.

She nodded.

"You are all from the same convent?"

She nodded again.

"Did you know Sr. Mary Ignatius well?"

She shook her head, and then opened a door to a cell-like room.

It was too small for all of us to enter, so Reid and I stood by the door as Holmes went in. As I stood beside Sr. Julius I was conscious of the pleasant scent of her perfume.

The room contained a narrow bunk, a chair, a small table and a thin wardrobe. Holmes glanced inside. It contained her spare habit and underwear. On the desk were a writing pad, ink and blotter. The blotter was new and unused. Holmes picked up the pad and held it up towards the window so that the light would reflect off the page. He grunted as if he had just discovered something significant and put the pad down.

"Nothing here I'm afraid," he said turning around, his words belying his previous manner.

The nun led us silently back to the front door where we were once again joined by the Mother Superior.

"Find anything helpful?" she asked.

"Unfortunately, no," replied Holmes with a sigh. "Thank you for your time, Mother Superior."

* * * * * * *

On the drive back to town, I asked, "Did you learn anything useful, Holmes?"

"Quite a bit," he replied enigmatically.

"I don't see how. The Mother Superior wasn't overly helpful."

"It is not what they said, Watson, but what they omitted to say," Holmes explained, then changing tack, asked, "Did you notice her hands?"

"Yes. She had very elegant hands," I stated, and Reid nodded in agreement.

"Exactly," said Holmes, sitting back on his seat as if he had just made a point.

"Anything else?" I prodded.

"Did anything strike you as unusual about Sr. Julius?"

"No—not really."

"You're not even trying, Watson," complained Holmes disgustedly.

I concentrated, recalling all I could about the nun.

"The...uh...wedding ring...?"

"No! The Mother Superior already explained its presence."

"She was very attractive for a nun," I offered rather tentatively.

Holmes scowled at me. "There is no law that says nuns have to be ugly," he countered.

Reid gave a little snigger at that, but said nothing.

Unfortunately, it brought Holmes's attention to him. "What about you, Sergeant, did *you* notice anything?"

After a long moment of thought, Reid shrugged. "I'm sorry. She just looked like an ordinary everyday nun."

Holmes shook his head. "A good investigator uses *all* his senses," he hinted.

"Perfume!" I exclaimed suddenly. "She was wearing perfume!"

"If a man waits long enough," said Holmes with a long-suffering theatrical sigh. "Yes, Watson, she was wearing perfume."

"That's hardly significant though, is it?"

"How many nuns do you know that wear perfume?"

"Um...well, actually, I don't know any nuns. Is that important?"

"It could be," replied Holmes.

Looking at him, I was struck with a sudden thought. I poked a finger at him and accused. "You don't know, either!"

Holmes' lips quirked into a faint smile of acknowledgment, before he confessed, "I'm afraid I am not personally acquainted with any nuns either, but I am pretty certain that they do not wear perfume, not French perfume at any rate."

I smiled to myself. Holmes always gave off the aura of all-knowing, even when he wasn't certain of his facts. This was the first time I had actually caught him in an uncertainty.

"I need to send a wire, and I want to visit the prison," Holmes said to Sergeant Reid.

"It's getting late, Mr. Holmes. The prison doesn't allow visitors at nightfall and it'll be dark by the time we get there."

"In that case, I'll go tomorrow. Meantime I would like to see the local doctor and the station-master instead."

FIVE

At the post office, Holmes scribbled out a telegram. While he did so I noticed that Sergeant Reid seemed a little edgy and kept checking his watch, however, as he did not say anything, I felt it prudent not to ask. I assumed it was the call of nature that was causing his agitation.

Our next stop was to the train station. The station-master had been absent when we arrived; else I'm sure Holmes would have questioned him then. He proved to be a stocky little man with a phenomenal memory—much to Holmes's delight.

"Yes, Mr. Holmes," he replied in answer to Holmes's question. "Only one nun boarded the train that night."

"What did she look like?" asked Holmes.

"Scared."

"Really?"

"Yup. Like the devil hisself was after ha'."

"Did she say anything to you?"

"Just—'one ticket to London, please'."

"What other passengers boarded the same train?"

"Just Mr. Crabtree—the local chemist, and a young lad with red hair."

"Crabtree goes up to London every second month and visits his brother, sir. Been doing that for the last three years," interjected Reid.

"And the boy—did you recognize him?"

"Nope. Can't say as I did. But then I don't know ever' one aroun' here. Could be some farmer's lad."

"Has he returned?"

"Nope."

"On the following day, how many people disembarked here?" asked Holmes.

"Two. Mr. King, visiting his sister over at the post office, and Mrs. Philmore, the dressmaker. She goes up regular like to buy material and stuff, she does."

"What day did they leave?"

"Mr. King doesn't live here—he's from Oakland, and Mrs. Philmore took the mornin' train and came back on the last."

"Only two passengers disembarked for the whole day?" I asked in surprise.

"We're not exactly a bustlin' metropolis," grinned the station-master.

"Let me test your memory a bit more," said Holmes. "On the day we arrived, there were five other passengers besides ourselves. Did you know any of them?"

"Sure did. There was Bart Hayes—he's a farmer. My wife buys our eggs from him. Duncan Martin, he works for Hayes. The other was Crabtree on 'is way home again and then there was Tom Werner, bar tender at the Criterion."

"That's the pub," elaborated Reid, as if we couldn't figure that out for ourselves.

"What about the woman?"

"What woman?" asked the station-master, stumped for the first time.

"The attractive blonde-haired young woman that alighted

here same time as us," I said.

"No woman came through the gate, sir," said the Station-master.

Holmes glanced along the platform. It was open to the country at either end, and in fact, all around. "She could easily have left without going through the gate," he pointed out.

"Yup, sure enough. Many do it, if they've got folk waiting for them. It's only if they're headed for town that they'll come through the gate," replied the Station-master.

"Do people board the train the same way?"

"Nope. They have to come to the ticket window. Can't board without a ticket, you know."

"Actually they can," I said. "Anyone could sneak on."

"I s'pose, and some 'as tried it, but they don't stay on," countered the Station-master. "See, I always make a ticket check on the train just before it pulls out. There ain't no conductor on the late run, it's our job to check the tickets. There was only one nun, Crabtree and the boy that boarded here that day; I'd stake me life on it. And there were only seven other folks on board picked up from other stations."

"I see," said Holmes. He tossed a sovereign to the Station-master, and nodded his thanks.

"Home now?" asked Reid eagerly.

"Not yet. I want to talk to the doctor," replied Holmes, oblivious to the other's agitation.

Reid led us to the doctor's house at a brisk pace. The doctor was having his dinner but did not mind our intrusion.

"I just want to know about Mother Superior Capuano. What did she die of?" asked Holmes after introductions had been performed.

"Heart failure," came the prompt reply. "That's why she was retiring. It's unfortunate that she never had a chance to go to the convent in London. She was really looking forward to that."

"Was her death unexpected?"

"Not really, she was three and eighty after all, and with her heart the way it was, it could have happened at any time.

The excitement of the impending move could quite easily have brought it on."

"What did her hands look like?"

The doctor blinked in surprise. "Her hands?"

"Mmm."

"Like a nun's. Worn from years of hard work, gnarled and arthritic. Does that answer your question?"

"Perfectly, thank you."

As we left, I noticed Reid checking his watch again. "Can we go home now?" he asked plaintively.

"Certainly—is something wrong Sergeant?" asked Holmes, finally deigning to notice his obvious discomfort.

"It's just that I'm usually home for dinner by six; my wife was expecting us around then."

"Oh—and the time now?"

"Nearly eight." That explained his anxiety. He was worried about how his wife was going to react to our being so late for dinner. She would not be pleased.

SIX

We hurried to the Sergeant's house after a quick detour to the police station to pick up our bags. When we entered his house, he went quickly to the kitchen, while we followed along at a slower pace.

Mrs. Reid was sitting at the kitchen table. She was a plump, fluffy honey-blonde. She was crying.

Reid hastened over to her, apologizing furiously.

She looked up at him: "It's ruined," she cried. "All ruined! I wanted it to be perfect and now it's spoiled."

Holmes always claimed to have no penchant for dealing with distraught women, but when he wanted to he could be irresistibly charming—calming even the most waspish woman with his suave manner. He decided to turn on the charm now. He stepped forward:

"My dear Mrs. Reid—a thousand apologies. If I had known such a charming and attractive a hostess awaited our arrival, I would not have dallied so. Your distress is entirely due to me and I am disconsolate." He took her hand and kissed it with a flourish and a courtly bow.

Her tears dried instantly. She was not accustomed to being greeted with such vigor and panache. "I am just upset, Mr. Holmes, because I wanted dinner to be perfect and now it's ruined."

"Ruined? Surely not." Holmes went over and peeked in the oven. "You exaggerate, my dear Mrs. Reid. In fact, I think you've been talking to Mrs. Hudson. How else would you know that I prefer my roasts to be overcooked? I have an aversion to raw meat."

"Th-then you don't mind?" She looked hopeful.

"Mind? Not at all. It's cooked to perfection. Give us a moment to wash up and we will not tarry anymore. I am ravenous."

The lady smiled and wiped her eyes, her mood brighter.

"I'll show you to your room," offered Reid, his voice reflecting his relief. As he led us up the stairs, he said: "Thank you, Mr. Holmes. We don't often have such important visitors and my wife wanted everything to be perfect."

There was a twinkle of amusement in Holmes's eyes. "Far be it for me to be the cause of marital discord."

We entered our room. There was one ordinary bed and a camp bed set up. Holmes tossed his bag onto the camp bed, leaving me the other.

"You're a faker, Holmes," I said, taking off my coat.

"Oh. Why do you say that?" He eyed me curiously.

"You pretend to be cold, emotionless and indifferent to others, but really you are just a big softie inside."

"I see, and what brings you to that conclusion?"

"How you treated the Sergeant's wife."

"Oh that. We are staying in their home, and I for one, have no desire to listen to them fighting. My motives were purely selfish."

"You can't fool me, Holmes," I replied. "You do realize that you'll have to eat whatever she dishes up now, don't you?"

Holmes made a face, and then smiled suddenly as a thought occurred to him. "You'll have to eat it all too. It would be rude not to."

"Thanks for nothing," I replied sourly, while at the same time giving thanks that I thought to bring my medical bag with me. It had a good supply of digestives and antacids in it.

We washed quickly and returned downstairs. Mrs. Reid had tidied up her appearance and the table was set. She piled our plates with burnt and dry roast beef, accompanied with burnt and dry roast potatoes. We required frequent sips of wine to wash the food down.

Holmes, who had never been a big eater, cleaned his plate, and with effort I managed to do the same, though every piece seemed to stick in my throat. The Sergeant gamely followed our example. None of us dared not to.

An excellent dessert followed the main course. We complimented the lady profusely on her culinary expertise. By the end of dinner, I believe Mrs. Reid thought Holmes was the most wonderful man on the face of the earth, as he entertained her with humorous anecdotes of some of his cases.

We retired at ten-thirty, claiming fatigue from a long journey and hectic day. Once in our room, I was quick to break out the antacids and other aids to digestion. Holmes was rubbing at his sternum. I handed him a dose, which he drank gratefully.

"I hope Reid appreciates our sacrifice," he said.

"I'm sure he does. As long as you don't run off with his wife."

"I'm not about to run off with his wife."

"No, but she's about ready to run off with you. Don't tell me you didn't notice. She thinks you're wonderful," I said, half-serious, half-teasing.

"I *am* wonderful, Watson," replied Holmes immodestly. This statement was followed by a burp that set him to rubbing his sternum again.

SEVEN

Next morning after a light breakfast, Reid drove us to Princeton Prison. The Governor was delighted to meet Holmes, happily listing all the prisoners that were current residents thanks to Holmes's efforts.

"Really, sir," said Holmes, when the other stopped to take a breath. "I had no idea there were so many."

"You've been busy," he said.

"Indeed I have," agreed Holmes pleasantly.

We made our way to Governor Snowden's office. Once we were all comfortably seated and puffing away on his cigars, Holmes brought up the object of our visit.

"Tell me, Mr. Snowden, has the new Mother Superior from the convent visited and introduced herself?"

"Yes, she certainly has. Her first week here, in fact. A most charming woman she is. Almost a pity she's a nun," replied Snowden.

I thought to myself that it was lucky she was a nun or he would probably be chasing her, if his enthusiasm were anything to go on.

"While she was here did she speak to any of the prisoners?"

"No—not really."

"Not really? Elucidate please—what exactly do you mean by not really?" Holmes fastened his gray eyes intently on the other man.

"Well, she wanted to view the inmates during their exercise period. We were in the yard. As we were passing a couple of inmates she stumbled. She would have fallen, but one of the fellows caught her and helped her up. She only thanked and blessed him. She didn't actually converse with him or anything like that."

Holmes frowned. "Did they touch?"

"He held her arm momentarily."

"What about her hands, were they in your sight at all times?"

The governor thought for a moment, a little puzzled by Holmes's questions. "I can't say I noticed."

"Have any nuns been here since?"

"No. There's been no need. We only call them if someone is sick or dying. The men like to see a woman at times like that. I don't trouble the good sisters otherwise."

"Who was the prisoner that she stumbled into?"

"Hastings. He was standing nearby—him and his son."

"Hastings...." Holmes closed his eyes as he searched his memory. "Ah, not John Hastings that raided the Bank of England's vaults four years ago?"

"Yes, that's the one. Scotland Yard nabbed him and his son for the job. The rest of the gang got away with the money. Hastings never talked. They killed a night watchman during the robbery."

"Stabbed wasn't he?"

"Yes, I believe so."

"I'm surprised they weren't hung," I said.

"They should have been, but the law is hoping that they may change their minds eventually and tell us where the money is or who their accomplices were."

"Have they had any visitors since their incarceration?"

"Young Hastings' wife comes every three months. John Hastings' wife has come a couple of times, but not recently.

"What about the women? Have they been kept under surveillance—presumably their husbands have told them the whereabouts of the money," said Holmes.

"I believe they were watched for a time, but I doubt if Hastings told them. Could any man trust his wife to stay faithful once they've got their hands on half a million pounds?"

"Wait a minute," I interrupted, a little confused. "Did you not say, sir, that the accomplices got away with the money?"

"I did, but that was only conjecture at the time of the robbery. No trace of the money has shown up. If it was in circulation—and it would be by now—some bank would have come across some of the notes. The general theory is that Hastings had it and hid it. That's why he refuses to talk. I think he's hoping those same accomplices will find a way to free him."

"Has any attempt been made?"

"Yes. They were in Dartmoor originally. Almost escaped from there. Clothes were smuggled in to them. That's why they were transferred here. We have higher security."

"How long a sentence did they draw?" I asked.

"Life. They were offered a deal in exchange for the whereabouts of the money, but refused it," explained Snowden.

"I'd like to have a look at the exercise yard if I may?" said Holmes, standing up, abruptly ending the conversation.

"Er...certainly," agreed Snowden, a little startled by Holmes's manner. As we walked along the stone corridors to the exercise yard, I reassured him that this was just Holmes's way and urged him not to be offended.

Holmes took a walk around the exercise yard, which was empty at this time—all the prisoners being occupied at various tasks inside.

"Does that wall lead to the outside?" asked Holmes.

"Yes, but as you can see we have armed guards patrolling the perimeter. If somehow a prisoner managed to breach the wall, they wouldn't get very far before they were shot. We have an excellent view for some five miles all round."

"Hmm." Holmes looked around him. "That gate—where does it lead?"

"To the front entrance. No prisoner could escape that way."

Holmes nodded then held out his hand to Snowden. They shook.

"Thank you very much. This has been a most instructive visit."

"Anytime, Mr. Holmes. You're always welcome here."

* * * * * * *

On our way back to town, Holmes was silent and thoughtful. As we reached the outskirts of Sherbrook, he said: "You can drop me off at the Post Office, Reid."

I alighted with him and waited outside whilst he went in. The telegrapher handed him a telegram that had just come for him. Holmes read his message as he walked out to join me.

"What now, Holmes?" I asked.

"I think...," he began only to cut off his words when he spied the Mother Superior from the convent walking towards us on the other side of the street. He crossed quickly to meet her, and I hurried along in his wake.

"Good afternoon, Mother Superior Augustine," he greeted.

"Mr. Holmes. How is your investigation proceeding?" she asked pleasantly.

"Quite well. I'm returning to London on the last train," he said much to my surprise. "I have a meeting this evening with the Mother Superior of your old Convent—Morevale isn't it?

"Yes. Please send her my regards won't you? It was she that recommended me for this post." She smiled disarmingly at him. "Are you any closer to finding the reason why Sr. Mary Ignatius went to London?"

"Yes—she was coming to see me." Holmes watched her like a hawk studying a worm.

"Goodness, I wonder what she wanted with you?" Her manner remained charming, but her eyes were surprisingly cold and calculating.

"I know what she wanted," Holmes replied still watching her.

She smiled at him and replied, "I see. That's good. The sooner this business is over the better for all concerned. You've informed the police of your suspicions of course?" She was still cool, but I thought I detected a note of concern in her voice.

"Not yet. I never work like that. If you have read any of Watson's stories you would know that I like to have all my facts at hand before presenting a completed case to the authorities."

"Oh, so you are missing some facts?"

"One or two minor ones."

"Interesting, I must find the time to read the good Doctor's stories. I'm sure they're fascinating. You're going on the evening train you said?"

"Yes."

"Well, I wish you a pleasant trip then," she smiled, nodded and left us.

"I didn't know we were going back to London, Holmes: and what use is it visiting the Mother Superior of Morevale Convent?"

"Merrivale Convent, Watson," corrected Holmes.

"But you said Morevale," I pointed out.

"Yes. You would think she'd know the name of her previous convent, wouldn't you?" he replied, his voice dry.

"Well, whatever the name of the convent, why are we going there?"

"We're not."

"But you just said...?"

"Head on over to the Reid's house and pack our bags, will you, Watson?" he asked, ignoring my confusion.

"Will we be there for dinner, or should I make our apologies?"

"No we'll eat first, as long as we can catch the seven o'clock train."

EIGHT

Holmes returned to the Reid house with Sergeant Reid in tow at five-thirty. As Mrs. Reid was setting the table for dinner, she asked, "Must you leave so soon, Mr. Holmes?"

"Unfortunately, yes. I have to continue my investigations in London. However, we will probably be returning in the near future, and I must say, my dear Mrs. Reid, that the food and hospitality we have received here exceeds even that which the best hotels in London provide."

She smiled warmly at him. "I will look forward to your return, Mr. Holmes. It's been an honor and a pleasure having you here."

"The pleasure is all mine, Madame," responded Holmes smoothly.

"I'm already anticipating your next visit here. I will always make *you* welcome," she said, still smiling at him.

My eyebrows went up at that for her tone was suggestive. Lucky her husband wasn't in the room. As for Holmes, if he picked up on the tone of her comments, he chose to ignore it and sat down at the table instead.

The dinner of shepherd's pie was excellent—she really was a good cook. We collected our bags, thanked our host and hostess and walked to the train station.

"It is just as well we are leaving, Holmes. A couple more days in that house and Mrs. Reid would be divorcing her husband for you."

"Nonsense."

"No, true. She is smitten with you."

"It is just an infatuation, Watson. She is unaccustomed to gentlemen."

"No, it's more than that, trust me. I can tell these things." I insisted.

"Well, Reid's marriage is safe. I am not in the habit of chasing other men's wives. In fact, I'm not in the habit of chasing any women, married or otherwise—as you very well know, Watson."

"I didn't say you were doing the chasing, Holmes. But your speech was very flowery. Women like that sort of thing."

"In that case, we will make any future visits here brief and not overnight, for that is the sort of situation I prefer to avoid."

I smiled, and when we reached the train station, I bought the tickets while Holmes wandered out onto the platform. There was only one other traveller besides us—a young man, who seemed intent on studying his shoes.

Holmes went over to him and said, "Excuse me, young man, but were you perchance on this train on Monday night?"

The fellow gave Holmes a fleeting glance before returning his gaze back to his feet, mumbling his answer in a husky voice. "I ain't never bin on a train afore."

"I see, terribly sorry to bother you, then," apologized Holmes, moving away.

When the train arrived we boarded and the station-master came on with us, checking tickets. As he drew level with us, Holmes asked softly. "'Scuse me—is that the boy who was on the train Monday?"

The station-master glanced at the boy and frowned. "Looks a bit like him, 'cept that lad had red hair and this 'uns dark."

"Thank you."

The station-master went on his way and checked the tickets of the other nineteen passengers on board. We moved out of the second-class carriage to first-class once the train started to move.

As we made ourselves comfortable, I said, "Too bad it wasn't the same boy."

"Hair color can be easily changed, Watson."

"So you think he's the same one?"

"As I never saw the original one it is hard to say. Curious coincidence though, is it not?"

"Not really. There must be a thousand boys travelling trains at any given moment. It would only be a coincidence if there was a boy and a nun—and Mr. Crabtree." I replied.

"You're so pedantic Watson," said Holmes without rancor. He lit his pipe and closed his eyes. I soon followed his example— without the pipe—and dozed for a bit. In fact I was still dozing when Holmes left the carriage. I was dreaming. In my dream I heard a cry of, "Watson!"

My eyes flickered open and I woke. I blinked in confusion for a moment and looked around, noting Holmes's absence.

"Holmes?" I stood up and looked out into the passageway. There was no one there. I walked along, feeling a sudden gnawing of apprehension in the pit of my stomach. Where was Holmes? He couldn't just disappear. I came level with the side door and stopped to eye the passing terrain. I automatically placed my hand against the doorframe as I put my nose to the window. Then I took my hand away I stared stupidly at the red stain upon it for a moment.

Blood!

Visions of Holmes being stabbed and shoved from the train brought strength to my legs and thought to my brain. I leapt toward the emergency cord and pulled with all my strength. The train came to a screeching halt, almost toppling me over.

There was no conductor on the train so it was left to the irate driver to come storming along demanding to know who pulled the cord. As soon as I saw him, I demanded, "You need to shunt the train back up the tracks. Sherlock Holmes has been attacked and pushed off the train."

"Sherlock Holmes—the detective?"

"The one and only. I fear he has been murdered."

"You got it Guv'nor," he said, his eyes alight with excitement.

Within minutes, ignoring the queries of the other passengers, I hurried out onto the platform at the back of the train and held up the powerful lantern that I found in the guard's carriage when I passed through. As the train began to shunt backwards, I scanned the terrain. Fortunately the moon was out, so it wasn't quite pitch black. My heart was heavy. Was this the end of our partnership—our friendship? I dreaded the thought. Could Holmes be so easily defeated? More to the point, how could it have happened? He was on his guard. He was always on his guard. To be knifed and pushed off a train so easily, it just did not seem possible.

As I held the lantern up I continued to study the topography, while I fingered the whistle the engineer had given me in my other hand.

We shunted for some fifteen minutes before I espied a dark shape by the side of the tracks. I gave three quick blasts on the whistle and leapt from the train before it had stopped, hurrying to the shape.

I recognized the familiar hounds-check cloth of his Inverness.

"Holmes!" I cried as I dropped to my knees and rolled him. There was blood on his head and the handle of a knife protruded from between his ribs. His eyes fluttered open.

"Angel face," he muttered before passing out again.

The engineer and fireman joined me. "He's alive," I said. They helped me carry him back onto the train and into our carriage. I unearthed my medical bag, being glad for a second time that I had brought it.

"Please get to London as quickly as you can," I requested. The engineer grinned in anticipation and we were soon speeding along—the train breaking its own speed record.

I was oblivious to all this though, concentrating all my efforts on Holmes. I pulled the knife out and checked the position of the wound, heaving a sigh of relief as I did so. Favor smiled on Holmes. The knife had missed his vital organs, but he had bled heavily. The damage was minimal in surgical terms, only if I hadn't noticed him missing when I did, he would almost certainly have bled to death before he was found. Just as the nun had.

I heaved a sigh of relief. He would recover from the knife wound and the loss of blood. At this stage I was more concerned with his head injury. Head wounds were tricky at the best of times. He must have received it when he fell. I was surprised that he had broken no bones in the process, for the train had been travelling at full speed.

I tried to rouse him with smelling salts but was unsuccessful. His pupils were equal and reacting to light, but for all I knew he could be bleeding intracranially. I dressed the cut on his head and sat back and worried.

I had known Holmes for five years now, and yet I still knew so little about him, while he knew probably everything about me. What of his relations—his next of kin? Did he even have any? Who should I notify if he died? I didn't even know who Holmes' lawyers were or even if he had made a will. He never spoke of his parents, so I assumed they were dead. He never mentioned any siblings, so I assumed he was an only child. These were the thoughts that went through my mind. Why, I didn't even know what religion Holmes was—if any.

Looking at his ashen face, as he lay on the seat breathing

raggedly, I determined that whatever the cost, whatever it required, I would not let Holmes die.

NINE

As soon as the train stopped, the stoker ran for the police and for a cab for me. Meantime, the engineer, calling for help from the platform porters ensured that every door was guarded to make sure none of the passengers disembarked before the police came and questioned them. It was my belief that the murderer was still on the train, for we had travelled non-stop. He couldn't have got off anywhere and we were moving too fast for him to jump off.

While I was waiting for the stoker to return with the cab, an elderly constable approached me. I told him what happened as quickly as I could and mentioned that Holmes had been suspicious of a young lad. I gave him a description of the boy and asked him to investigate him thoroughly. I also mentioned that the attack on Holmes was exactly the same as the attack on the nun—the case that we were currently probing. He promised to get details on all the passengers. I referred him to Inspector Hopkins and told him that he was handling the nun murder case, and to notify him at once of this attack on Holmes. I was about to issue further instructions when I spied the stoker waving to me.

"I have to go now, Constable. Holmes needs urgent medical attention. Inspector Hopkins knows where to find me." With that and the help of a couple of porters, I carried Holmes to the waiting cab, thanked the stoker and was soon on my way.

At Baker Street, the cabby helped me carry Holmes upstairs and I wasted no time in putting him to bed.

Mrs. Hudson fluttered around me in a great state of anxiety, eager to help. She acted as my nurse as I stitched the knife wound and applied a dressing.

Through the long night, I continued to monitor Holmes' vital signs and his neurological state, which remained unchanged. He wasn't exactly in a coma, but he was deeply unconscious. He did respond to some stimuli, but was not opening his eyes or able to speak.

As I sat there by his bed in the dimly lit room, I pondered on those words he had muttered to me out by the railroad tracks. Was it from the ravings of concussion or was he trying to tell me something? I doubt very much if he was calling *me* angel face. Was he merely confused? Or perhaps he was seeing things? Or was it a vital clue as to the identity of his attacker?

It was at moments like this that I wished I had his quick wit, and was the actual light, instead of the illuminator as he often referred to me. Obviously it meant something to Holmes, but it was a complete mystery to me. I decided to try a different tack.

How did the killer know we would be on the train? Holmes had only decided when he was talking to the Mother Superior in Sherbrook. She knew we were going and so did Sergeant Reid, his wife and the station-master. The station-master wasn't on the train and I felt I could rule out the Sergeant and his wife—especially his wife. That only left the Mother Superior. She wasn't on the train though, nor was there any nuns. Nuns were often called angels of mercy. Was Holmes referring to them? Surely a nun didn't stab Holmes? That seemed too remote a possibility to even contemplate.

* * * * * * *

I managed to doze at intervals throughout the night, but was still weary and bleary-eyed come morning. Mrs. Hudson came in with coffee at six, and she too looked as if she had slept little. She stood by Holmes' bed looking at him, not realizing that I was awake and watching her. She gazed at him with a fondness, not unlike that of a mother for her son, and I realized just how much she cared for her erstwhile, temperamental and exceedingly difficult tenant. He was more than a tenant to her and she fussed over him like a mother, putting up with all his moods, odorous experiments and even indoor target practice without complaint.

I also understood Holmes' attitude towards her now. He was always respectful and polite to her even when he was moody. Perhaps he thought of her as the mother he never had. It was an interesting situation and one that I promised myself I would pay more attention to when he recovered.

I yawned and straightened up in my chair, stretching the crick out of my back.

Mrs. Hudson turned around at that and looked at me anxiously. "How is he Doctor?"

I made a quick check of his vital signs. "Stable." Neurologically he was unchanged, although it appeared to me that his breathing was more natural and regular than it had been—more like that of a person sleeping deeply. I checked his pupils; they contracted rapidly in the light.

"He doesn't seem to have deteriorated. If anything, he appears to be sleeping now, rather than unconscious." I explained to her—perhaps needing to hear the words out loud to reassure myself. Mrs. Hudson appeared to be very near to tears. I patted her shoulder reassuringly. "He's a survivor. You know that as well as I."

She nodded.

I took up the bottle of smelling salts and held them under Holmes's nose. His eyes flickered in response. They opened but were unfocused.

"Holmes...can you hear me?" I asked.

His eyes met mine. I took hold of his hands and instructed: "Squeeze my hands, Holmes—as hard as you can."

To my great relief he complied. His grip was weak, but that would be due to the loss of blood, not to any paralysis. The fact that he responded and obeyed was proof that despite his obviously dazed state, there was no brain damage. He closed his eyes again and was soon asleep. I turned and smiled at Mrs. Hudson.

"I think he is going to be all right," I said.

She hugged me in an unexpected display of emotion, apologized for it and then left the room hurriedly, no doubt to have a cry in her kitchen.

At seven, Stanley Hopkins arrived. A tall, corpulent man, who did not introduce himself, accompanied him. Hopkins also neglected to introduce him. This man said little but listened attentively to everything I said.

"What happened, Doctor?" asked Hopkins.

"We were on the train, returning from Sherbrook. I was dozing in our carriage and never heard Holmes leave. I woke to Holmes's cry. I ran out into the corridor and there was no sign of him. That's when I found the trace of blood on the exit door's frame. I stopped the train immediately and had them back up. We found Holmes about five miles back. He'd been stabbed." I stood up and handed Hopkins the knife. "You will note that this is identical to the knife we found in the nun."

Hopkins nodded in agreement studying the knife with interest.

"How is he?" asked the fat man, speaking for the first time. I noticed that he had light gray eyes, similar to Holmes' when he was concentrating intensely.

"He was lucky with the knife wound. It missed all his vital organs and did little damage. He bled heavily of course. If we hadn't found him as quickly as we did, he would have bled to death. My main concern however, is the head injury he received falling from the train," I explained.

"Head injury?" There was concern in the fat man's voice.

"Yes, but I think he is going to be all right with that, too. He's been unconscious all night, but woke up and responded a little this morning. I am hopeful that he will make a full recovery."

The fat man nodded.

"Did he say anything—anything at all?" asked Hopkins.

"Just...well...it sounded like 'angel face'. I've been racking my brains trying to figure out what he meant by that."

"It doesn't ring any bells?"

"Nary a one." I replied. "What about you, did you question

the boy?"

"What boy?" asked Hopkins.

"Why, the boy on the train of course," I was surprised at his apparent ignorance.

"There was no boy on the train. There were seven women and twelve men, not counting you and Holmes. They were all questioned. What's this about a boy?"

"The day the nun was killed one of her fellow passengers was a boy with red hair. The station-master did not know him and he hasn't returned to Sherbrook, or so we thought. Yesterday at the Sherbrook station, a boy—roughly the same age as the previous one—also boarded the train. He had dark brown hair, but I know Holmes was suspicious of him. He insisted that it was more than a coincidence. Claimed it was easy to change the color of one's hair," I explained.

"But if he was suspicious of this boy, surely he would have been on his guard if the boy approached him," said the fat man.

"I know," I agreed. "That's what I thought. He was suspicious. He was wary. I have no idea how it could have happened. Holmes is a man perpetually on his guard." I felt perplexed and I showed it.

"Well, there was no boy on the train when it reached London, which means he must have jumped off when you stopped the train to pick up Holmes," said Hopkins.

"May we take a look at him?" asked the fat man.

I nodded.

He entered Holmes' bedroom without asking directions to it, and stood by the bed, looking down at the sleeping form.

As Hopkins made to follow him into the room, I grabbed his sleeve and whispered: "Who is he?"

"Uh...a friend of Holmes'."

The fact that he still refrained from mentioning his name made me wonder if he was somebody important, someone whose identity had to be kept secret for security reasons.

After a long moment, the fat man turned, fastening his steely gray eyes onto me and offering his hand.

I shook it.

"Thank you, Dr. Watson," he said simply. "I appreciate all you have done."

"Notify me the minute he wakes and is capable of talking—day or night," instructed Hopkins.

I nodded in agreement.

TEN

It was nearly lunchtime before I got around to reading the morning papers. The headlines glared at me.

SHERLOCK HOLMES ATTACKED!
GREAT DETECTIVE AT DEATH'S DOOR!
SUPER SLEUTH CRITICAL!

God only knows where they got their information from for I certainly hadn't spoken to any reporters. I dozed in my chair until nearly five o'clock. I roused when I heard a sound coming from Holmes' room. I hurried in. He was awake. His eyes were clear and reasonably alert.

I smiled at him. "Hello, Holmes. Do you know where you are?"

He looked around the room and replied: "My room. My bed."

"Which is—where?"

"221B Baker Street." His voice grew stronger with every word.

"What year is it?"

"1886."

"Who am I?"

"Dr. John H. Watson. My friend and doctor."

My relief knew no bounds at his replies. I quickly checked his limb strengths and reflexes, before asking, "Do you know what happened to you, Holmes?"

He looked at me, his eyes clouding slightly. "That's what I

was going to ask you."

"You don't remember anything?" I prodded.

"My head hurts. My side hurts. I feel generally weak all over and you are treating me like a patient. I am assuming that I have been in some kind of accident. As to what that accident was, I have no recollection."

"We were on the train returning to London from Sherbrook," I said, trying to jog his memory.

"And?" he looked at me expectantly.

"And you left our carriage and were stabbed and pushed off the train."

"By whom?"

I shook my head. "Not sure. We think it was a lad of some six and ten years. He was on the train, but had disappeared by the time it reached London. You had been suspicious of him, Holmes."

"Was I? I guess I had a right to be if he was the one who did this to me." Holmes smiled weakly at me, but I knew it troubled him that he could not remember the incident.

"What were we doing in Sherbrook?" he asked after a moment's thought.

"Investigating the death of a nun—don't you remember?"

"She was stabbed and thrown off a train?" he answered, his voice doubtful.

"Yes, yes! You do remember," I cried excitedly. "She was from the convent in Sherbrook."

"I see. Actually, I don't remember. I just deduced that."

My excitement died. His abilities had not diminished; he just had no recollection of recent events. This was not uncommon with head injuries.

"Never mind, Holmes. I have it all written down. You can read it when you're feeling better. It will come back to you, I'm sure."

"Are you?" His eyes met mine with his unflinching gaze.

"Yes, quite sure. Amnesia is common after head trauma. You bumped your head when you fell off the train. It is not unusual for people to forget recent events in such cases. The fact that your long-term memory is unaffected proves you suffered no lasting damage. It's only a matter of time before you regain your memory.

"When you are feeling stronger, you can read my notes. It will help to jog your memory. In the meantime, it is more important that you get your strength back. Do you feel up to taking some nourishment?"

He nodded. I notified Mrs. Hudson and she insisted on feeding some broth to Holmes personally, even though he protested that there was nothing wrong with his arms. While she was doing that I sent a telegram to Hopkins telling him Holmes was awake but had no memory of the attack. I also added to the message a warning not to bother Holmes until he was stronger. I didn't want him coming around and pestering Holmes. Badgering him would only increase his anxiety over his loss of memory.

* * * * * * *

The next day, Holmes still in bed, but taking more of an interest in his surroundings, asked for the afternoon papers. I brought in several. The news of his attack had been relegated to the second page. The headlines for this day were full of news of the massive jailbreak at Princeton. Apparently someone had dynamited the side wall of the exercise yard at the prison. The prisoners had run for it. Ten had been shot; three guards had been killed, and police were still rounding up the escapees. At this time thirty-four had been apprehended and twelve were still missing.

"Watson," said Holmes, "I seem to recall visiting Princeton Prison."

"That's right, Holmes, we did. You showed an interest in the exercise yard and in a couple of prisoners named Hastings— father and son."

"John and Robert Hastings—the Bank of England job of '81," replied Holmes, though I noted there was still some uncertainty in his voice.

"Yes, you're exactly right," I agreed.

He smiled with satisfaction. "Send a message to Hopkins will you, Watson. Ask him to come round when he can. I want to know more about the breakout."

"Certainly." I hurried to do his bidding, and then returned to his room and helped myself to some of the papers.

* * * * * * *

It was nearly eight before Hopkins put in an appearance.

"Mr. Holmes, I'm glad you're feeling better," he said.

"Ah, Hopkins, good of you to come. What can you tell me about the breakout?"

"We have recovered all but four," said Hopkins.

"Two of those four being John and Robert Hastings," stated Holmes.

Hopkins sat up straighter on his seat, a look of surprise on his face. "How did you know that?"

Holmes smiled and for the first and last time in our acquaintance admitted, "Lucky guess. Watson told me I had shown an interest in Hastings when I visited the prison last week."

This from the man who swore he never guessed!

"Do you know why you were interested in them?" asked Hopkins eagerly.

Holmes frowned. "I'm not sure, but I believe I feared that someone would attempt to break them out. After all half a million pounds is a tempting lure."

"It's been tried before," agreed Hopkins. "Unsuccessfully."

"Until now," pointed out Holmes. "Tell me, were there any nuns at the prison when the breakout happened?"

"Not at the prison, but there was one with a wagon along the road. In fact, she had seen some of the fleeing prisoners and pointed the police in the right direction."

"Was her wagon searched?"

"No, of course not. She would know if a prisoner climbed on

board."

"Yes, she would."

"Surely you don't think she was hiding prisoners in her wagon?"

"I don't know what to think," sighed Holmes, lying wearily back against his pillows.

"Do you remember anything from the train?" asked Hopkins.

"It's still a complete blank, although I am starting to recall a few bits and pieces from the last few days."

"What about the words 'angel face'? Does that mean anything to you?" persisted Hopkins.

"Angel face?"

"That's what you muttered to me when I found you, Holmes," I said.

"Angel face." Holmes repeated, thinking with effort. "I'm sorry. I have no idea what I could have meant. Are you sure I said angel face?"

"That's what it sounded like," I said, feeling rather doubtful now that I heard right.

"Have you found the boy, Hopkins?" asked Holmes.

"No. We've scoured the villages near where the train stopped in case someone spotted him walking in, only he seems to be invisible."

"Just like the one that was on the train with the nun," I commented.

Holmes slithered down in his bed and pulled his blankets up to his chin. He closed his eyes, and just before sleep claimed him said, "The easiest way to become invisible is to change your identity."

I escorted Hopkins out. Holmes's comment had triggered a thought.

"Inspector, the seven women that were on the train—what did they look like?"

"Like women," he replied.

"No. I mean did any stand out—in looks, character, behavior?"

"Well, there was one," Hopkins smiled almost dreamily. "Blonde she was. Sweet and angelic. What a woman."

"Angelic? She had a face like an angel?" I prodded, suddenly excited.

"You could describe her like that," agreed Hopkins.

"Don't you see—face like an angel, angel face! Holmes was stabbed by a woman—that woman!"

Hopkins' eyebrows went up a notch.

"If you'd seen her, Doctor you wouldn't say that. She was such a pretty, sweet little thing."

"That's just it. No man would be on his guard in her presence. Not even Holmes. He was on the lookout for a boy. It is easy for a woman to disguise herself as a youth, and I remember he kept his face turned away so we never saw it clearly. She probably wore a wig, and then once the train was moving, changed into her female garb and took Holmes by surprise. That is the only way anyone could get close to him."

Hopkins was nodding now. "There is a certain logic to that, Doctor. We have her address at the Yard. I'll check into it." "Don't be surprised if you find it's false," I cautioned.

Hopkins left, as optimistic as I was that we were on the right track.

An hour later I received a telegram from him saying simply: *Wrong Address. No trace. Hopkins.*

I smiled. Now I knew what Holmes felt like when he made a breakthrough on a case. I resolved to spend some more time in contemplation. I helped myself to tobacco from the Persian slipper, and, with pipe billowing, made myself comfortable in an armchair, endeavoring to emulate Holmes.

ELEVEN

I recalled the vision of loveliness that had passed us on the train and disembarked the same time as us on our trip to Sherbrook. She had made sure that no one at the station would see her. It all made sense to me now. Disguised as a boy she boarded the train with the nun and murdered her. That's why the 'boy' never returned to Sherbrook, but a woman did. Then again a boy boarded with us and attempted to murder Holmes while disguised as a woman. She escaped unhindered and unsuspected while the police wasted time looking for the non-existent boy. She had probably already returned to Sherbrook by now.

I puffed for a moment on the pungent shag, watching the smoke spirals. Where would a woman of uncommon appearance hide in a small village? Holmes always said the easiest way to hide something was to leave it where everyone could see it. Where would you not notice a woman—amongst other woman of course! And where was the biggest collection of anonymous women? The convent!

I almost leapt out of my chair. Holmes had been suspicious of the nuns at the convent—two nuns anyhow. The Mother Superior and Sr. Julius. Sr. Julius wore perfume, which he considered odd. Now what was it about the Mother Superior that aroused his suspicions? I puffed furiously.

Her hands! He asked if I had noticed her hands. There had been nothing noticeable or remarkable about her hands, yet Holmes considered it a significant point. I knew him well enough by now to know that he did not bring things to my attention for no reason. The fault was not his but mine that I repeatedly missed seeing what he did. I tried to remember what I'd seen that first day. Her hands were white and smooth with manicured nails—a typical lady's hands.

My eyes widened and I spluttered on the smoke. That was it. They were lady's hands! Not a nun's. The local doctor had said the old nun that died had gnarled, work-roughened hands. If the new Mother Superior had been a nun all her life, her hands should have been the same.

I jumped out of the chair and went over to where Holmes' coat was hanging and pulled a telegram from its pocket. It was the reply he had pocketed before speaking to the Mother

Superior about us returning to London. It said: *Mother Superior Augustine and three sisters left Merrivale convent June 6th. No rings. No scents. Hopkins.*

Three nuns. Four in all. I remembered now. Sergeant Reid had mentioned that. We had only seen two. The angel-faced woman could be one of the other two. Maybe Sr. Mary Ignatius found out that they were impostors and that's why she was trying to contact Holmes. My elation grew. I knew I was on the right track. It was all clear before me. Holmes had already deduced all this, but had forgotten it after the blow to his head.

Another thought struck me as I walked over to my desk. The Mother Superior had lied about the name of her previous convent. Holmes had tested her. Is that why he told her we were leaving and on which train? Perhaps he expected to be attacked. No doubt he thought he would be more than a match for any woman, but it seems he underestimated the enemy for once.

I sat down at my desk and wrote out my reasoning. I decided that I would return to Sherbrook on the morrow to confront the impostors and find the murderer posing as a nun. I suppose I could have informed Hopkins, but where would the glory be in that? He would take the credit. Holmes was indisposed, so that left me. This was going to be my case, solved by my own reasoning. It was going to be a nice surprise for Holmes, too, and perhaps he would be a little less critical of my deductive reasoning ability in the future. I finished writing, blotted the letter and slipped it into an envelope. I emptied my pipe and had a quick sherry before going into Holmes' room.

He was sleeping soundly. I smiled. He was sure to be astonished when I apprehended the impostors and captured his attacker. I savored the thought. I was always a step behind him when I accompanied him on an investigation, but not this time. Thanks to his amnesia, I was a step ahead. It was my turn to shine.

I went to bed feeling rather light-hearted. I would catch the eight o'clock train first thing in the morning. Should have the whole case wrapped up by lunchtime. I slept the sleep of the just, dreaming of my impending triumph. I suppose I was feeling a bit cocky and pleased with myself, but then, how was I to know?

TWELVE

Next morning, I was up early and had breakfasted by seven. Holmes was still sleeping. At this point in his recovery, sleep was what he needed most, and considering how little he slept normally; I believed it would do him no harm. I took care not to disturb him. Before I left, I propped the envelope with my deductions and plan of action in it on the breakfast table, donned my coat, checked that I had my revolver in my pocket and made my way to Paddington Station.

I reached Sherbrook at ten thirty. As I disembarked, I hesitated for a moment, wondering if I should seek Sergeant Reid's assistance or go it alone. After a moment's deliberation, I decided that his presence would make my visit official. I walked to the police station and found a sign tacked to the door.

HUNTING PRISONERS

Of course! I had forgotten about the prison breakout from Princeton. It looked like I was on my own. I went to the local blacksmith, who recognized me from my previous visit. He was more than happy to supply a pony and trap for my use. With transport organized, I was soon on my way to the convent, firmly resolved as to what I would do.

At the convent, I had no sooner walked up the steps than Mother Superior came out to greet me.

"Dr. Watson," she said. "What brings you here?"

"I am on a commission from Sherlock Holmes," I replied, thinking that his name would bear more weight.

"Mr. Holmes—why...I thought he was at death's door?" she said, sudden concern on her face.

"It was a near thing," I admitted. "However, he is recovering."

"So Mr. Holmes didn't actually send you?" she asked, the relief in her voice evident.

"I often pursue my own line of inquiry when we work together," I replied a trifle pompously, a little put out by her manner.

"Has he been able to pass on his knowledge to the police yet? I seem to remember him saying something to the effect that he hadn't...prior to his accident," she said.

"Madam—that was no accident. It was a vicious attack by a woman. A woman whom I believe is hiding here at the convent." I announced, forgetting for a moment that she was also under suspicion.

"Really? My goodness! So Mr. Holmes saw his attacker then?"

"No, but I did."

Her eyes narrowed, then she smiled pleasantly at me and said: "If that woman is hiding here, the only way for you to find her is to search the convent."

"That is exactly what I mean to do, and I will tolerate no hindrance," I said as sternly as I was able.

"Dr. Watson, I am as anxious as you to find Sr. Mary's murderer, and I am absolutely horrified by the thought that it could be one of us. You may search as much as you like, and be welcome," she said warmly.

Now I was confused. If she were an impostor hiding a murderer would she want me to search the convent? What if I had done her an injustice? Just because she had smooth hands did not necessarily make her a villain. What if she only ever did administrative work, rather than field work and heavy labor like the other nuns? Her hands would stay soft then. There was always the possibility that she was completely innocent; certainly her attitude wasn't that of someone with a guilty conscience. She seemed so obliging and concerned for Holmes's welfare....

"I want to see all the nuns," I began.

"Yes, of course. If you'll follow me, Doctor, you will be able to see them when they come out from Morning Prayer."

She motioned to a door and I walked in ahead of her, as she brought up the rear. I had perhaps taken ten steps up the hall when her words came back to me like a thunderbolt: *'I'm as anxious as you to find Sr. Mary's murderer.'* I had said I was looking for the woman who attacked Holmes, not Sr. Mary's murderer. How did she know they were one and the same? No sooner had the thought crossed my mind, than I began to turn, and in that instant everything went black and I collapsed.

* * * * * * *

When I revived, my head was pounding and I found myself tied to a chair in the Mother Superior's office. I was face to face with a woman of angelic appearance dressed as a nun. I shuddered for there was a look of anticipation on her face that was unsavory taken with her appearance, that and the fact that she played with a knife.

"Back off, Ida," ordered the Mother Superior, and the blonde moved over and to the side of me. I could see now there were six women in the room, all dressed as nuns.

"Why stop her," said one of the nuns in a deep masculine voice. "Let Ida finish him off, and then we'll set fire to the church and be on our way. We have no reason to hang around here any longer. He might have talked."

"He hasn't," she replied confidently.

I saw the face of the nun that had spoken before then. It was actually a man dressed as a woman.

"Who are you?" I asked in surprise.

He smiled at me. "Don't see why I shouldn't tell you, your time's fast runnin' out. I'm John Hastings."

"The convict?"

"Ex-convict," he corrected. "Soon to be wealthy tourist."

Now, I understood Holmes' interest in the prison, and his questions regarding the Mother Superior and if she had had any contact with Hastings. He surmised that she was here to break him out. If only he had shared his knowledge. Now it was too late. I was in one hell of a pickle, brought on by my own care-lessness. So much for my moment in the sun. I was a miserable failure, just like always. I silently berated myself, paying little attention to my captors. I barely heard their conversation, so wretched was I. Hastings was saying something about going to Lord Nelson to pick up the money, but I didn't catch it all.

I heard the cry of a whippoorwill and looked up. It is fortu-nate I was tied to the chair, else I would have fallen out, for there was Holmes' face peeking at me through the window. He winked at me and disappeared. *All was not lost!*

I decided to distract the killers, to give Holmes a chance to get in and affect a rescue. Though I didn't see how he would be able to manage so many, but then again, I considered it impos-sible that he could even be here at this time when he should have been home in bed. It was so like Holmes to do the impossible.

"Actually, Hastings," I said a little more loudly than normal. "The police know where I am. I left a message for Sergeant Reid, asking him to bring reinforcements here. He's had more than enough time to organize his forces. I doubt very much if you will be going anywhere but back to prison. As for these women, I will see them hang."

There came a hiss from behind me. A hand gripped my hair and pulled my head back, exposing my throat. I felt the prick of Ida's knife against my neck.

"What did you write in your note?" demanded Hastings.

"Why should I tell you?" I returned.

"If you don't I'll let Ida finish you off. It's a sickness with her. She has the face of an angel, but she just loves to kill, don't you Ida love?"

She moved the knife from my neck and caressed its tip. "I love to see them bleed. Let me slit his throat, Dad. We don't need him."

"Later, sweetheart. If the police are on their way, we may need him as a hostage. We don't need the other nuns though. Robert, go set fire to the church. Clara," he turned to the Mother Superior—his wife no doubt, and said, "Is everything ready?

We can't afford to waste anymore time here."

"Yes the wagon is at the back, loaded and ready."

"Good. Untie the good doctor, will you Julia?" he ordered the woman I knew as Sr. Julius.

As soon as she untied me, I stood up. It was at that moment that Holmes burst in, gun at the ready. Hopkins and Reid, both armed, followed him in. Hastings, gentleman that he was, pushed Ida towards Hopkins and fired his revolver at Holmes. Holmes returned fire and he did not miss. Hastings dropped, his head bloody. Hopkins, meantime, fought with a crazed Ida, who slashed at him with her knife, managing to wound him in the process. Despite her attack he was still hesitant to shoot her.

Holmes struck out with the barrel of his gun and knocked her to the ground. The Mother Superior dropped to the ground beside her husband. I moved over quickly and picked up his fallen gun. Reid covered the others, his weapon unwavering.

"I can't tell you how pleased I am to see you, Holmes."

He smiled wryly in return. "And I you, Watson. I should congratulate you on your deductions. You were quite right." He looked down at the unconscious woman by Hopkins' feet. "It was she who attacked me. She boarded the train disguised as a boy, then changed to herself after the train left the station. She did the same thing with Sr. Mary."

"I wasn't quite right," I said ruefully. "I never connected them with the Hastings."

"You were hardly to know that Hastings had a wife and two daughters, and his son had a wife. There was no gang when they robbed the bank of England; it was just this lot—one big happy family. It was our knife wielder here that murdered the guard. I suspected it was his womenfolk posing as nuns as soon as I heard that the Mother Superior had made contact with him in the prison. Her hands were out of sight. She no doubt slipped him a message with their escape plans on it. It was all very clever, and they might have got away with it if they hadn't killed Sr. Mary Ignatius."

Clara Hastings glared at Holmes. "How did you know we

killed her? How could you know?"

"You removed the top page from her note pad and read the letter she sent to me. You knew she was coming to see me and you also missed her presence at evening prayer; that's when you sent Ida to stop her."

I nodded in confirmation and he continued. "When I looked at her notepad, I saw that the sheet was unmarked, it shouldn't have been. If she was crazy as you claimed she was, there should have been an imprint of the letter she wrote to me on it. That there was not, told me that you knew she had written to me, and what she had written. All you had to do was stop her talking to me and I would be no wiser—or so you thought. Ida murdered her, pushed her body off the train and returned the next day to Sherbrook."

"You can't prove that," muttered Clara Hastings.

"I think I can. I am afraid, my dear Mrs. Hastings that you, your daughters and daughter-in-law are for the gallows. You're responsible for seven deaths that I know of."

"Seven?" I looked at him in surprise.

"Yes, seven. The real Mother Superior Augustine, and the three nuns that accompanied her. They murdered them and took their clothing and identification. Mother Superior Capuano was also murdered. No doubt she realized you were an impostor so you smothered her in her sick bed."

"She died of heart failure," insisted Clara.

"Heart failure, smothered by a pillow; it is difficult to tell the difference," shrugged Holmes. "Then of course, there was the night watchman during the robbery, and we mustn't forget Sr. Mary. Not to mention the attempt on me."

"Too bad about the last one," she muttered sullenly.

"Yes, she slipped up badly didn't she? Didn't count on Watson finding me so fast and treating me so expertly. Had I been alone she would have been successful."

"Our cover was perfect!" cried Julia Hastings—wife of Robert.

"Not really, Mrs. Hastings. You left on your wedding ring,

and although Mrs. Hastings Sr. tried to explain that away, I knew it was a falsehood. You also wear scent—expensive French perfume if I'm not mistaken. I have never heard of any nun that did. Then there were your hands; you all have smooth hands as opposed to the real nuns. The day we were here, Sr. Agnes told me you were liars and impostors...."

"Sr. Agnes?" Clara Hastings looked up at him. "How could she? She didn't say a word to you."

"Yes, I must admit, Holmes, I don't see how you can make a claim like that," I said, agreeing with the criminal on this one.

Holmes smiled. "She didn't speak, but she wrote me a message. You thought she was fidgeting, Watson, when in reality she was writing a message."

"Ah, that's why you pretended to drop your pipe, you were reading it?" I said, understanding dawning.

"Exactly. She wrote the word 'no'. I had asked her if what Clara here said was true, she had nodded under the watchful eyes of her captors, but wrote no in the dirt. That commotion that broke out just before we went in to see Sr. Mary's room was some of the nuns wanting to come to us for help."

"What I don't understand is how only four women could keep the other twenty or so prisoner. The others outnumbered them. Surely they could have overpowered them?" I said.

"Unless I am mistaken, Mother Superior Capuano was murdered for two reasons; one, to silence her, the other to set her up as an example to the others. I have no doubt whatsoever that there were several nuns held in captivity with Ida guarding them, to ensure the continued good behavior of the others. They could not act for fear of risking their lives."

"Sr. Mary did though," I pointed out.

"She tried. It cost her her life."

At that moment we heard the approach of someone. Clara Hastings tensed, perhaps thinking it was her son, Robert, but to her disappointment it was a young police officer. He saluted Hopkins and said: "We've got Robert Hastings, sir and we've found the nuns. They were all tied and gagged and locked in the chapel. The floors, pews and some of the nuns were drenched in paraffin. He was about to set fire to them."

Hopkins shook his head in disgust. "Money or no money, he'll hang this time. All of you will."

More policemen entered and handcuffed the survivors. Lovely Ida was just starting to rouse from the clout Holmes had given her. It was a shame that such a demented mind hid behind that sweet face.

The real nuns, once freed of their bonds were quite eager to talk and tell their story. It was much as Holmes had said. Several nuns were held hostage to ensure their cooperation. They were not a silent order and only had to pretend to be, as Clara Hastings did not want any of them being given the opportunity to talk. She bragged of killing Mother Superior Capuano to the nuns and threatened to do the same to them if they disobeyed. Sr. Mary had managed to smuggle her letter to Holmes out by putting it in the letterbox by the road. The postman collected it and posted it for her as he often did for the nuns when he found outgoing mail in their box. Mrs. Hastings was unaware of this practice and had thus been fooled.

I admired the courage of Sr. Mary Ignatius in trying to seek help for the other sisters. It was a shame she did not live to see this day.

THIRTEEN

On the journey back to London, I said to Holmes. "How was it that you arrived so fortuitously, Holmes?"

"I woke up around nine o'clock when Hopkins arrived. I invited him for breakfast. Your letter had slipped down and I did not find it until Mrs. Hudson cleared the trays away. When I read it, my memory came flooding back. I remembered everything. You were on the right track, Watson. I'm proud of you."

Praise from Holmes was rare indeed. My heart warmed to him.

"Unfortunately, I realized that you were walking into danger, for it was obvious you had not made the connection between the prison escapees and the nuns. Still, I was most impressed with your deductions. Hopkins commandeered a train and we came to Sherbrook post haste. Sergeant Reid met us at the station with reinforcements and we made our way here. We advanced cautiously when we saw the wagon at the back. We weren't sure if we were in time, or if they had already left. You bought us that time, Watson. We would have been too late to catch them. You know the rest."

"You have no idea how I felt when I saw your face looking in the window," I said.

"I think I might," he returned, smiling faintly.

"There's just one thing that puzzles me, Holmes."

"That is?"

"How did that woman manage to stab you and push you off the train? You were expecting an attack weren't you?"

"Yes I was. That's why I told Mrs. Hastings that we were leaving. I thought sure she would make some sort of an attempt."

"And you suspected that the boy was really a woman?"

"Naturally."

"Then how did she manage it?"

"Easily. Yes, I knew the boy was a woman and I was watching for him. I was standing in the corridor by the exit door, when a soft female voice said: 'Excuse me please.' I turned to let her pass. As she passed I glimpsed her face and recognized her as the woman that disappeared from the train at Sherbrook. I was about to make some comment, when she swung round suddenly and stabbed me. The shock of that blow disorientated me for a moment. She opened the door and tried to push me out. I hung onto the doorframe with a bloody hand, until she stamped her foot against it causing me to let loose and fall. It happened so fast, Watson. I underestimated her deadliness."

"I'm sure a lot of men have," I returned.

"Not anymore. She'll hang, along with the rest of her family."

Back at Baker Street, I urged Holmes to return to bed as he was looking pale and exhausted. The activities of the day had placed a strain on him in his weakened state. The fact that he went without argument and without a final pipe of the night was proof of this. I was glad to be home. For a while there I thought I would never see it again.

* * * * * * *

Two days later, Holmes was up and about and more his usual self. He grumbled repeatedly about Mrs. Hudson fussing over him and urging him to eat to get his strength up.

"Say, Holmes," I began. "When you were unconscious you had a visitor who did not introduce himself."

"Oh? What did he look like?"

"He was as tall as you, perhaps a little taller and a great deal wider. He had curious pale gray eyes and didn't say much, but he did seem concerned for your welfare. Who was he?"

"He's the executor of my will, Watson," replied Holmes, the tone of his voice brooking no further questions. However, he took pity on my hangdog expression and added, "He is an interesting fellow. Perhaps I will formally introduce you to him one day."

"Thank you, Holmes," I said and meant it for I knew how jealously he guarded his private life.

That afternoon, Stanley Hopkins stopped by for a visit. We plied him with brandy and cigars, and he made himself comfortable by the fire.

"Its good to see you looking so well, Mr. Holmes," he said.

"Thanks to Watson, Inspector," returned Holmes, generous as always.

"It's a shame we weren't able to recover the money. Robert Hastings refuses to talk, his Mother, wife and sisters don't know where it is and John Hastings of course, is dead."

"They didn't happen to say anything while you were held captive, did they Watson?" asked Holmes.

I frowned, my brow furrowed in thought. I wish I'd listened more closely to their conversation. I had been too preoccupied with my own self-pity.

"I seem to remember Hastings saying something about picking the money up from Lord Nelson." I said finally.

Holmes turned to Hopkins. "Where were the Hastings' apprehended?"

"Near the state Library," he replied.

"Do you think the money is in the library?" I asked eagerly.

"Hardly. Too many people going in and out. They needed a hiding place that was unlikely to be disturbed." Holmes put down his pipe. "Gentlemen, fancy an expedition to Trafalgar Square?" His eyes were shining and I could see he was excited.

"Don't tell me you have figured it out already, Mr. Holmes?" said Hopkins, also putting out his cigar.

"Possibly, Hopkins. Quite possibly."

* * * * * * *

We were soon on our way to Trafalgar Square. This late in the day, traffic was mild and no crowds thronged the streets. Holmes went straight to the statue of Lord Nelson and studied it. After a few minutes he gave up on the statue and studied the base. He gave a grunt of satisfaction and took out his penknife. With this he started to chip at the mortar around one block of stone. After some five minutes, the block came loose and Hopkins and I gasped in surprise. For instead of being the thickness of the other stones it was no more than one inch thick, leaving a cavity. Holmes reached in and pulled out an oilskin bag. He held it up, smiling with delight at our expressions.

"How did you know, Mr. Holmes?" Hopkins was full of praise.

Holmes tapped the piece that he had removed. "It's not stone. It's wood, carefully made up to look exactly like the other stones. They must have planned on hiding the money here in case the police came by. At some stage prior to the robbery, they came and removed a stone and replaced it with this replica. The Bank of England is only two streets down from here. After the robbery, the men came here while the women went home. That is how they were caught because they returned later. That is also why the women were never arrested, because there was no proof that they had gone out. They had been seen near the bank by the guard in another building. It was a stroke of bad luck for them, but they did have time to hide the money. They always thought that their womenfolk would break them out of prison, which is why they never talked. Perhaps Robert is still keeping his mouth shut in the hope that someone else will get him out."

"No hope now, I can guarantee that. As soon as word gets out that the money has been found, there will be no takers. He's on his own." Hopkins shook hands with Holmes and myself. "Thank you, Mr. Holmes, Dr. Watson. It is always a pleasure to see you in action."

He left us clutching the oilskin sack jubilantly, and we returned to Baker Street.

* * * * * * *

"Well, Watson, that was an interesting case wouldn't you say—and profitable too."

"Profitable, how can you say that? Your client is dead. She's hardly going to pay you."

"No, but the Bank of England will for recovery of the money. I think we will be able to afford a holiday out of it. Fancy a trip to the Riviera, Watson? It should be rather pleasant this time of year."

"I say; that would be excellent!" I agreed with enthusiasm.

The Riviera was a place usually beyond my budget. It would be an absolute delight to go there, and it was not often that Holmes suggested going on holidays. It was usually all I could do to drag him away from Baker Street."

"As your doctor, Holmes. I would highly recommend it."

IRENE AND THE OLD DETECTIVE

BY RICHARD L. KELLOGG

Irene walked slowly down the country lane and tried to remember what Mr. Holmes had told her. The old man said that most people don't pay attention to the little things which make life so exciting. To understand our world, he felt that we must learn how to look, listen, touch, taste, and smell.

The little girl stopped and thought very hard. She saw the strange designs made by the clouds in the sky. She heard the soft rustling of the leaves in the trees. Noticing some red berries along the hedgerow, she gently touched the bushes and then ate some of the delicious fruit. It was early fall and she smelled the faint odor of a wood fire drifting in the breeze.

"My friend is right," she thought. "It is more fun to wander through the woods when you notice everything around you. I am glad that Mr. Holmes taught me so much."

Irene lived with her parents on a small farm in the southern part of England. A lively girl with blond hair and blue eyes, she was often lonely until she met a new neighbor named Holmes. He lived with his housekeeper, Mrs. Hudson, in a cottage near a sandy beach on the English Channel.

Mr. Holmes was a retired detective; a tall, thin gentleman with white hair and a crooked nose. He spent a great deal of time taking care of his bees, working in the vegetable garden, and reading the many books in his library. The old man was lonesome and enjoyed the company of children. He liked the little girl and often told her that he had once been fond of another pretty girl whose name was Irene. The two became the best of friends and he taught her a lot of the things he had learned during his long life.

Irene wasn't sure what detectives did, but she knew the old man was good at solving problems. He would help her solve a difficult problem, chuckle softly, and say that the answer was "Elementary, most elementary." This meant that it was a simple problem to work out.

As she came out of the woods, she saw her friend pacing around the lawn in front of the cottage. He was puffing rapidly on a large pipe and clouds of smoke were curling like a halo around his head. Taking off his battered hat, Mr. Holmes wiped his brow and shouted, "Hello, Irene. Come and join me. It is quite warm for so late in the year."

Irene waved a greeting in return and hurried down the lane to his house. She saw that he had planted flowers around the yard since her last visit. The blossoms would attract more birds and bees to his home.

"How are you today?" asked Irene. "I haven't visited you in quite a while."

"I'm feeling fine, thank you. It is time for tea and biscuits after a busy morning in the garden. Can you stay for lunch?"

"I would love to," said the little girl. "I have missed the hot tea and your delicious honey."

After their meal, they went outdoors to sit in chairs on the front porch. The old man told her how he had been feeding the birds and that they perched on his hands when he sat quietly. He showed her some pictures he had sketched of the birds. Irene clapped her hands with joy when he gave her one of his best drawings to take home.

As Irene was preparing to leave, the old man asked softly, "Is there anything I can help you with? You appear to be upset over something."

"Oh, it's nothing for you to worry about. Besides, I didn't say anything about being upset."

"No, you didn't," replied Mr. Holmes. "However, I noted that your right eye was twitching and that you were rubbing your hands together. It is also obvious that you have recently been chewing your fingernails."

Irene took a deep breath and laughed. "You are up to your old tricks again. I can never keep a secret when you are around."

"Friends should not keep secrets from each other," noted the old man. He put the pipe back in his mouth and puffed away with a very sad expression on his face.

"Well, I guess you should be told," said the little girl. "I am not doing well at school. My grades are poor. My parents and my teacher are not pleased with me."

Mr. Holmes saw that Irene was close to tears. "Come now, don't cry about it," he said. "This is a little problem we can solve together. I haven't had such an important case in years."

"But older people seem to know everything," complained Irene. "Children are never as smart as adults. I feel bad whenever I think about it."

Mr. Holmes just grinned. "It seems that way to children but grown-ups don't have all the answers either. They have just lived longer and had more time to learn things. You are a bright girl and don't you forget it."

"But how can I get better grades at school?" the little girl asked. "You are the best and wisest man I know. Everyone knows that. Can you show me how to be as smart as you are?"

Mr. Holmes scratched his chin and thought for a moment. He suddenly snapped his fingers and his gray eyes twinkled. "We can do it together. Let's have a meeting tomorrow. We will talk about the best way to learn. I know you can do much better at school."

When Irene returned the next afternoon, the old man was feeding the birds behind his cottage. He called each bird by name and smiled as they ran around the lawn between his legs.

"Welcome back," he yelled. "I have a fine lesson for you today. Come and join the class."

The little girl could see that he was in a cheerful mood. They sat in chairs beside the house and felt the warmth of the sunshine. It was a wonderful day to be outdoors with a friend.

"I have some problems for you today," stated Mr. Holmes. "I will pretend to be the teacher and you can pretend to be the student. The lawn will be our classroom."

"This will be great fun. I hope that I know all the answers."

"We will see," replied the old man. "Here is my first problem: How many animals of each type did Moses take on the ark at the time of the great flood?"

"What an easy question! He took two of each kind. I learned that last year in church. Two is the answer."

"Are you sure of that answer?" asked Mr. Holmes.

Irene said, "I am absolutely, positively sure."

The old man smiled with an impish look on his face. "I am sorry to disappoint you but Moses didn't take any animals on the ark. That was Noah's job."

"Oh, you fooled me," cried the little girl. "I guess I wasn't paying attention."

"Try another one," continued Mr. Holmes. "A train goes off the rails and crashes into a bridge during a terrible storm. The passengers on the train are from England, China, and Australia. In which one of the three countries should the survivors be buried?"

"Let me think," said Irene. "England, China, and Australia. How strange. It seems they would be buried in their own countries."

"My questions are pretty tricky," the old man admitted. "The people who survive would not be buried. After all, they are still alive."

"Of course," said Irene. "The problems are really simple ones when you listen carefully."

"That is just my point. You must pay close attention to what the teacher tells you and to what you read in your textbooks. Every fact is useful when you are trying to solve a mystery."

Irene said, "You are probably right. Sometimes I look out

the window or whisper to my friends during class. I promise to work harder on my lessons."

The little girl tried to do what Mr. Holmes suggested. She listened closely to everything her teacher said and put extra effort into her lessons.

* * * * * * *

Several weeks later, Irene visited the old man again. She wanted to tell him that she was doing much better at school. As she knocked on the door, she heard the sound of a violin. Mr. Holmes was practicing the musical scales.

He opened the door and asked her to come in. "It's good to see you once again," he said.

"I see that you have new kittens at home," he continued. "How many do you have to play with?"

"There are three but I don't remember telling you about them. They were just born last week."

Holmes nodded his head and chuckled. "No, you didn't have to tell me. I see cat hairs on your blouse and fresh scratches on your hands. Kittens love to bite and claw people. Of course, it's all in fun."

"You usually know things before I tell you. I suppose you already know I am here to report about my better grades at school."

"No, I didn't know, but I am delighted to hear about it," said the old man.

They went into the living room. Mr. Holmes placed his old violin on a stack of books near his favorite chair. He agreed to play some music before she had to leave for home.

After sitting down, the old man told Irene that he was quite concerned about the health of his dearest friend. He had just received a letter from Dr. Watson, who was residing in London. He passed the letter to Irene so that she could read it aloud.

"My dear Holmes," Watson had written. "Thank you for your kind invitation to the country. I need time to recover from a broken limb before making such a long trip. In fact, I just walked home from the doctor's office. I was taken there today after falling down some stairs at a home on Baker Street. I pray this finds you well. Most sincerely yours, Watson."

"That is too bad," said Irene. She slowly read the message again and thought for a few moments.

Her eyes brightened as she spoke. "It is too bad that Dr. Watson broke his left arm. My arm was broken when I fell out a tree last year so I know how it feels."

"Wait just a minute," interrupted the old man. "How do you know if it was the right arm, left arm, right leg, or left leg? Watson didn't provide any details of his injury."

Irene started to laugh. "You taught me how to pay attention. Since Dr. Watson walked home, he must not have broken his leg. I also remember that he writes with his right hand so it must be the other arm which was broken."

Holmes leaned back in his chair and placed his fingertips together. He reached out for the violin and said, "Nice work, Irene. You solved the puzzling mystery of the broken limb without any help from me. It appears that we are ready to form our own detective agency."

Irene was proud of herself. She knew there wouldn't be any more problems with her work at school. Her friend had taught her how to be a good student as well as a good detective.

For Caitlin Jonas, who likes
to pretend that she is a detective.

ACKNOWLEDGMENTS

A number of these pieces have been previously published, in whole or in part, and are reprinted by permission of their authors or agents:

"The Mystery of Ogham Manor" by Stan Trybulski appears here for the first time. Copyright © 2012 by Stan Trybulski.

"The Dentist" by Magda Jozsa appears here for the first time. Copyright © 2012 by Magda Jozsa.

"The Fury" by Lyn McConchie appears here for the first time. Copyright © 2012 by Lyn McConchie.

"Death and No Consequences" by Richard K. Tobin appears here for the first time. Copyright © 2012 by Richard K. Tobin.

"Murder at the Diogenes Club" by John L. French appears here for the first time. Copyright © 2012 by John L. French.

"The Adventure of the Night Hunter" by Ralph E. Vaughan appears here for the first time. Copyright © 2012 by Ralph E. Vaughan.

"The Adventure of the Devil's Father" by Morris Hershman was first published in *Red Herring Mystery Magazine*, 1996. Copyright © 1996, 2012 by Morris Hershman.

"A Memo from Inspector Lestrade" by Marvin Kaye was first published in somewhat different form in *Sherlock Holmes Mystery Magazine* #6, 2011. Copyright © 2011, 2012 by Marvin Kaye.

"The Button Box" by Lyn McConchie appears here for the first time. Copyright © 2012 by Lyn McConchie.

ABOUT THE AUTHORS

STAN TRYBULSKI is a Connecticut writer who is the author of the crime novel *The Gendarme*, and the popular Doherty Mystery series which includes *The Ides of June*, *Forty-Deuce*, *One-Trick Pony*, and *Case Maker*. His short stories have appeared in *Hardboiled, Sherlock Holmes Mystery Magazine* and many other periodicals. Stan can be contacted via email at ftrybulski@sent.net.

MAGDA JOZSA is an Australian author who says she was bitten by the writing bug at the age of fourteen when *The Australian Woman's Weekly* magazine published a short story written by her. She makes her home in Ballarat, Australia and is a huge fan of the Sherlock Holmes tales. As Ballarat and the goldfields feature in several of Doyle's Sherlock Holmes stories, it's only natural she graduated to writing Sherlock Holmes pastiches. She is the author of the novel *Sherlock Holmes on the Wild Frontier* (available on amazon.com) which is a terrific tale of Holmes and Watson in the American West. A sequel *Return to the Wild Frontier* has recently been completed. She has also written some twenty-three books in her Neptune King detective series and many other fine works. Magda's two stories here are top-rate traditional Holmes tales, she can be contacted via email at shwildfrontier@yahoo.com.

LYN MCCONCHIE hails from New Zealand and has written novels published by Tor and Avalon Books as well as a volume of fourteen Sherlock Holmes short stories with the common theme of someone either from one of the original stories, or sent by them, who has come to Sherlock and Watson asking for help. She writes her Holmes tales unapologetically in the original style, no sex, no undue violence and I am happy to have two of her fine tales in this book. You can find out more about Lyn at her website www.lynmconchie.com.

RICHARD K. TOBIN is a Canadian author from Nova Scotia who began life as a farm boy. He recently worked as an employee of the Department of National Defense. In 2002, Richard took over the care of his elderly, widowed mother and in his spare time began to teach himself the writer's trade. After writing and selling many short stories and poems, Richard's first book, *The Cuban Connection*, saw publication from Bio Publishing in 2012, available at Amazon and other online bookstores. This is Richard's first short story about Sherlock Holmes.

JOHN L. FRENCH in the real world is a crime scene supervisor with the Baltimore Police Department Crime Laboratory. As a writer of crime, pulp and horror fiction for many years, his stories have appeared in *Hardboiled, Alfred Hitchcock's Mystery Magazine*, and *Best New Zombie Tales*. He is the editor of the hard crime anthology, *Bad Cop, No Donut* (Padwolf) and of the forthcoming *To Hell in a Fast Car. Paradise Denied*, a collection of his short stories will soon be published by Books of the Dead Press. "Murder at the Diogenes Club" is John's first official Sherlock Holmes story. John can be reached via email at jfrenchfam@aol.com.

RALPH E. VAUGHAN makes his home in California and is the author of several Sherlock Holmes tales, many of which involve Lovecraftian themes. His first was the well-regarded, *The Adventure of the Ancient Gods* which has the minor distinction of being the first pairing of Sherlock Holmes with H. P. Lovecraft. Other Holmes volumes include *The Coils of Time*,

The Dreaming Detective, *The Terror Out of Time*, and *Professor Challenger and the Mystery of the Dreamlands*; many of these books originally were published by Gryphon Books in the US but he has also been published in Germany and Croatia. Ralph can be contacted via email at ralphy1@gmail.com.

MORRIS HERSHMAN is a legendary author who lives in Queens, New York. He is one of the original writers from the great days of vintage paperback pulp fiction. He has written almost every kind of book and every type of short story you can think of, though he has particular talent in writing thrilling crime tales. Morris is one of the original writers for the 1950s digest crime magazine *Manhunt*, and many others of that era, all of which are so collectible today. Morris also wrote many novels for Midwood Books and other outfits under his pseudonym Arnold English.

MARVIN KAYE is a renowned writer and editor who has been writing fine books in the fantasy field for decades. He has written one excellent pastiche novel of interconnected Sherlock Holmes stories, *The Incredible Umbrella* (Dell Books, 1980) and edited three terrific Sherlock Holmes anthologies of all new stories by top writers for St. Martin's Press: *The Game Is Afoot* (1994), *Resurrected Holmes* (1996), and *The Confidential Casebook of Sherlock Holmes* (1998). He is currently the editor of the popular crime fiction periodical *Sherlock Holmes Mystery Magazine* and the new, revived *Weird Tales*. He is a terrific writer, but he is also one of the best editors I have ever encountered.

GARY LOVISI is a Brooklyn-based author and big-time Sherlock Holmes fan and collector who writes both fiction and non-fiction about The Great Detective. He is the founder of the small independent press Gryphon Books, and editor of *Paperback Parade* and *Hardboiled* magazines. His Sherlock Holmes books include *The Secret Adventures of Sherlock*

Holmes (Ramble House, 2007), which contains three long pastiches including his MWA Edgar Award Nominated Best Short Story "The Adventure of the Missing Detective"; *More Secret Adventures of Sherlock Holmes* (Ramble House, 2011) three more pastiches; and the new novel, *Sherlock Holmes: The Baron's Revenge* (Airship27, 2012) which is a sequel to Doyle's classic story "The Adventure of the Illustrious Client." His Holmes pastiches have appeared in various anthologies as well as *Sherlock Holmes Mystery Magazine* and *The Strand Magazine*. Editing this anthology of new Sherlock Holmes stories is a dream come true for him. You can contact Gary at his website www.gryphonbooks.com.

RICHARD L. KELLOGG lives in upstate New York and is a Professor Emeritus of Psychology at the SUNY College of Technology in Alfred, New York. He has received grants from the SUNY Research Foundation to develop instructional materials on the Sherlockian model of problem solving and has delivered conference presentations on Sherlock Holmes at Alfred University, Colby College, and the Stevens Institute of Technology. Richard is also a frequent contributor to *The Baker Street Journal* and *The Serpentine Muse*. His most recent book on the Great Detective is the collection of insightful articles, *Vignettes of Sherlock Holmes* (Gryphon Books, 2008). Richard delights in introducing young readers to the magical world of Holmes and Watson and his story in this volume is no exception. He can be reached via email at rkellogg8@stny.rr.com.

LUCILLE CALI, our cover artist for this book, is a Brooklyn gal born and bred. She has done book and magazine cover art for Gryphon Books and *Hardboiled* magazine that recreate the best illustrations from popular pulp ficton vintage paperbacks. Her special cover for this book was the result of her original painting done on a wooden box recreating a classic British Sherlock Holmes paperback cover of the 1950s. She has been married to Gary Lovisi for the last thirteen years and is an avid Holmes fan. Lucille can be contacted vai email at lalovisi@ gmail.com.

Lightning Source UK Ltd.
Milton Keynes UK
UKHW041819150719
346204UK00002B/60/P